DROP DEAD RED

Alice,
Congrats! You won a
copy of Drop Dead Red.
Enjoy!
Glenda

DROP DEAD RED

Glenda Carroll

Author of *Dead in the Water*

Glenda Carroll

BEACHBREAK PRESS

Marin County, California

2017

Also by Glenda Carroll
Dead in the Water

Acclaim for *Dead in the Water*

"DEAD IN THE WATER is....so well written you just can't put it down...If you're like me, you'll be trying to figure out who committed the murder while you're working out."
　　—Lynne Cox, *New York Times Bestselling author, "Swimming to Antarctica," "Open Water Swimming Manual," "Swimming in the Sink: An Episode of the Heart."*

"Carroll combines a skill for mystery writing...with her sports journalism and Masters swimming background by nailing the details of what it's like to race in open water...I liked Carroll's characters immensely, but it was the story that kept me up late reading."
　　　　　　　　　　　　　　—Swimmer Magazine

"(This) is a swim-centric mystery that will keep you turning pages while you think about your strokes. It's the first open-water-detective-novel that I know of, and it's great fun to read."
　　　　　—Lynn Sherr, *a broadcast journalist and writer, was an award-winning correspondent for more than thirty years at ABC News. She is the author of "Swim: Why We Love the Water."*

"It is a great first novel for the author and the main character has secrets to be explored in future books. It is a fast read and will appeal to open water swimmers, athletes and mystery lovers."
　　　　—US Open Water Swimming Connection

"DEAD IN THE WATER is a fast-paced thriller set in San Francisco Bay where it is open season on open water swimmers."
　　　　　　—Daily News of Open Water Swimming

BEACHBREAK PRESS
Marin County, California
beachbreakpress@gmail.com
glendacarroll.com

ISBN 10: 0-9991109-0-X
ISBN 13: 978-0-9991109-0-4

Cover Design: Richard Burns

To my sister, Rebecca Salazar

ACKNOWLEDGEMENTS

With many thanks to all the friends and professionals that encouraged me during the writing of Drop Dead Red.

The CSI Division (Crime Scene Investigation), Marin County Sheriff's Office, walked me through their job at a crime scene and offered valuable local information. Editorial analyst Martha Engber was the first to look at the manuscript and offer suggestions to make the characters come alive. Diana Verhalen took out her blue pen and found many errors in my early manuscript. Eight drafts later, Molly Giles was my mentor during the editing process. She made me believe that with just 'a few more changes' I had a story people would want to read. Special thanks to my cousins -- Charlee Ganny and Joan Ganny--both authors, and my sister, Rebecca Salazar, who were always on my side.

Richard Burns and Karen Brigando created the cover with the right amount of creepiness.

But, I have to say that it was my teammates at Tamalpais Aquatic Masters and my co-workers at the San Francisco Giants who kept me moving forward. The only way I could answer "Is it done yet?" was to finish Drop Dead Red.

CHAPTER 1

I was speeding across the lower level of the Richmond–San Rafael Bridge, a span almost low enough to shave the tops off the white caps on San Francisco Bay. The water below was as grey as the pre-dawn sky above. Lena, my sister, was in the passenger seat next to me. At thirty-five, she is eight years my junior. That makes me...well, I'd rather not talk about it. Lena was always the cute one. With her cinnamon corkscrew curls, wide-set grey eyes and dimpled chin, she invites a second, even a third look. She is small, about 5'3", with a solid swimmer's body. That morning, she was wrapped up in her knee-length swim parka, staring out the window. I smiled as I glanced at her. Since our mother died, I've always felt protective of her.

We were headed east, away from the foggy Pacific and into the heat of the Livermore Valley. It was 5:30 a.m. on a Saturday and there were only two other cars on the five-mile span. Erector-set steel arms zigzagged past us on either side.

"Ever think about the bridges in the Bay Area? How lucky we are to have them?" I asked, glancing at a massive container ship moving through the Bay below.

"No. I don't care, Trisha. Come on, I'm tired."

"This bridge, for instance...," I said.

"Stop. Just stop."

●

11

"Without it, we would have to drive an hour more to get to Lake Caldwell."

"Enough, Trish," said Lena, plugging in her white ear buds and disappearing beneath the hood of her parka into a world away from me. Normally my sister was sassy, smart mouthed and talked non-stop. Not today. Now that I thought about it, not for the past few months. Something was bugging her and my concern was growing.

I reached over and pulled out an ear bud.

"What?" she asked.

"You are awfully quiet," I said.

"I don't have to talk all the time, you know."

"Come on Lee, you've been too quiet. That's not like you. What's up?"

She glanced out the window. "It's my friend, Shari. I'm worried about her."

That took me by surprise. "She's running this swim clinic thing we're going to today, isn't she?"

"Yeah."

"Well, why are...?"

Lena cut me off. "It's probably nothing. She's always been the over-achiever of my friends. I'll talk to her once we get there." She settled back into the seat and then looked over at me.

"Before the bridges, there used to be ferries," she said.

"What?"

"Before the bridges were built, people took ferries all the time. You're not the only one who knows about local history." Then she disappeared beneath the hood of her parka, a wise-ass smile on her face.

"Well, Ms. Smarty Pants...," I said as I accelerated off the bridge onto the near-empty freeway.

I have always been the responsible sister. I had to be. Our mom died of cancer when we were young. And dad? Well, he walked out of the house once I hit 18 and graduated from high school, leaving me to raise Lena.

I looked at the highway in front me. It was all so familiar. This is what we did, my sister and I, many times each summer. We'd drive to a lake or river, sometimes the Pacific Ocean. My sister would gather with hundreds of other swimmers behind a starting line and when the horn blared, she'd hop into the water, race around big triangular buoys and sprint toward the finish line. I'd sit on the beach listening to the San Francisco Giants games.

I was the chauffer in my old tan Honda. She was the competitive swimmer. In the last few years, she'd moved from the hectic, pressure-packed world of pool competition to what she called the 'Zen' of the sport...competing in open water races around Northern California.

Today we were headed to a lake tucked into Lake Caldwell Regional Park about 70 miles east from our San Rafael home. Actually, it was Lena's home. I was only there temporarily. This morning, we had volunteered to staff an open water swim clinic, led by her childhood friend Shari Grantner. Let me put this another way, Lena volunteered me. I should have been annoyed. I was somewhat. But I owed her.

Lake Caldwell Regional Park is in a valley between wide rolling straw-colored hills and graceful oak trees. It is miles away from neighborhoods, schools, traffic lights and people. Goats and some cattle graze on the tinder-dry slopes.

Lena finally stirred as I rolled down the last hill and stopped at the brown wooden kiosk to pay the entrance fee.

"Anyone else here for the clinic?" I asked the ranger, handing her five dollars.

"A few people," she said. "Have fun."

This clinic was the second in a series of three with a specific purpose: to prepare swimmers for Northern California's first open water carnival. This wasn't my kind of carnival with rides and cotton candy. Instead it was all about swimming. In a few short weeks, there would be two long swims––a 10k and a 5K on the first day. The following day, there would be three more swims, starting from longest to shortest––a two person, 5K relay (each swimmer swimming 2.5K); a one-mile swim, and a 500-yard sprint. The carnival would end with a big barbecue on the beach––that's if anyone could even stand or lift their arms to pick up the after-race food. My sister and her swim buddies thought this was the greatest event to take place in Northern California. I thought they were all nuts.

Lena pulled out her phone. "Wonder if Shari showed up yet? Oh...right. Phone reception is sketchy." She dropped it back into her pocket.

We followed the curving road past empty parking lots edging the long man-made lake.

"Turn there," said Lena pointing at the next entrance.

"I know. I've driven you here before." I glanced toward the end of the parking lot next to the shuttered snack bar. "I see a few cars. Must be..."

"Our fearless clinic leader, Shari Grantner."

"The redhead. I haven't seen her in years," I said as I slowed down. "She has a younger brother and sister. Twins, right?"

"Right. Mia and Mitch."

"And their parents are dead. Something tragic, if I remember."

"Yeah, about 10 years ago. Car crash. Hit by a drunk driver."

"Terrible," I said. Life is never easy, I thought, thinking of my family.

"Now Shari's in charge of the family fortune. And I do mean fortune. That family is rich."

Except for three cars near the snack bar, the wide meandering lot was deserted. I drove past row after row of empty parking spots and pulled into a place nearest the beach. Cool air blew off the lake and filtered into my stuffy car. The morning sun was still hidden behind the hills and a low mist hunkered down over the greenish-brown water.

I turned the engine off when Lena stretched across me, looking out my window. My sister's mop of curls blocked my view. "There's Shari and Mitch, her brother. Wonder why he's here?"

"From the looks of it, he didn't come to help," I said.

Like impatient boxers getting ready for a match, the sister and brother shifted their weight from one foot to another. They leaned in until their foreheads almost touched. Their shoulders were hunched, eyes locked. Shari was the tallest, close to 6'; Mitch was a head shorter. Next to them stood Mia, a doughier version of her siblings with light brown wispy shoulder length hair. She put her hand first on her sister, then her brother, trying to separate them.

Their voices were tense and loud, easy to hear in the still air.

"You can't cut me off. I need that money," said Mitch. About 28-years-old, he was wearing black bike shorts. His multi-colored cycling jersey was stretched tight across his chest and muscular arms. A vein pulsed on his smooth forehead beneath wavy copper hair. His eyes narrowed as he glared up at the long-legged Shari standing directly in front of him, her hands on her hips.

"I can't give you an advance. The estate is about to be audited. That money is your inheritance, not an open bank account," said Shari.

"You don't understand."

"Oh, I do. Your playboy lifestyle is coming to an end. Go get a job like the rest of us."

Mitch lunged forward and gave her a shove. Her head jerked to one side. She took a step in and put her hands on his chest, leaning closer, closer still, until her face was inches from his. She said something quietly to him. His cheeks flushed a bright red, almost the same color as her waist length hair. Then she pushed him, hard, and he stumbled backwards losing his balance.

"Whoa, someone has to stop this." I said, opening the car door and looking around for help. There was no one.

"Shari can handle herself," Lena said, grabbing onto my arm. "That brother of hers is a lazy trust fund douche...a good looking douche...but a total creep. Always was."

"Hey! Hey! Knock it off or I'm calling the police," I said walking toward them. Mia looked in my direction and then stepped between her sparring siblings.

"Come on guys...there has to be a better way to work this out," she said. "Mitch, stop. Walk away. Leave, okay? Shari, we have work to do. In about an hour, there will be more than 50 people here for the clinic. We have to get ready."

I came up behind Shari and put my hand on her shoulder.

"Everything okay here?" I asked.

She jumped, then nodded and took a step back.

"Who are you?" said Mitch.

I was about to answer when Shari moved closer to Mitch again, who stood there, jaw set, right eye twitching, fists clenched. "I'll talk with you later––that's a promise. But my mind is made up. No more money," she said.

"If I had a gun, I'd shoot you," said Mitch. He wheeled around on the cleats of his biking shoes and peeled out toward his bike leaning against the snack bar.

"Shari, remember me, I'm Trisha, Lena's sister."

She looked at me blankly, then a slight smile crossed her face. "Sorry, Trish, for a minute it didn't register. I forgot you were helping out today. You guys are here early. This is my sister, Mia." She nodded at me. "The guy who ran out of here with steam coming out of his ears, is my younger brother and Mia's twin, Mitch."

"He just threatened you," I said.

"Not the first time," said Shari.

"Hey Shar," called Lena, walking toward us. Her voice echoed across the sweeping green lawn down to the sloping pebbly beach. A few geese huddled together on the lawn snapped their grey and black heads in her direction, then they settled back down in the damp grass and stared out at the water.

Shari waved.

"Are you hurt?" asked Lena.

"No."

"What was that all about?" my sister continued.

Shari shrugged her shoulders. "You know Mitch. Never happy. Come on Mia, we have to empty the car."

The two women walked back toward the parking lot, pointing to different areas of the venue as they moved. Lena started after her, but I grabbed hold of her arm.

"He threatened her and she doesn't seem to care," I said. "Am I the only one that thinks he is dangerous?"

"Look, according to Shari, this family fights all the time," said Lena.

"We fight all the time," I said, "but I don't go pushing you around."

"Shari doesn't seem worried. So why are you?"

I rolled my eyes. "You really don't find this odd? Two minutes ago, her brother wants to shoot her and she moves on like nothing happened?"

"Nothing did happen. I once dated him."

"You didn't? Him?"

Lena ignored me. "He can be explosive when it comes to family and then Mia steps in to calm things down. If this is a fight about money, I bet you they've had it before. Need to let it go, Trisha. You're here to work, not be a family therapist."

Shari looked over from her black SUV in our direction. "You guys," she shouted, "come on Swimmers will start showing up soon."

With that we walked quickly to her vehicle. Two more

cars of volunteers pulled up next to Shari. "Right on time," she said. "Let's get these things on the beach."

The eight of us picked up boxes full of swim caps, goody bags, colored coded agendas for different groups, name badges, and a megaphone. I grabbed two easels and Lena took the self-stick white easel pads.

The only thing left in her trunk were two stand-up banners. I unrolled an edge of one and saw the long legs of a male swimmer kicking in cobalt blue water.

"Nice."

"From our sponsor, Swimnetics."

"Hope your swimmers aren't expecting nice blue water like that."

Shari smiled. This is the first I'd seen her in about 12 years. She had grown into a beauty, a tall red-haired stunner who exuded confidence. Lena was about two years younger than her friend. They met on a swim team years ago. Back in the day, Shari was a strong, fast swimmer, a sprinter with a powerful kick. Unlike many female swimmers, even after years of training, she remained willowy, dainty almost.

"It is going to be a beautiful day," Shari said. "Water temp is about 70 degrees. Before I forget..." She stopped, put down her boxes and pulled a tube of sun block from her pocket. She squeezed out a quarter-sized blob and smeared it on her face. The white zinc oxide sat on her skin like a geisha's makeup.

"You look lovely," said Lena.

"Need to do it. The dermatologist gasps every time I walk into his office. He wants me to coat my face with industrial strength sunblock. No wimpy sunscreen for me." She pulled a hair tie out of her pocket and pushed her long hair through it.

"That is so not you," said Lena, staring at the camouflage browns and greens of the tie.

"It was a gift. My boyfriend. Camo is not my style. But it does the job. Need to put on my swim suit before the crowd gets here."

As we carried the rest of the equipment to a wooden picnic table on the grass, Shari moved off to the side and wrapped a towel around herself and began to strip off her clothes underneath.

"Shari, there are changing rooms," Lena called out. Shari looked over her shoulder at my sister, smiled and then dropped the towel exposing a muscular back and round bottom.

"Oops," she said, as bent over to pick it up. "Oh why bother," I heard her say. She flung off the towel and pulled on her swim suit.

"Shari," Lena, Mia and I called out simultaneously. "What are you doing?"

But she ignored the comment, tugged on a pair of board shorts over her suit and walked to the SUV.

"This isn't the Shari that I remember," I said to Lena standing next to me. "When did she become an exhibitionist?"

"Beats me," said Lena.

It took no more than 30 minutes before everything was in place. Attendees would stop first at the registration table, then they were split up into two groups. Finally, they would meet together at the tall lifeguard chair next to the water's edge.

Under a nearby tree was the food table. The volunteer in charge of feeding everyone was unpacking bagels, cream cheese, bananas, tangerines and containers of hot coffee. I couldn't wait to get a cup. The morning air was chilly and I had goose bumps on my legs and arms.

I jogged back to Shari's van, picked up the two stand-up banners. These would mark the finish line of the short open water swim that concluded the clinic. I hoisted the two long bulky carrying cases.

"Over there," yelled Shari to me, "close to the ramp." She pointed to a spot where the trees grew almost into the water.

"Got it."

Shari turned to Mia and they both looked at a clipboard

full of papers. Mia said something. The older sister laughed.

I watched them and thought of my relationship with my one and only sister. I was used to being in charge, at least of her. After dad deserted us, I gave up thoughts of higher-education. I was interested in criminal law, but, I had to shut that book. Those were tough times. However, I am proud to say Lena went to college on a swimming scholarship. Then I got married. Brad, my husband, and I moved to Colorado. I worked as an office manager for a health organization. He was in computers. Then I got unmarried. Moved back to California into my sister's Marin County home, shell shocked.

Things are a little better now. I have a part-time job and I can pay rent––well, partial rent. And, last year––although I almost got us both killed––I solved my first mystery. A well-known open water swimmer had died during a race in a Sierra lake. I knew it wasn't an accident and I proved it, much to everyone's surprise.

I laid out the parts of the banners and went to work, fitting one metal pole into another, sliding on the banner and standing them up. It was dead calm and the banners sagged. They would be totally useless unless the wind picked up. No one would see them from the water.

I started back up the sloping beach. The pale early morning sun had finally scaled the hills that bordered the lake. It filtered through the trees and painted long dark shadows on the beach. I glanced out to the parking lot, now with about ten cars parked close to mine. Probably the instructors and in-water assistants. No sign of Mitch. He had taken off pedaling like his legs were on fire and had disappeared around a corner.

"Hey Trisha," Shari called. She waved for me to come over. "This is where I want registration to be."

Shari was standing by a cement picnic bench underneath a circle of stately old growth oaks. I grabbed a knit cap out of my jacket pocket and pulled it over my head.

"Chilly," I said with a smile.

"Right," said Shari. She looked up at the lake for a minute, lost in thought.

"Anything special I should know?" I asked.

No response.

"Shari, anything I should know?"

"Oh, sorry...okay. It's pretty simple. Check off the swimmers' names as they come in. Make sure they sign the safety waiver. Everyone gets an information packet. Tell them to find a spot on their corner of the beach. That's it. Questions?"

I had questions. Plenty of them. All about her brother.

"This is somewhat off topic, but are you concerned that Mitch will be back?"

Shari looked up from the registration papers on the table. Her eyes were amber. I could see a scattering of freckles on her nose. "A little. Well, honestly, a lot. Do me a favor and keep an eye out for him. Let me know if you see him."

She looked toward the beach and switched on the megaphone she was carrying. "Okay, let's get everyone together for our pre-clinic briefing."

I started to get up. "No Trisha, you can stay here. Get your things organized." she said with a smile. "You know, you're a star...a celebrity in the open water swim community since you figured out who was hunting down our swimmers last year. I'm so glad you are on our team."

Then she walked off to a picnic table closer to the beach.

Lena was standing behind me and had overheard the whole interchange.

"Can I have your autograph, Ms. Celebrity?"

"Nobody has ever called me a star before."

"You did good on that case. But, that was last year. Don't go looking for mysteries where they don't exist. Why were you asking about Mitch?"

"Shari needs help. She even said so. I have a feeling that something bad is going to happen. What if Mitch shows up again? Still angry? With a weapon? He was certainly mad enough."

"Seriously? Do you hear yourself? What were you watching on tv last night?" Lena headed down to the picnic table with the other volunteers. At one point, she looked back at me, raised her eyebrows, pointed a finger toward her head and made a circular motion. Then she pointed at me.

"I am not crazy...just concerned," I said to the geese sitting near my registration table.

It didn't take long to organize my material. Everyone was pre-registered and pre-paid. I scanned the list of names. One group of swimmers all listed the same work number. Must be an employee team of some sort. More cars were driving across the lot and finding places to park. The athletes climbed out of their vehicles, stretched, pulled out their gear––beach chairs, swim bags, sweat shirts––and headed for the walkway.

"Here they come," Mia called to no one in particular. She greeted the early arrivals with a smile and a welcome and sent them over to me. I watched Mia as she interacted with the swimmers. Lena had mentioned that Mia was an interior designer. Cheerful, encouraging and friendly. She and Shari couldn't have been more different, not only in physical appearance but in attitude. Shari was determined...focused. She didn't smile much. There was a 'let's get it done' air about her.

Lena had told me that besides running the open water clinics in her spare time, Shari was a powerful labor lawyer in San Francisco. She was known for taking care of details, organizing to the point that some thought compulsive. Mia, on the other hand, was soothing with a gentleness about her. Perfect for the welcoming role she was now playing. According to Lena, she was the family mediator. The way I saw it, she was the blanket on the family fire.

A 12-passenger white van pulled up near the snack bar and a group of laughing men and women tumbled out and bustled toward the table. They were all wearing royal blue tee shirts with a blue and gold logo. A few of them turned around and waved at the driver of the van who slowly pulled into a parking place shaded by a nearby tree.

"See you later Andy," called out one of the women waving a towel at him. I stretched around the group to see who she was talking to. I caught a glimpse of the back of his head and a military salute.

"He's not swimming?"

"Nope," said one of the men. "Not his thing."

"Are you all from the same swim team?" I asked.

"Not really," said the tallest man in the group. "Unless you consider our employer a swim team."

The six of them crowded in front of me attempting to get closer to the table. If I could, I would have moved back, but the concrete bench I sat on didn't budge. I looked up and six nervous faces stared back at me. They were like anxious kindergarteners, peering over each other's shoulders.

"Most of us work for the same healthcare organization, Mercy Health," said a skinny, blonde woman. I wondered how she would take to the cool lake water.

"And we all signed up for one of the fitness programs... swimming," said a slightly overweight balding man.

"The royal blue shirts are from your employer, Mercy Health?" I asked.

"Yes. Well, no. Some of us are healthcare workers and members of NSEU, National Service Employees Union. Others like Phil back there..."––a tall muscular Asian man waved his hand––"work for the union," she said pointing to the logo on her shirt.

"They are supporting you, too?" I asked.

"Yeah, both NSEU and Mercy Health are hoping we come out of this as competent, lightning fast, open water swimmers," said the thin blonde. The heads around her bobbed in agreement.

"Why is that?" I asked.

"We signed up for the swimming leg of a healthcare triathlon in two months and none of us know what we are supposed to do. We can swim but we haven't raced in open water before," said the balding man.

"I haven't raced at all," said a dark-haired man in the back.

"Well, you're in the right place," I said.

"Sharks. We want to be sharks," said a short chubby woman with purple and black hair.

Energy to burn. I smiled up at the group and signed them in. I pointed out the changing rooms and the spot on the beach where they needed to gather.

A cup of coffee was put down in front of me.

"I brought you something. You'll need it after dealing with that bunch."

"Well, that's nice of you." In front of me was a guy with a pony tail and tattoos running up and down his arms. "If you're swimming, I'll sign you in," I asked.

"Not me. I'm only the driver."

"For the union group?"

"Yep." He looked out at the lake. "Nice place. Gonna take some pictures and I think I'll start with you."

"Oh, please, no." A professional looking camera hung around his neck and while I was protesting he clicked off a few shots.

"Very nice. Cute, even. You're cute."

I started to blush.

"Well I'm going to check out the beach, then head back to the van and watch the proceedings from there. See ya," and he walked away.

From that point on there was a steady stream of swimmers

heading for my table. Most of the athletes attending today had never raced in open water. They were excited, but also apprehensive. It wouldn't take long before they realized that Lake Caldwell wasn't a pool. There was no black line running along the bottom or a pool edge nearby to grab if they became tired. Add to that the murkiness factor––they couldn't see the lake's bottom or the wildlife in the water with them.

"I can't believe I signed up to go out in the middle of a lake where I can't stand up," said a woman picking up her registration packet.

"Don't worry," I said. "There will be instructors with you the whole time. In fact, my sister is one of them."

About 50 swimmers had pre-registered and forty-five had signed in. Skittish athletes walked around, poured cups of coffee, grabbed bagels, and headed down to the water's edge chatting––or not––with the others.

Mia walked by and looked at the sign-ins. "The rest will show up. They always do," she said and continued down the slope.

"Excuse me," said a handsome man standing in front of my table. He was probably about 6'4" with thick dark eyebrows, brown eyes and a full head of brown hair. His oval face showed the signs of teenage acne. He was wearing a royal blue jacket.

"The rest of your group already arrived. Let me sign you in. Name?"

"No, I'm not here to swim. I'm looking for Shari."

"She's down by the lake, talking to the lifeguards."

The man walked away.

Lena was walking up the path when I called her over.

"Who's that?" I asked. "He is gorgeous."

"Shari's boyfriend, Duncan Sinclair, business agent for NSEU," she said.

"Yum. He has that dark mysterious air to him," I said.

Duncan ambled across the pebbly beach to the water's

edge where Shari was huddled with the supervisor for the East Bay Lifeguards. He stood slightly behind her. The supervisor looked up when he approached but then re-focused on Shari and they continued talking.

Duncan tapped her arm. She glanced at him and even from a distance, I saw her eyes widen in surprise. She held up one finger as if to say, 'give me a minute.' He tapped her arm again. This time she didn't look at him; just brushed his hand away. Duncan moved from the group and headed toward the edge of the beach. He found a picnic table near the NSEU group and sat down, arms crossed, legs stretched out. The skinny blonde came over and sat next to him. She saw Shari turn and look in their direction. With a big smile on her face, she leaned close to Duncan and put her hand on his arm. He didn't seem to notice, but Shari did. She jogged up to the two of them, looked at the blonde and said, "You can't participate in the clinic unless you can swim at least a half mile. This isn't for beginners."

"I'm not a beginner," the blonde said.

"I hope not, because I don't want to fish you out," said Shari. "Go sit with your group."

The blonde glared at Shari but she stood up and walked over to some swimmers sitting on the sand.

Shari stood there with her hands on her hips looking at Duncan when one of the volunteers called her name. She turned away and the boyfriend was forgotten, for now. She glanced quickly over to the blonde and then she switched on the megaphone.

"Welcome everybody. Let's get started."

Parkas were beginning to come off as the sun rose in the sky and heated up the beach. It took close to an hour to get through the on-land chalk talk. The participants listened carefully, took notes and asked questions. In the beginner's group, once the basics were covered, goggles and thermal caps were passed around and examined. An instructor demonstrated the fastest way to pull on a wetsuit for the majority of swimmers who would be wearing them.

I stood behind them listening.

"You know there's a right way and wrong way to enter and exit the water for a race," said the instructor.

"You got to be kidding," said a man sitting toward the back.

"We'll teach you how in the drills," the instructor said.

The other group had raced in open water before. They talked about acclimation to cold water, the pros and cons of a warm up swim and the best way to draft--swimming to the side or behind a lead swimmer while being pulled along by their wake--and how to pass another swimmer during a race. They finally got around to everyone's favorite topic-- panic--the anxiety and fear that flooded through their body during the first leg of a race.

"Being squeezed between other swimmers, getting kicked, maybe hit, is no fun," said a woman wearing a blue knit cap. "That's when I can't breathe."

The athletes nodded in agreement. I saw some concerned faces.

Mia moved from group to group, watching the clock, giving time cues. She stood next to me during the 'I can't breathe' discussion.

"No matter how many times I've watched the start at these open water swims, I never understood the in-water combat," I said.

Mia smiled. "I think some swimmers wear their bruises as a badge of honor." Then she called out. "Ten minutes more before the drills." She glanced back up the sloping beach toward the food table and waved. I turned. A man on a bike was heading for the back of the snack bar.

"Is that Mitch?"

"No. Someone in a blue shirt. Probably one of the union folks who is doing the biking leg of the triathlon," Mia said.

I looked back, but the man was gone.

The dryland talks finished up and the swimmers moved into the lake. For the next 45 minutes, I watched as they practiced swimming straight, not the easiest thing to accomplish when your face is in the water most of the time, rounding buoys and drafting off of each other. One group of eight packed together in the shape of a pyramid and swam elbow to elbow...an opportunity to duplicate the dreaded first leg. Another group stood close together on the shore and when the instructor blew a whistle, ran into the water up to their knees, threw themselves superman-style into the lake and paddled like crazy for about 60 seconds. After a brief rest, while they floated on their backs or treaded water, the swimmers turned around and swam back to shore. When their fingers touched the sandy bottom, they stood up and sprinted out, lifting their knees high, feet skimming the water top.

Finally, it was time for the open water swim. Using a megaphone, Shari gathered the swimmers together in the shallow water.

"Don't worry about your speed," said Shari. She described the course and which way to round the large yellow rectangular buoys out in the far reaches of the lake. "Concentrate on what you have learned." With a loud buzzer and a few cheers, the swimmers began to churn toward the first mark, arms flying and legs kicking. Drops of water sparkled like diamonds over the group.

One woman had an abrupt change of heart and came running back up the beach, followed by Lena. "You can do this," I heard my sister say. "I'll be right at your side." Lena grabbed her arm and before the retreating swimmer could refuse, she guided her back to the water's edge. Within minutes, both were swimming.

I stood in the hot sun and watched the swimmers, stretched out like beads on a thread, following each other to the first turning buoy, then the second and finally turn for the beach. It didn't take long before they ran out of the water, knees pumping, toward the banners now moving in a gentle breeze. Relief was the common emotion. There were high-fives and smiles all around. They had done it. They were happy and they were hungry. Wetsuits, caps and goggles were forgotten as the athletes hopped on tiptoes across the hot pebbly beach and headed to the snack table in the shade.

"You did great. Hope you enjoyed it," Shari said over and over. "I want to see all of you at one of the swims this season. You can do it. I saw that today. Thanks for coming."

From a shady spot by the food table, Duncan watched as Shari moved among the swimmers, congratulating them and answering their questions. Two women in royal blue tee shirts sat on the grass next to him eating strawberries and chocolate chip cookies. Within thirty minutes, the food table was picked clean, swim bags were packed and the swimmers were headed for the parking lot.

It had been three hours from start to finish.

"All done," Shari said to the volunteers cleaning up. Then, she walked over to Duncan. He put his arms around her and gave her a big hug. She gently pulled away from him, taking a step back. I watched them from the finish line while taking the stand up banners apart. Lena walked over to give me a hand.

"Wanna hear my take on their relationship?" I said.

"When did you become 'Dear Abby'?"

"I know what I know."

"Now you're psychic."

"Here is what I think is happening. Tall, dark and handsome Duncan likes tall, smart and very pretty Shari. Shari likes Duncan, but not as much as she used to. But she's not ready to pull the plug on the relationship, especially since skinny blonde is inching closer waiting to pick up the spoils."

"And you can tell all that from a hug?"

"Just watching. What kind of man is Duncan? He doesn't look much like an athlete."

"Duncan is an odd pick for her," said Lena. "He's intense,

like Shari. He's gorgeous, that's for sure. But, he doesn't have her pizazz, if you know what I mean. He's a stable guy and, from what she says, very responsible. But I think he's about as exciting as an old sponge. Dull, dull, dull. All he talks about is work...union stuff."

I glanced over at the couple again. "So he's good in bed? Eye candy? What? I didn't remember Shari being so shallow."

"He is a business agent specializing in healthcare. Known as being tough, really tough in negotiations. He came here from Michigan where he was involved in the 'right to work' campaign. You remember all that, don't you?"

I shook my head.

"Union busting is what I've heard Duncan call it. You know, you are right about their relationship. Shari mentioned to me that her feelings for him had changed. But she didn't know how to tell him. How'd you figure that out?

"I could tell from her lackluster response to his hug. There was no smile, no 'gee, I'm glad to see you' look. And then there was the way she brushed him off earlier when he tried to talk to her. But the skinny blonde has made her rethink things."

Lena and I walked up the beach one more time. Actually, Lena bounded up like a happy puppy. I followed behind. My thighs were aching...too much back and forth for me. Also, a little bit too much weight. After my husband disappeared, I put on 35 pounds. That doesn't look good on someone 5'5". I have been dieting but the scale isn't moving in the right direction fast enough. Sweat dripped down my sides. My shorts stuck to my legs. I held my shoulder-length brown hair off my neck. Duncan nodded at Lena as he walked toward the parking lot.

"Okay, Red, I'm off," he called to Shari. "I'll pick you up later for dinner." He stopped to chat with the other NSEU folks leaning against the van.

"A successful clinic, I would say. You've got this down to a science," I said.

"Well, I've run about five of them now. We've developed

a smooth well-oiled package that takes beginners and gives them the confidence to compete." Shari looked over at Lena. "I want to show you something. I've been scouting out locations for other clinics later on in the season."

"Really? I thought this beach was perfect."

"I'm always looking around. There's another beach, still in this park, but on the other side of the lake. Follow me over there."

"I hope there's shade," I said, fanning my face with a leftover agenda.

Shari got into her shiny black SUV. We headed for my dusty old tan Honda. Although the grounds surrounding the lake were empty when we arrived early morning, it was now close to noon and packed with families. Beachgoers covered the grass, sat at the picnic tables and played in the roped off swim area as up-tempo Mexican pop music blared from oversized radios. Outside the roped off swim area, paddle boarders struggled to stay upright on oversized surf boards.

We followed Shari out of the parking lot, up the winding road toward the park entrance, past more lots almost completely full. Turning right, we headed over a bridge that led to the campsites.

"I've never been this way," said Lena. She stuck her bare feet up on the dashboard and hung her right arm out the window.

The SUV turned right and we followed. Then Shari turned right again onto an unpaved dusty road. Three minutes later, she finally stopped next to a small chained off parking lot. A film of dust was still settling around her car as she jumped out and practically skipped down to the beach.

In front of us was an empty, protected lakefront. It was in a small cove that angled to the right. Two points of land on either side of the beach made it a perfect 'u' shape. Unless someone was on the beach or in the water directly in front, this little beauty of a lagoon was invisible, hidden by a forest of oaks.

Lena and I walked down to the still dark green water.

Shari was already wading knee deep into the lake.

"This is Caden's Corner. What do you think?" Shari asked looking over her shoulder at us.

"The proverbial secret spot. How did you find it?" Lena asked. "I've been coming to Lake Caldwell for years and didn't have an inkling this was here."

"The park rangers told me about it," said Shari. "There really wasn't a beach area until a few months ago. Trees and shrubs had to be pulled and they trucked in tons of sand. The result is this lovely, remote beach in the middle of a very busy regional park. It will take another few months until the bathrooms and changing area are finished, but the rangers said I could be the first to reserve it, if I wanted."

"And I'm sure you do," I said.

"Yes, I do. It's perfect." Shari walked back up the beach sat down on the sand. "This may be the best spot yet. I'm checking out another place later today in Marin, but it won't match..." Shari spread out her arms. "This."

Lena and I sat down next to her. I ran my fingers through the hot sand.

"My legs are burning. I'm going in the water." With that I kicked off my sandals and bunny-hopped to the water's edge. Lena and Shari followed. There was a joint audible sigh when we walked into the cool water.

Shari looked at Lena and then me. "I need to apologize to the both of you for my brother's behavior. I'm so sorry you had to see us fighting."

"What was that all about?" I asked. Lena grimaced but Shari answered.

"Money. It's always about money when it comes to my brother. Mia and Mitch will receive their inheritance next year when they turn 30. I'm not supposed to but I've been giving Mitch some cash...well, a lot of cash, each month. I learned that the estate account is about to be audited. I'm not sure how I will account for the funds that have been dispersed.

"He doesn't care. He's demanding his whole inheritance now. He's involved with a start-up tech company—or at least, that's what he tells me—and venture capitalists have turned down his request for funding."

"Does a year make that much of a difference? Can't you give him the money and get him off your back?" asked Lena.

"I did advance him a sizeable amount, $250,000 three months ago. It's gone. I don't know where it went. He won't give me any accounting of it. My parents worked hard for their money and I don't want it thrown away. They loved Mitch but they knew he could be impetuous when it came to handling money. He is a financial zero.

"You don't need to hear about my family woes," said Shari as she waded further into the water. The edges of her shorts were wet. She readjusted the camo hair tie to hold her long red mane off her neck. With one quick movement, she ducked down under the water and popped back up with a big smile on her face.

"Shari, did I ever tell you about Trisha's redheads?"

"Don't go there," I warned, lunging through the knee deep water toward Lena.

"Did you know that my sister had a thing for men with red hair?"

"Knock it off."

"How many were there? One?" she said splashing water at me. "Two?"

"Bitch," I said.

"Oh, that's right. There were four."

With that I tackled her and we both tumbled beneath the cool water.

Lena surfaced spitting water but still talking.

"And they all drove white Camaros."

I was laughing when I grabbed her around the waist and pushed her down in the shallow water. She grabbed my legs and I followed with a splash.

"I thought each one would be better than the last," I said finally standing up, water streaming down my face.

"But you were so wrong," laughed Lena. "And if that wasn't bad enough, last year she was crushing on a psycho. You heard about the guy that was killing open water swimmers?"

Shari nodded.

"Well," said Lena.

"Enough," I shouted.

"No," said Shari. "That was the crush?"

"No one else," said Lena.

I dove for her legs and knocked her over while Shari stood there watching us, grinning. From a distance, there was the muted sound of tires rolling along the dirt road. Then a pickup truck moved slowly into sight followed by a curtain of dust.

"It's Duncan," Lena said. "What is he doing here?"

Duncan pulled his pickup close to Shari's car. He slid down the window and smiled.

"Hey, Red," he called.

"I thought you were leaving," she asked. "How did you find us?" I haven't told anyone, even you, about this beach."

"Not that hard," he said. "Can you spare me a few minutes?"

"Must have forgot something," said Shari as she walked out of the lake, up the beach and over to the now dusty truck. I could hear Duncan's deep laugh when Shari stuck her head inside the cab and shook it like a wet dog. They said a few quiet words and then she stood back up.

"Guys, talk to you later."

"Well, that must be our clue to leave," I said to Lena. "I need to get home anyway and get ready for work."

"We have another clinic coming up, don't we?" Lena asked Shari as we headed for my car.

"Right, in two weeks. Same place. But with a little luck the location will change soon," she said. "Thanks for helping, Trish. It was good to see you again."

Lena walked around to the passenger's side of the car and

pulled open the door.

"You have a towel to sit on?"

"A little water might clean up your car seats," she said.

"You do have a towel, right? These seats are burning hot."

She reached into the backseat into her swim bag, pulled out three towels and waved them around like flags.

"Just get in," I said.

She dropped one towel on her seat and one on mine. She threw me the third one.

"You'll need this. The steering wheel has probably reached its melting point."

On any normal ride home after an open water swim, Lena would fall asleep. Instead, she was looking out the window as we cruised down the freeway heading for San Rafael. "I can guarantee you this new beach will be a favorite open water swim spot," she said. "Something wrong?" She looked over at me. "You are quiet even for you."

"No. Just thinking."

"How come you aren't listening to the baseball game?"

"Because it's a night game. I'm working. Remember?" I stared at the cars in front of me. "How did Duncan know about Caden's Corner?"

"Probably Shari told him," said Lena, closing her eyes and relaxing back into the seat.

"That's not what she said. Caden's Corner is a *big* secret. I think we were the first she showed it to."

"So what?"

"The men in Shari's life are strange," I said, adjusting the sun visor to keep the glare out of my eyes. "Her boyfriend shows up unexpected. That's not such a big deal. But then there's her hothead brother who spits nails every time she says 'no' to him."

"Sister, you think too much. And, by the way, thanks for driving."

"All part of the Big Sister Care Program." I glanced at Lena. Her eyes were closed but she was smiling. "You take good care of me."

It was my turn to smile. The car was quiet except for the highway noises around us.

"If I were Shari––,"

"You're not. This is none of your business."

"Well, Shari did ask for help. Just saying…if someone threatened me, I'd take it seriously."

CHAPTER 2

By the time we reached home, I had about an hour to shower, change into my work clothes and drive to the nearest freeway exit to meet my carpool. My co-workers were only working a four-hour shift, so I'd be taking a a bus home after the game. We had to clock in by 4 p.m. at AT&T Park, a gem of a ball-park anchored on the edge of San Francisco Bay. My job with the San Francisco Giants was part-time, but it gave me the first steady income I'd had in almost two years. Unfortunately, it was seasonal. By the end of September––maybe October if the Giants made it to the post-season––I would be out of work. It was completely different from my office-bound job in Colorado. But I liked the interaction with the fans and being in constant motion for close to five hours.

We reached the employee parking lot behind the ballpark in about an hour. "Are we going to be late," I asked the park-ing attendant from the back seat of the car.

"You have plenty time," said the small Asian woman who took our money and pointed the way to a long row of parked cars. We found a spot and jogged through two connecting lots beginning to fill up with fans, around the back of the ballpark, past the Marina Gate, though security, and down the high-ceil-ing tunnel until finally we reached the bank of time clocks.

My work assignment had me checking tickets at the main entrance, the Willie Mays Gate. This was the biggest and busiest gate in the ballpark. Crowds already filled the huge sidewalk plaza with its 24 towering palm trees. One of the pre-game network television sports show was being broadcast from the plaza and there were fans crowded around the sides and back of the set waving black and orange Authentic Fan placards.

Tonight's game was against the Arizona Diamondbacks and the gates would open at 5:05 p.m., about ten minutes from now.

"Will you look at that fog hanging at the top of the hill," said an older ticket scanner with short grey hair, eyes focused over the heads of the fans.

"It will be down here soon enough," said another.

"Gonna zip up my jacket now," said the scanner standing next to me. "I can already feel the wind picking up."

Weather and the best way to dress for it was always an important topic of conversation since we spent hours outside and had to keep warm. I was listening to what these veteran employees had to say when I heard my name.

"Trisha. Hey Trisha."

I looked around but only saw the crowd in orange and black packed in front of the gate. There were so many people. They stretched back to the street. It was hard to pick out a single face. I stood on my toes and tried to locate the voice.

"No, right here. Here, look here."

Standing with his faced pressed against the tall black gate was Jon Angel, a man I'd met last year when I was working at Fort Mason, a sprawling San Francisco Bay waterfront complex that hosts art events, drama, ballet, and even gem shows.

"Jon? Hey, good to see you."

The National Park Service security guard smiled. He put both hands up on the gate and peered through at me. "I'm going to a game," he said, shifting his weight from one foot to another. He waved a bright orange, "We're Number 1" foam finger above his head.

"I can see that," I said.

"I wondered what happened to you," he said. "Looks like

you were right all along about the man who died last year. If only you hadn't waited so long to go to the police."

I could feel my face flush. I'd been fired from a temporary job at Fort Mason last year when I wouldn't––couldn't––stop asking questions about the death of an elite open water swimmer. Jon was the security officer who took away my office key and escorted me out of the building.

Next to me, another ticket scanner overheard part of the conversation.

"Police? Want me to call security?" he said with a smile. It was loud enough for the other workers to chime in. "Hey don't bother Trisha, we'll come after you." There was a lot of laughter behind me.

My supervisor called to me. "Trisha, the crime stopper. I knew it all along. You're an undercover cop."

"Interesting bunch that you work with," Jon said. The crowds behind him were getting louder. One of the security guards walked by talking into his radio. "Five minutes," he said. The gates were about to open.

"Can't talk anymore. Have to get ready to work. Where are you sitting?"

He showed me his tickets, View Box, Section 315.

"I love the View. You can see everything, the whole field, the boats in McCovey Cove, even across the Bay to Oakland. I'll stop by if I can," I said moving away from the gate.

He waved and disappeared toward the back of the crowd.

Will not happen, I said to myself. I liked Jon. He had been a steady, protective, force who examined everything without judgment. But, even a year later, I was still humiliated when I thought of him walking me to my car and waiting for me to drive off the property.

As the towering black gates were pulled open in front of me and the other ticket scanners, the crowd erupted in cheers. From then on, it was a constant, unending stream of baseball fans anxious to get in. When fans come this early, they're here to watch batting practice. Maybe snag a ball or an autograph.

"Thank you. Enjoy the game," I said over and over as I checked their tickets and answered questions about seat location, garlic fries and the World Series trophies display.

Coming toward my gate was a guy wearing a full orange body stocking that even covered his face.

"Can you see in that?" I asked.

"I live in an orange-colored world," he said pushing past me and high fiving the two guys with him.

As the crowd poured by like a river rushing downstream, I could feel my phone vibrate in my back pocket. It stopped and started again. Whoever it was would have to wait.

It was three hours later when I checked my cell. There were two messages from Lena and a text from her that said, 'CALL ME' in all caps. The phone messages were about Shari. Lena's voice went from conversational to concerned with each message.

Message 1. "Mia called. She wanted to know if Shari mentioned where she was going after the clinic. She never came home this afternoon. Duncan said we were probably the last ones to see her. He was supposed to pick her up at 6 p.m., but she wasn't at the condo."

Message 2. "Another call from Mia. Her anxiety level is spiking. She's upset and getting me upset. She can't reach Shari by cell phone or text. Wasn't she going to check out a beach in Marin? Duncan's on the other line. Got to go."

There was one more text waiting for me when I finished my shift and was walking out of the ballpark to catch the streetcar that would take me to the Marin bus stop.

"Still no Shari. Mia & I at her condo. Come here ASAP."

CHAPTER 3

Shari's condo was about a mile from AT&T Park...a long walk after standing on concrete for the last six hours. Although it was almost 11 p.m. and the sky was dark, people were still leaving the ballpark and stopping into bars and restaurants before they headed for home.

Lena had mentioned that Shari spent millions for her South of Market Street condo between the San Francisco Bay Bridge and the stadium. I turned a corner on King Street and followed the directions Lena had sent. In 15 minutes, I walked into a dark street with a single patch of white light spilling onto the sidewalk from the lobby of Shari's building. I walked up to the glass front door and pushed it open. Duncan was pacing back and forth by the elevator.

"Here, here, come in," he said. "I've been waiting for you." Then he looked at me. His eyes scanned my clothes. "What are you wearing?"

"My work clothes." I guess I did look a little odd if someone didn't know that I worked for the Giants. But the Guest Services San Francisco Giants logo on my black stadium jacket and my employee badge hanging on a lanyard around my neck should have been a clue.

"Is she back?"

"No."

"Did she call?"

"No."

"Did anyone talk to Mitch?"

"No."

"I was supposed to pick her up at 6. She wasn't here. She hasn't answered her phone. She's not responding to my texts, nothing. That's not like her. She always calls when she is going to be late or can't make it."

"From what I know, Shari is a very responsible woman. Maybe she had car trouble or lost her phone or..."

He didn't respond. We stood by the elevator waiting for the door to open. I watched Duncan's distorted image in the reflection of the door. He gazed at his feet, then over his shoulder, then back at his feet. He let out a sigh when the elevator opened. The ride up to the fifth floor was in complete silence. I'm not sure either of us took a breath. It wasn't much better in Shari's apartment. Mia was pacing back and forth. Lena was sitting on a low modern coach that looked extremely uncomfortable.

"Glad you're here," Lena said.

"Anything?" asked Duncan.

"No," Lena and Mia said in unison.

I unzipped my work parka and sat down on the edge of couch next to Lena. I took her hand which was trembling. I hated to see her upset. I always did. She leaned into me like she used to as a little girl.

I glanced around the room. Shari's apartment was metallic cool. Brushed metal tables, stark low chairs. No colors really, just black and white and hard wood floors. Not my taste, too austere. But there was a knockout view of the Bay Bridge lit up with piercing 25,000 white LEDs off the deck of her living room. The 1.7-mile workhouse of a bridge was a pulsating light sculpture stretching from the shores of San Francisco to the East Bay.

"Look at this," I said to Lena trying to distract her from the disappearance of her friend. I walked over to the sliding glass doors leading to the deck. I opened them and walked out on the deck. Lena followed. "If the lights were still on, you could see the ballpark, including the seagulls flying around."

Lena slid the glass door shut behind her.

"Are you okay?" I asked.

She nodded and a surge of relief flowed through me. My shoulders relaxed and I took a deep breath. "You know she might not be missing. Maybe she bought herself a little me time."

"What do you mean?" asked Lena.

"You mentioned how busy she is. Maybe she's stressed, too and needed to get away."

"You may be right. These days when I do get a chance to talk to her she tells me how much pressure she is under. From work, the open water clinics, her brother––who is driving her crazy––and then there is Duncan, the potential ex-boyfriend. But why wouldn't she let someone know that she is okay?"

I shrugged. "I can't answer that one."

Lena had visibly calmed down. She turned her back to the night time view and stared through the sliding glass doors, her eyes following Mia as she walked back and forth.

"I can't tell you how often she said, 'That's it. That's all I can take. Tomorrow I am going to get in my car and drive, as far away from here as I can and not tell a soul.' I never expected her to act on it, that's all."

"That's what Dad did," I said. Lena winced.

"Sorry. Didn't mean to bring it up. But it is similar."

"Do you think she'll show up?" she asked.

Something told me she wouldn't, but I wasn't about to say that to Lena.

"I do."

"Let's go back in and reassure these people as best we can. Then let's go home. I'm tired and my feet hurt. It was a really long game, extra innings..."

"Please don't talk about baseball right now," said Lena

sliding open the glass door on the deck.

Mia and Duncan were as we left them, Mia pacing and Duncan leaning against the wall, arms crossed, eyes almost closed.

"I've tried to get a hold of my brother, but he's not responding. Not that he ever does," said Mia.

"Did you ever think that Shari might be taking a––how do I put this––a timeout?" I asked.

"From what?" asked Mia.

"From all of this. From work. From the clinics. Maybe from all of us. Lena says she is under a lot of pressure. Maybe she is needs a break."

"Not Shari," said Duncan. "She thrives under the pressure. You know that, Lena. Right? She wants more to do, not less."

Mia stopped pacing.

"Do you think I pressure her? I'd never do anything like that. At all. All I do is try and help her. I'm the good sibling, not like my brother."

"My advice, for what it's worth, is let's sleep on it. She'll be here tomorrow. Maybe she lost her phone or her car broke down. There are lots of possibilities. But if she's not, call the police and report her missing," I said.

Lena and I walked toward the door.

"I'm staying here tonight," said Mia.

"What if Shari decides to come by your house," said Duncan. "Won't she wonder where you are?"

"Maybe. So I should go home? Stay here? Oh, I don't know what to do."

Duncan walked over and patted Mia on the shoulder, then walked into the kitchen.

"We're going to leave," I said to no one in particular. Then, I opened the door and Lena and I almost ran through, heading for the elevator.

"I bet neither of them sleep tonight," I said.

We walked into the elevator, the door closing behind us.

"So where did you park?"

"Are you going to chip in for gas?"

"You want me to chip in for gas?"

"Why not?"

"I can't believe it. After all the time I've driven you to open water swim after open water swim. I pay for gas, bridge tolls, park entrance fees parking and...and...I know there's more."

"Blah, blah, blah," said Lena. The elevator stopped at the first floor and she quickly walked out in front of me. "Don't forget you've been living with me almost free of charge for the past year."

She pushed open the glass door in the lobby and moved into the shadows of the dark street. A warm flush crept up my neck and flooded across my cheeks.

"Where did that come from?"

The sidewalk was dimly lit by the amber light of a street lamp halfway down the block. We were walking side by side––each of us trying to move faster than the other, trying to get ahead––something we used to do as kids. Lena's car was at the end of the block.

"Lena? Lena. Talk to me. What's wrong? You asked me to move in, remember?" I said, climbing into the passenger's seat.

Silence on my sister's part.

"Do you want me to leave? I can do that. I'm earning some money now. Tell me, do you want me to move?"

Lena started the car and we headed for The Embarcadero, the picturesque roadway that skirts San Francisco Bay. We drove across the streetcar tracks and passed under the San Francisco Bay Bridge. I could see its dancing, sparkling lights through the car's side mirror. Lena was silent.

"Do you?"

Lena's spare bedroom in her Marin County became my home after my husband disappeared. I looked for him. I really did. I contacted the police, his employer, his gym, his brother on the East Coast, and checked his credit card statements. After six months, I gave up. I didn't know what else to do. It was a frustrating mystery I couldn't solve. My only clue was from the brother. "He doesn't want to be found." I didn't know what happened, how my marriage fell apart under my nose and why the men in my life always seemed to leave.

By then, I'd stopped going to work, lost my job, collected at least one DUI and was sinking into a deeper and deeper financial hole. I'd stand by the kitchen sink in the dark and eat and eat and eat. I couldn't sit down at the table since it was covered with past due bills. At one point, I stared into the mirror and started to laugh. My life had become a cliché; something you see on reality tv. Those were terrible times, but now, I was slowly getting back on my feet, thanks to my sister's generosity. I had started to diet and I was trying to exercise.. The truth be told; I really didn't have enough money put aside to move out. Not just yet.

"I'm sorry. That was tactless, even for me. Forget about it," she said. "This Shari thing has stressed me out."

"You sure that's all?"

"Positive."

"Really? That's it?"

"Really." She let out a sigh and while focusing on the road ahead, punched me in the arm.

Maybe Shari's disappearance had rattled her. Or I had become a financial burden. And she didn't want to say. Did she need her privacy? Her boyfriend, the Emergency Room doc, Terrel Robinson was a semi-permanent guest. And her house wasn't that big. This was giving me a headache. I planned to hash it out with her tomorrow.

We rode in silence for a while until we came to the Golden Gate Bridge. Heavy fog draped over the tops of the South and North Tower. It drifted down over the suspension cables like a filmy curtain. The flickering navigation lights on Alcatraz to my right and the Pt. Bonita lighthouse, at the end of the Marin headlands overlooking the Pacific Ocean on my left, blinked on and off, patiently, but insistently. Below, San Francisco Bay was the color of murky charcoal.

"Where do you think Mitch is?" I asked.

"He's never around when you want him, according to Shari."

"Doesn't sound like she wanted him around," I said.

"I don't know who would. We hung out together back in the day."

"You mentioned you two went out a few times."

"The most self-centered guy I ever met. His one good quality was his affection for his twin, Mia. Other than that, he was a jerk." Lena pushed her foot down on the accelerator and we flew off the bridge on to Highway 101 heading for the Robin Williams tunnel and San Rafael.

CHAPTER 4

It was past 1 am when I fell into bed, but I was up, wide awake around 7 am. My mind was working overtime. Money never was a concern for Lena before. Why now? And then there was Shari. And her missing brother, Mitch. My gut said something was wrong. I headed down the hall to the kitchen. A soft chime came from Lena's phone sitting on the table. A text from Mia popped up on the dark screen.

"Shari's found. Call me. Now."

I was thrilled. Lena would be relieved. I couldn't wait to tell her. I walked into my sister's bedroom. "Wake up," I said. Her head was under the pillow, one arm hung off the side of the bed, one leg was on top of the covers. Next to her was her boyfriend, Dr. T as we both called him. He was longer than the bed and his brown feet were barely covered. T was the product of a black father and a white mother. With his long lanky frame, his professional interest in classic cars, and his passion for basketball, no one guessed he was an emergency room doctor in San Francisco. But he was whip smart and the go-to guy for tough medical cases.

"What? What's happening?" Lena said eyes still closed.

Dr. T sat up. "This had better be good. I finally have no call for 48 hours and you wake me up at...at? What time is it anyway?"

"Good news. Text from Mia about Shari. Sounds like she's back."

Lena's eyes popped open and she sat straight up, throwing the covers to the floor.

"She's home?" asked Lena.

"I don't know. Call Mia," I said.

"Make that call somewhere else, okay?" said Dr. T, his voice muffled by the covers.

Lena grabbed the phone and as we walked out of the bedroom back to the kitchen, she punched in the phone number. I could hear a wail when Mia answered the phone. There was silence as my sister listened, tried to ask questions, but was cut off again and again. Then, Lena hung up and looked at me, tears in her eyes.

"What?" I asked. "Where is she? What happened?"

"Not good. Not good at all. Shari is dead."

CHAPTER 5

"What happened?"

"Some kind of awful accident, I think. Her body was found at China Camp. Here in Marin. Rangers found her on the edge of San Pablo Bay," Lena said.

"She drowned?"

"I guess. I don't know. Mia was almost incoherent. Would you call her back? Maybe you can understand her."

The call went to voice mail. "Mia, this is Trisha, Lena's sister. Please call us back as soon as you can." I looked at Lena who was pacing around the kitchen. "What exactly did she say to you?"

"Mia was so upset. It was hard to follow. She said that the Marin County Sheriff's Department had telephoned. And then something about Marin County rangers working with the sheriff's office. She mentioned the location of her body––by the water at China Camp. They thought it could be a drowning. She was crying so much I could barely understand her. They took her body to Napa."

"Napa?"

"That's what she said."

"Why in Napa? What's in Napa?"

"Stop asking me questions. I don't know."

"Well I am going to find out." I picked up Lena's phone,

but she grabbed it out of my hands. "No," my sister said. "I'm going to call Mia again."

I left the kitchen while Lena repeatedly hit redial and left message after message.

"Text her," I called out as I walked into my small bedroom. My phone was on the dresser where I left it when I came home from work last night. I looked through my contacts and found the name of a friend who was a dispatcher for the Marin County Sheriff's Department. I recognized her voice immediately when she answered the phone.

"Carmela, this is Trisha Carson. Remember we met at the hair salon in San Rafael a few months ago? We talked about your job and you had heard that I helped solve the death of that swimmer?"

"Trisha, this is an emergency line."

"I know. But this is an emergency."

Dr. T was in the kitchen talking softly with Lena and holding her hand when I came back.

"Where you able to reach Mia?" I asked.

"No. She didn't pick up or answer the texts. I feel like my head is about to explode. I mean, we just saw her yesterday. From early morning to early afternoon, we were all together."

"I have a little more information," I said. "I called a friend at the Sheriff's office." I paused. Both Dr. T and Lena stared at me.

"And?" said Lena.

"Right before dawn, a runner was on the hill above China Camp Village. He saw a body on the beach, face down, right along the tideline, so he called the Sheriff's Department. Emergency personnel came out. Rangers from the park were there. Deputies couldn't move the body until someone from the Coroner's office showed up. He was the one that made the decision to send the body to the Coroner's office in Napa."

"Why Napa? Why couldn't her body stay here in Marin?"

I didn't want to say anything else, but I had to. "I asked the same question to my dispatcher friend. According to her, bodies are sent to Napa when there is something suspicious about the death."

"Are you saying what I think you're saying," said Dr. T.

"Yes. They are not sure that Shari died of natural causes."

"Meaning, she was killed?" asked Lena in complete disbelief.

"It's not definite. My friend couldn't...maybe, wouldn't... tell me anymore than that."

"And they are definite it's Shari?" Lena asked again, looking for a way around the inevitable.

"Yes."

"T, how do they know?"

Dr. T with his years of emergency room experience at a busy San Francisco hospital had seen it all and often talked about funny, unusual and even tragic cases. But now he seemed reluctant to say anything. He started slowly.

"If she drowned like Mia thinks and her body was in the water less than 24 hours, it wouldn't have deteriorated..."

"Don't call her an 'it.' She isn't...wasn't...an it. Her name is Shari," said Lena.

Dr. T started again, speaking quietly, calmly. "Shari's body wouldn't have deteriorated very much. They could take her fingerprints and run them through their computer. Her DMV records would have popped up. Or she could have had some id, her driver's license, maybe, tucked in a pocket."

"When we were at Lake Caldwell, she said that she was checking out sites for future clinics. And that she was going to visit a place in Marin," I said. "Do you think the place she was checking out in Marin was China Camp?" I asked. I stood up and walked over to the sink. I turned on the tap and watched the cool water run, circle around the drain and disappear.

Lena thought for a moment.

"We never talked about that location for a clinic. We did discuss McNears Beach right around the point from China Camp. McNears is a county beach and has everything that the clinic would need: parking, bathrooms, changing areas, wide grassy lawn. It's used for swim events. But the water's cold and murky, not the most inviting spot for new open water swimmers. China Camp couldn't be much different."

"But since it is a mixture of salt water from the Pacific and fresh water from the melting snow packs in the Sierras, the swimmers would be more buoyant. They'd like that, right? Shari wouldn't go at night to check it out, would she?"

Lena started to answer, but I cut her off.

"And if she did, she certainly wouldn't go into the water. She knows better than to swim by herself," I said to Lena.

"What does it matter, now? My friend, my longtime friend, is dead." Lena stood up and Dr. T gave her a hug. She moved quietly out of the kitchen, down the hall.

T took her spot at the table.

"T, tell me about drowning?"

"Now? Right now?"

"What happens when you drown?"

"Do we have to have this discussion so early in the morning? The woman is deceased. Learning about drowning won't bring her back."

"Please."

"Okay. First, the Hollywood take on drowning when someone thrashes around is untrue. Most people slip quietly below the surface and that's it. If they have the presence of mind to keep their mouth shut in seconds their chest gets tighter and tighter. Desperate to take a breath, they open their mouth and the lungs fill up with water. It becomes harder for the body to transfer oxygen into the bloodstream. Water is forced into the sinuses. Oxygen level falls. In a few minutes, he or she is unconscious. The heart stops soon after." Dr. T stared at me. "That is basically it."

"What a horrible way to die."

"Yes. It is. You okay?" he asked. T's knees bumped against the table as he stood up, and started to leave the kitchen.

"Trisha, you have a pretty good sixth sense when it comes to these things. What do you think happened?"

"I don't know. We left Shari yesterday talking to Duncan, her boyfriend. She was going to check out a beach, then go home and out to dinner with him. I can't say how she ended up dead at the water's edge 70 miles from where we left her. Maybe Duncan can help. She might have said something to him."

"You think he's involved?" asked Dr. T.

"If I was going to call out anyone, it wouldn't be Duncan. It would be her brother, Mitch. I don't know if he is behind this, but I'm going to find out."

CHAPTER 6

Later that day, I stood at the living room window and saw Lena coast into the driveway with Mia sitting in the passenger's seat wearing dark glasses. I could only imagine what she was feeling. I was glad I wasn't her. She and Mia had driven north to Napa, home to rolling vineyards and charming wine tasting rooms, to identify the body.

A local news feed appeared on the blank screen of my cellphone and a short piece on a woman's body found at China Camp popped up. They didn't mention Shari by name, but it had to be her. I couldn't believe the press had the story already. It was only a matter of time before they released the name and tracked Mia down for an interview.

The two women trudged wearily through the front door, not talking. Mia tumbled onto the couch and covered her face with her hands.

I glanced at Lena and whispered. "What happened?"

Mia answered. "They have to do an autopsy to come up with a definite cause of death. And autopsies take time. Weeks, sometimes."

"Couldn't they do that here in Marin?" I asked.

"Seems they have so few reasons to perform an autopsy locally, they don't do it at all. They outsource, so to speak, to Napa and their brand new facility."

"I saw the body," said Mia. Her hands started to shake. "It was Shari. Beautiful. She was beautiful. Her skin was white as paper next to her long red hair. I expected her eyes to open and she would sit up. But..."

"Did they say that she drowned?" I asked.

Mia began to cry quietly. "That seems to be part of what happened. Her body was found at the water's edge and her lungs were full of water."

"Her face and upper torso were on the sand; her legs were in the Bay. The tide was going out. So they think she might have washed up on the beach," Lena continued.

"You said part of what happened? What else did they tell you?"

Lena walked over and sat by her dead friend's sister. She draped an arm around her shoulder and Mia started to sob. "There were marks on her neck."

"What kind of marks?" I asked.

Lena took a deep breath and said, "There is bruising around her neck and a huge bump on the back of her head."

"I saw her hands," said Mia. "The coroner said there was debris under her nails, like she was clawing at the sand."

"Like beach sand. Could they tell where it came from?"

"They are checking it out," said Lena.

"Sounds like Shari was in a fight or some type of struggle and held under water until she died," I said. "So this wasn't an accident. She was really killed."

"It gets worse," Lena said. "The deputy had this plastic bag. Inside was Shari's camouflage hair tie. It was still damp. Remember, yesterday, I told her it wasn't her style."

I nodded. "But, I'd expect the sheriff's office to have her clothes and things." I stopped. "What exactly was she wearing?"

"She had on a swim suit under the shorts and tee shirt. But that's not the important part," said Lena. "When they turned Shari over at China Camp, when they found her...that tie...the one Duncan gave her...was stuffed in her mouth."

CHAPTER 7

No one spoke. The words hung in the air until their weight became too much. They drifted down pressing against my shoulders. I began to sway under the pressure almost losing my balance. I grabbed hold of the doorframe. So Shari was murdered at China Camp, but why and by who? I kept thinking of Mitch, her brother. He had threatened her the last time they talked and now was nowhere to be found. He wanted money and Shari wasn't going to give it to him. Was he angry enough to kill for it? And if it wasn't him, who was it?

My heart went out to Mia. And to Lena. I remembered Shari as a 10-year-old sitting at the side of a swimming pool with my sister, both of them kicking their legs in the water and giggling. She was all skinny arms and legs and red hair pulled back in a ponytail. What a sad ending.

I suggested that Mia stay at our house for the night. She could take my room. I'd sleep on the couch. Her face was ashen; her stare blank. She nodded.

"Why don't you give me your keys? I'll drive by your apartment and pick up some clothes. Anything else you might want?"

She looked over at me like she was seeing me for the first time.

"No, just something to sleep in and maybe a clean blouse

and some underwear. Thank you for doing this." She reached into her purse and pulled out a key ring with the letter 'M" on a dangling charm. It was loaded down with six keys.

"See these two keys, the ones with the American flags on them, they are to my house. The rest are for Shari's apartment and Mitch's apartment. Oh, in my bedroom, in the top drawer of my computer desk, there's an old cellphone of mine. Would you bring it back here? It might have more contact information of our relatives around the country. I need to call and tell them about..." Her voice faltered. "Tell them about Shari."

Her eyes filled up with tears again.

"I'm happy to do that," I said, taking the keys and slipping them into my pocket.

"I'll leave now." I grabbed my backpack and walked out to the car. I reached into my pocket and felt Mia's bulky key ring. I ran my thumb over the "M" and then over each of the other keys.

Mia lived in the Marina District of San Francisco. I've called it Yuppieville for as long as I can remember. Although the actual houses have changed very little since the 1920's, the families and older residents fled after the 1989 earthquake. Moving in behind them were the 'marina people", trendy 20-somethings who liked to jog around the Marina Green, a 74-acre park that sits on the edge of San Francisco Bay. I'd seen Chestnut Street, the main shopping area, change over the years. And I'm not sure it was for the better.

While most of San Francisco thrives on diversity, the Marina has stayed white. And now it was for the rich, young, entitled. Mia fit that profile. According to Lena, her family indulged all three of their children. She easily could afford the $5 million price tag on a pleasant two-story home on Scott

Street. The flat front facade of her home and the empty, wide sidewalk were not unappealing in an old time family neighborhood kind of way.

Standing at her doorway, fumbling with her keys, I wondered if a neighbor might stop and question me. It didn't happen. There wasn't a soul outside, but me.

The interior of Mia's home was stylish and comfortable, what you might expect from an interior decorator. The furniture had the look of an upscale coastal cottage, with bright yellows, blues and stark whites. A telescope sat by the big picture window, although I'm not sure what she could see at this angle. San Francisco Bay and the Golden Gate Bridge were hidden behind the houses and apartment buildings across the street. I admit I was jealous. This was nothing like the milk carton crates and brick-and-board book shelves of my first apartment.

I found a cloth shopping bag imprinted with the local public radio logo and filled it with Mia's clothes. The computer room was off her bedroom. On the shelf of a bookcase were photos of her family and then pictures of the three siblings. Mia and Mitch looked like a close-knit pair. Shari was off to the side or in the background.

The old cell phone was just where Mia said it would be, in the drawer by the computer. It felt peculiar to be in some else's home, especially when they weren't there. I was about to turn and leave when her phone rang. Probably one of the few landlines left in the Marina. The caller ID said MG. Maybe Mitch was finally getting in touch. I stared at the phone. Why not? Mitch needed to know where Mia was and what happened to his older sister.

I picked up the receiver and coughed.

"You sick?"

Before I had time to answer, the caller continued.

"Saw that you're home," said the reedy male voice. "Glad that the bitch has left the planet, aren't you?"

"Hello?" I said.

The line went dead.

I listened to the dial tone for a few seconds before I put the receiver down. That had to be Mitch. Mia had been trying to reach him. She must have left a message about Shari. Families all have their problems. Certainly mine did. But to call his sister––who just died––a bitch was incomprehensible.

I headed for the front door, then stopped abruptly. How did Mitch know someone was in the house? He must be able to see Mia's home from where ever he was. Maybe he had a telescope like his twin. I shuddered. This family was frightening.

I pulled out the keys from my pocket ready to lock up the house. Besides Mia's patriotic house keys, there were four more keys. Two were decorated with dolphins swimming through blue water and the others had a red and gold Forty-Niner logo on them. They must be Shari's and Mitch's spares. I looked at each key for a second; turned them over in my hand. Then stopped. I had another place to visit before I drove back home.

CHAPTER 8

I headed back to the other side of the city to Shari's condo. I decided to drive along the Embarcadero, the route Lena and I took home last night. I bypassed Fisherman's Wharf and Pier 39––San Francisco tourist meccas––by taking Bay Street and then headed past the piers and wharfs jutting into the water. A light, drippy fog hovered over the long low buildings.

Although the morning commute had come and gone, San Francisco workers were still streaming off the ferries that docked at the historic nineteenth-century Ferry Building. They hurried through the restored grey arcades, past the Farmer's Market out to the Embarcadero. I managed not to hit anyone as they ignored the traffic lights and hopscotched their way across the street, clutching their jackets to their necks to ward off the dampness.

I was soon driving under the Bay Bridge. I'm not sure why I wanted to visit Shari's condo when no one was around. I only knew I had to be there. Off to my left was an enormous sculpture called Cupid's Span. Sitting on the edge of San Francisco Bay, the large sculpture was of a 60-foot bow belonging to the chubby little son of Venus and a vertical arrow, piercing the ground below. It sliced into a small waterfront park. I barely saw the tourists strolling around the structure snapping photos. I was thinking about Shari and what I might find in her condo.

The glass door entrance with its endless frosted suns and angular rays took me back to the architectural designs of the 1920s. The pattern of etched sun and rays was mimicked in the trim around the elevator. I hadn't noticed any of this last night when the elevator carried Duncan and me to Shari's condo.

The heavily-carpeted hallway that led to her apartment was quiet. Everyone was either at work or snug inside waiting for the sun to burn off the mid-morning fog. I knocked on her door. Nothing. Not surprising, but you never know. As I pulled out the keys, I created a story about who I was and why I was there, if a neighbor decided to appear. But I didn't have to bother. No one approached and the little noise that I did make was sucked into the dense carpeting in the hallway.

I opened the door and walked in. The living room was still. Even the noise from the street below was muffled. Less than 24 hours ago I stood in this same spot, sure that Shari would turn up. How wrong I was.

The fantastic view was still there, but a chilly stillness spread through each room. If someone killed Shari, as the coroner suggested, there might be something in the condo that would lead to her murderer.

I say 'us' since my last experience turned out to be dangerous, very dangerous. My sister and Dr. T made me promise to stay out of other people's business. Hard to do with a personality like mine. I call myself inquisitive; Lena calls me nosey, even pushy. No one understands me and my relationship with questions, puzzles really. I can't get enough of them. I like to examine things and see what happens. I start out being analytical, professional...or so I'd like to think. At some point, the cool scientific approach goes out the window. The questions are tantalizing. And I have to...have to...find the answers.

Anyway, the next part of the promise had me contacting

the police when necessary. I could...would...do that. Maybe.

Shari, unlike me, was a neat freak and an obsessive organizer. I opened a kitchen cupboard. Cereal boxes were lined up all facing the same way. Cans on the next shelf were divided into food groups. Nothing strange there. But she took it one step further: they were in alphabetical order. Baked beans were in the front; canned tomatoes were in the back of the shelf. The over-the-top order made me shudder and I quickly closed the cupboard.

There were no loose pieces of paper on the counter; no envelopes with notes written on the back. Her bedroom had that same austere look. Nothing was on top of her dresser, but a photo of Duncan, that was signed 'To Red, the girl of my dreams, D."

I couldn't help myself. I walked over to her closet and slid back the mirrored glass doors. Just as I thought. Her clothes were organized by type: blouses, skirts, pants, dresses. Then by color. Within each color, they were grouped by closings; buttons, zippers, hooks and eyes. It goes without saying that all hangers were facing the same way.

What puzzled me were her shoeboxes. Yes, they went by shoe type: sport, flats, work, heels, really high heels but they all had numbers on them that had nothing to do with the shoe size. I couldn't figure out what the numbers meant. I glanced at the rows of boxes so perfectly lined up. This was too good to pass up. All I needed was a quick look.

I picked up a pale green shoebox marked '4' and took the lid off, expecting to see a pair of brown leather flats. That was the description on the outside. But the description didn't match what I had in front of me. These weren't shoes. Not even close. They were copies of photographs from a desktop printer; erotic pictures of our girl, Shari. I wouldn't call them porn, exactly, but they were heading in that direction.

There she was naked; her long red hair draped across her body covering one breast, while she seemed to be massaging the other one. Her eyes were closed. In the next photo, that massaging hand had dropped to her stomach; then in the next, it was buried in her pubic hair. Now, her eyes were wide open staring at the camera.

The next photo was the most interesting. Shari was nude, sitting on a bed, her head thrown back, resting against the chest of a man. His arms were draped over her shoulders and were lost under the fall of her red hair. I couldn't see his face and could barely see his hands, but they probably rested on her breasts.

In the next photo, the man had his back to the camera and he was naked from the waist up. This was no one I knew and it certainly wasn't Duncan. He had what looked like shoulder length blond hair, pulled into a man bun that rested on top of his head. Hebrew letters printed in black ink stretched down his right forearm.

Maybe Lena could fill in the blanks. I wonder if she knew about this side of her friend's life. And Mia? Did she know? If not, how could I tell her? Carefully, is the only thought that came to mind.

I took the shoebox over to the bed, sat down and looked through the pictures again. Under the photos was a small silver thumb drive. That was going home with me, along with the pictures.

There may be a logical explanation for these photos. But, for the life of me, I couldn't think of one. I put the shoebox back on the bed and walked into Shari's small office next to her bedroom. There was her laptop. That was going home with me, too. I would think of a reasonable excuse for Mia. On the bookcase to the side were business check books that were linked to the family trust she was managing. It looked like brother Mitch received money on a steady basis––smallish sums––nothing over $500 a month for about five years. Then there was a check stub for $250,000 dated about two months ago. After that...the Bank of Shari had closed its doors to Mitch.

I walked back into the no-frills bedroom and looked at one of the photos again. This was the location of the photograph. No doubt about it. The bedspread with its sleek white and black stripes was the same one I was sitting on. From the angle of the picture, the photographer had been standing in the door to her office, next to the closet. I pulled out the rest of the photos and laid them on the bedspread. Yes, all the photos were taken in this room. Yes, she was on this bed. The angle in every one of them looked about the same, taken from the door to her office.

I tried to imagine Shari staring into a camera. She could see the glass doors of her closet and an image of herself off to the side. Next to the closet door was a narrow wall. Next to that was the door to the office. On the slim patch of wall were two landscapes of San Francisco in dark ornate frames. The frames were wide and deep.

I stared at the photos. The angles that the pictures were taken from weren't just similar, they were identical. I looked from my reflection in the mirrored door, past the landscapes to the study. No one gets the angle exactly the same every time they take a photograph…unless the camera is stationary. Maybe it was on a tripod, but possibly,there was a camera in one of the paintings, maybe behind or perhaps embedded in the large wooden frames. Still holding the box of photos, I edged toward the landscapes of Coit Tower and Ocean Beach. I focused on the dark wooden curly cues in the frame.

I stopped suddenly. There was a light scrapping sound coming from the front door in the other room. Then a series of creaks. Someone was opening the condo door. Then it closed quietly. Heavy footsteps shuffled into the living room; paused, then continued into the kitchen. I held my breath. My heart thudded in my ears. The refrigerator opened.

I stuffed the photos and thumb drive into my backpack and moved behind the bedroom door. I looked through the thin crack between the door and the wall. I couldn't quite see who had come in. But then the person moved into view. It was Duncan who looked like he hadn't slept all night.

"Hello?" I said.

The refrigerator door slammed shut.

"Who's here?" asked Duncan.

"Me, Trish." I walked into the living room.

"What are you doing here?" he asked.

"That's what I was going to ask you," I said.

"I talked with Mia about an hour ago. She told me what the coroner said. I can't believe someone would hurt Red. I had to be here, to be near her." He paused and smiled half-heartedly. "Or as near as I could be. So I...." His voice drifted off. He looked around the condo his gaze lingering at a small pile of papers by the kitchen. He walked over to them and started to leaf through them.

"Are you looking for something?"

"No," he said and wandered into the bedroom. His eyes stopped at Shari's desk and he stared at her laptop.

"Duncan?"

He turned around and looked past me into the living room.

"You know, Mia probably knows where Shari keeps everything. If you are looking for something in particular...?"

Duncan shook his head. "No, not really."

We walked back into the living room.

"I am picking up some stuff for Mia and for Lena like the open water clinic files. Shari was supposed to lead the next one." I waited. Duncan didn't say anything. His expression didn't change. Not sure if he bought the lie. Not even sure he heard me.

I sat down on an uncomfortable highly polished aluminum chair. Duncan moved back into the kitchen, pulled a beer out of the refrigerator and walked toward me. This was a man in pain. His gaze was on the floor. His shoulders slumped forward. His feet seemed weighted down by invisible concrete blocks. He collapsed onto the couch.

"I have a key, you know," he said. "I often stopped here in the evening and waited for Red to come home."

He stared out into space. Purplish-black circles hung under his eyes.

"I hope you don't mind me asking, but how did you and Shari meet?"

"We worked on the same union project. What a dynamo she was. Not afraid of anything or anyone. That was about a year ago and we have been together since then."

"So you spent a lot of time together?"

"Well," he smiled. "We did. But it developed into a kind of long-distance relationship although we both lived in the same city."

"I don't understand."

"We were busy with our careers. Sometimes, it was hard to connect."

"But you said, you waited for her in the evening. Probably had dinner together?"

"No, I was just here. Most of the time, she wasn't. She used to come home earlier, but her work had gone into overdrive and she often stayed late to meet with clients, other lawyers that type of thing."

Duncan shifted on the couch and slowly lifted his gaze from the floor to me. His eyes closed and he chewed the inside of his cheek. He shook his head slowly and his eyes reopened, then searched the empty space behind me. I wanted to ask more questions. But Duncan was standing up. The conversation was over.

There was a sharp rap on the front door. We looked at each other.

"Who could that be?" I said. But Duncan reached the door before me and pulled it open. There stood the skinny blonde I saw at the open water clinic. Her straight straw-colored hair was tucked behind her ears. A fringe of bangs almost reached her greenish-brown eyes. She was dressed exactly like Duncan, in khaki trousers and a NSEU blue polo shirt. But, on her the clothes looked trendy, like she was modeling the most fashionable work uniforms for women.

"I've been waiting in the car," the woman said. "You said you'd only be a few minutes."

"Sorry," said Duncan. "Candy, this is an acquaintance of Shari's, Trisha Carson."

"We met yesterday, remember, at the Open Water Clinic. I registered you and your friends. You wanted to be sharks?" I said.

"Of course." Her smile was forced. "So sorry to hear about your friend. I don't mean to push, but Duncan, we have a meeting in less than 30 minutes and it takes longer than that to get to Pacifica."

She took hold of his arm and not so gently pulled him toward the door.

"We have to leave. Now."

"Okay, sure." He turned to look back at me.

"Don't worry I'll lock up," I said. I couldn't believe he was working not more than 24 hours after his girlfriend died. No job was worth that kind of dedication.

His eyes moved across the room like he was memorizing each and every detail.

"Tell Mia that I'll call her later today."

I nodded. And with that he walked out of the condo and closed the door behind him. Something didn't add up. I believed his story about wanting to be close to Shari. He was in mourning. But his work friend changed all that. According to her, this was a quick drop in and leave. This wasn't an 'I miss you' visit. He lied to me. He was here to get something and he never expected to find me in the condo.

In case Duncan said anything to Mia about my unexpected visit to her sister's apartment, I would use the open water clinic as an alibi. I walked quickly into the office, picked up the laptop and after a hasty look around, found the files for the clinic. I thought of the photos in my backpack. Were they what Duncan was after? The man in the photo was definitely not him. Lena knew about facial recognition software. I bet she could find out who Shari's mystery groper was.

"Lots to think about," I said to the empty condo as I walked out the door. "Need to come back here, so I better have my own set of keys made."

CHAPTER 9

I was sitting in my car outside the condo with Shari's laptop and open water files next to me. I thought it wise to call Lena and tell her I had stopped by the dead girl's home. My story that I told Duncan should work for my sister as well as Mia. It did. All too well.

Lena was quick to change the subject. She decided that I––who had only been to one open water instructional clinic in my life––would be perfect to lead the next one.

"You have the files already. You understand the swims. Just a bit of prep. You'd be perfect."

"No," I almost yelled into the cell phone.

"Now that Shari's gone, we can't let her work stop. These clinics were her passion. You saw how the swimmers loved them. They have to continue," she said. She rattled on in her non-stop way that I was to take Shari's files for the open water clinic, digest them in a week, connect with the instructors, check in with the park rangers, email the swimmers and make sure that everything went smoothly on clinic day.

I looked over at the cream-colored folder labeled 'Open Water Instruction' resting on Shari's laptop.

"No," I repeated.

"You can do this. I know you can. You even have time. The Giants are out of town that day so you're not working." She sounded like she was in a car in the middle of traffic on a speaker phone.

"Where are you anyway? And where is Mia?"

"Right beside me. We're on our way to China Camp. We want to see where they found Shari's body." Lena's voice dropped. "The Sheriff's office feels this is a homicide and an investigation is underway."

"It was inevitable, I suppose," I said. "Mia, are you sure you want to go there?"

"Yes," Mia's subdued voice responded. "I need to."

There were a few seconds of silence.

"Look, Lena," I said, "I don't want to be in charge of the clinic. I'm not an open water swimmer. You are. Why are you even asking me?"

To be fair. I could run the clinic. Thanks to my sister, my last job was with the Northern California Swimming Association. Lena manages their website and helped me get part time work in their office. It had morphed into a full time job. And then, let's just say, it fell apart. At least for me. But one of my duties was to go to all the open water swim events and evaluate their performance. A clinic would be similar. Smaller even.

"Why don't you take it over?"

"I'm one of the instructors. I have to be in the water with the swimmers. It is simple. The whole thing...start to finish... is over in five hours. You can spare five hours out of your busy life. It's not like you have much else to do."

"Don't be sarcastic."

"The clinic...," I started.

"You'll do it?" Lena cut in.

"Let me think about it," and I clicked off.

I hit the redial button on my phone. Lena picked up.

"Yes?" she said.

"And I'll meet you at China Camp."

CHAPTER 10

At least once a month when I was 10 years old and Lena was about two, our family drove out to China Camp perched on the edge of San Pablo Bay. Once past the marinas on the San Rafael Canal and the bordering low-slung houses, the shallow Bay, with a shipping channel carved down the middle, disappeared behind a curtain of oaks. Dad always hit the gas on the narrow two-lane road that twisted and turned beneath the trees. Every time the speedometer inched up, Lena and I squealed and our mother threw her jacket over her head. She didn't want to see the oncoming traffic or the steep drop-off into the Bay.

China Camp was a popular beach for the locals. Like all areas in California, it has had different uses over the years. First it was home to the Miwok Indians. After the California gold rush, the picturesque cove grew into a thriving Chinese coastal fishing village with almost 500 residents. Mostly net fishermen, they caught shrimp––almost three million pounds of shrimp each year. Now it was a state park, with a pebbly beach made up of tiny pieces of clam shells, a museum that is housed in what was once a shrimp storage house, and a 300' fishing pier.

I hadn't been here in years, but nothing had changed. I drove down the steep incline and parked by the snack bar. I could see my sister's car a few spots down. Even on a warm sunny summer day like today, only a few people were on the beach. There were children playing at the edge of the Bay, not going in too far, since the water temperature was in the low 60's. Their laughter was muffled by the hills behind us. I wondered if Shari had called out. Did she scream? Did anyone hear her?

I stood on the old wooden boardwalk that flanked the parking lot. Parked nearby were five Marin County Sheriff's cars, white with green trim; a crime scene investigation (CSI) trailer and a four police dogs waiting patiently to be loaded into a van. Lena was right. An investigation into Shari's death was full steam ahead. At the northern end of the narrow beach, where it curves outward sharply into the Bay, I saw my sister and Mia standing outside an area cordoned off by yellow tape. The words 'Sheriff's Line Do Not Cross' repeated down its length.

"Lena," I called out, but she didn't turn around.

A slender, older man wearing a faded, long-sleeve blue tee shirt sat on top of a picnic table a few feet away and watched me. A shaggy fringe of silver hair circled his head. His eyebrows bleached bone white from the sun sat above sunken eyes that had squinted into the sun for a lifetime.

"Think she's too far away to hear you. Sound here gets soaked up by the hills and the water," he said nodding out toward the Bay. "Park just reopened. It was closed until about 30 minutes ago...an official crime scene is what they told me."

"What happened here?" Hopefully, he––whoever he was–– knew more than I did.

"Girl found dead this morning. Tragic. But you knew that, right?"

I glanced at him.

"You know those two girls down there? The one," he said pointing to Mia, "is the dead girl's sister, so I was told by one of the deputies."

"Who are you?" I asked.

"Volunteer with the park. I'm here most days; helping out and such. Who are you?"

"A friend. Do you know what happened?" I asked again sidestepping the question.

"Not me. But Frank might. He lives in the house up there on the hill, like his dad before him and his granddad before him."

"Really. I didn't realize that someone actually lives here."

"Oh, yeah, he's the third generation. Runs the snack bar."

I glanced from the cottage at the top of the hill back down to the two women at the far edge of the beach.

"You might want to talk to him or some of the guys in the snackbar."

"Thanks. I will." I walked quickly toward the yellow police tape. Who was Shari Grantner? A knock-out redhead that dabbled in porn. She had a boyfriend, who never saw her, a brother that hated her unless she wrote him checks, and a sister that would be lost without her.

Mia turned around when she heard my footsteps crunching across the broken shells. There were tears in her eyes.

"I can't believe she would come here at night. That doesn't make sense." She reached down and ran her hands over the crushed shells, picked up a few small pieces and let them fall back to the ground through her fingers. "Why did this happen?"

"The Sheriff's Office will find out. I'm sure they will," Lena said as she gently tugged at Mia's arm. She glanced over at me. "Right, Trish?"

For a minute, Lena sounded like the 11-year-old that I used to mother. She'd often ask a question about the future or even the past and end it with, "Right, Trish?" To put her at ease, I always said the same thing, just like I did now.

"Right, Lena."

The three of us walked back to the long gravel parking lot.

"I want to go home," said Mia.

"Okay, let me drive you to your car," said Lena. "You coming Trisha?"

"Not yet. Go ahead. Mia, I have the things you wanted me to pick up. Your clothes, the cellphone. Let me get them for you." I opened the trunk of the car and pulled out her cloth shopping bag. Here you go. And your keys."

She nodded. "Thanks. Trisha can you help find Shari's killer? Lena told me about the swimmer that died last year and you figured out who did it. Can you do that for me? For Shari?"

"The police will handle it," I said.

"Please."

"Well, if you think I can help, I'll do whatever I can," I said. She nodded. I had the go ahead to look into things. No one could call me pushy. I was properly invited to investigate.

I decided not to say anything about the phone call from her brother or my trip to her sister's condo. They climbed into Lena's car and drove slowly across the gravel parking lot. Then I retraced my steps and headed toward the shore. China Camp Point jutted into the water. I inched along, next to the police tape and the bluff until I could go no further. The tide was too high. I couldn't walk around the point to the other side. But I could get there from the picnic area up on the bluff.

I climbed the hill to the upper parking lot, made my way past the wooden picnic tables and followed a steep trail cut into the side of the bluff down to the water on the other side. I was now directly opposite the crime scene. This was Bullhead Flat, a shallow cove, around the point from China Camp Village. I stared up at the bluff. It would be hard to carry a body down the steep trail on the other side without being noticed. But there was an undeveloped boat launch in this cove; kayaks put into the water all the time. Maybe that's how Shari found her way to China Camp Village. Someone paddled around the point while it was dark and dumped her body.

"Sounds far-fetched, even to me," I said out loud to the empty sunny beach.

I trudged back up the trail and started down the other side. I headed for my car, one of a few in the parking lot, then I turned and walked toward the Gao Brothers Snack Bar. I pulled open the rickety screen door. Inside was a long narrow cozy diner straight out of the 1950's. I sat down at the counter on a red stool and glanced at the old movie posters on the wall. A few men sitting at the other end looked at me curiously. The gray-haired man wasn't among them.

"Excuse me, but are you Frank?" I asked the elderly Chinese man standing by the cash register.

The man stared at me. "Yes."

"I'm a friend of the woman whose body was found here this morning. I'm trying to figure out what happened. I saw her yesterday in the East Bay. She's a good swimmer. But I don't believe she came here to swim, especially not at night. Did you happen to see her or hear anything unusual?"

"I already talked to the detectives. They asked me the same questions. Talk to them."

"But..."

"Busy right now," he said, and disappeared through a door behind the counter into the kitchen.

"It was windy last night," said a short, stubby man with a sunburnt face and a glistening, bald head at the end of the counter.

"Would have made it hard to hear anything. Not the first time there's been a dead body on this beach. Last time was...Mike...you remember the young guy who committed suicide out on the pier? Found out later it was the son of my barber."

"You had a barber?" Mike said.

"That was back when I had hair. Do you remember when that ..."

"Sorry to interrupt...but...the girl who died...do you think she washed ashore or maybe, her body arrived by boat and then she was dumped in the water near the beach?"

"Why would someone do that?" asked the man.

"I don't know. But could it happen?"

"Possibly. The boat...the one you are talking about...would need a short keel because these are shallow waters. I can guarantee you that it wasn't launched from here. Had to be from somewhere else along the coast. Could have come from a marina in San Rafael or Sausalito, even Richmond, across the Bay. Maybe San Francisco." He shrugged.

"Just an idea. Thanks," I said, looking at the memorabilia on the wall. There was a faded movie advertisement for Blood Alley, a thriller shot here in 1955, starring John Wayne and Lauren Bacall.

"Where the seas run red with danger," said the sunburnt man pointing a thick finger at the poster.

His friends around him started to laugh.

"What? What did you say?" I asked.

"That's the line they used to advertise the film. China Camp was famous when the movie came out."

I nodded; unfortunately, the tag line was too close to the truth.

"Got to go. Thanks for talking with me." I pushed open the screen door and was greeted with a low tide smell of rotting kelp. My cell phone rang.

"Hey Trish, as usual I can't reach Lena," said Dr. T. "Do you know where she is?"

"Taking Mia to her car. A question for you. Do you know the coroner in Napa?"

There was a long silence.

"Why exactly do you want to know?"

"Well, Shari had bruises around her neck. He seems to think that she was dead before she drowned."

"Seriously?"

"And her hair tie was stuffed in her mouth."

"No way. Trisha..."

"I know what you're going to say. But this time it is different. Mia asked for help. Anyway, I'm only passing along information. They're going to do an autopsy. I was hoping you might give the guy a call and see what he finds out."

"Trish, we have had this conversation a number of times. I don't care what Mia wants you to do. If there is something that needs police involvement, that's where it will go. You... must...stay...out...of...it. Last time you stuck your nose in places it shouldn't be, you ended up in San Francisco Bay and Lena almost died of an allergic reaction. So I'm not inclined to do any favors for you."

"Come on, T. It's only a phone call. Just a simple phone call."

"Autopsies take time, Trisha. He won't have any information yet."

"I bet he knows something. Think about it, okay?"

"If you talk to your sister, tell her I have to stay at the hospital tonight."

"T? Please."

The line went dead.

The lower parking lot at China Camp Village was all but deserted when I walked back to my Honda. The sheriffs' cars, the van and the dogs were all gone. So were most of the children and their moms.

I pulled open the trunk and dug around in my bag of 'keep with me' stuff, like sweat shirts, leggings, jeans, energy bars and bottled water. I needed something to drink and trunk-warmed H_2O would have to do. To one side, stuck underneath a windshield sun shade was one of Lena's wetsuits. Not sure how long it had been there, but the neoprene had that ripe, 'I never fully dried' smell. Part mildew, part skunk. I picked it up and shook it out. I thought of tossing it into a nearby trash can to teach my sister a lesson, when I had another idea. I was going to put it on.

"Need some help?" asked the grey-haired man I talked to earlier. He stood there with his arms crossed, a slight smile on his face, looking at me.

I took a step back and put my hand on the door handle ready to make a quick escape.

"Sorry. Didn't mean to startle you. I'll leave you alone," and he began to walk toward the snack bar. I didn't want to end up like Shari but my gut said he was okay.

"I need more than help," I said, struggling to pull up the black wetsuit over my hips, my much wider hips than my sister's. "I think I'm supposed to put the bottom half of this on like pantyhose, one leg at a time and pull. But it's not working."

Sweat had broken out on my forehead.

"You're almost there," he said. Then, he reached over and gripped the two sides of the wetsuit and yanked it up.

"Whoa."

I coughed and glanced at him. He almost jerked me two feet off the ground. But, the wetsuit, or at least the bottom half was now in place. I stuck my arms in the arm holes and worked the top half over my shoulders.

"Why are you wearing a tee shirt? Most wear swim suits or nothing under a wet suit. Oh, by the way, I'm Earl."

"Trisha, Trisha Carson. Can't shake hands right now. Not quite sure where they are, to tell the truth." My hands were covered with the stretchy neoprene and freeing them meant inching them forward. Not an easy task since the neoprene was sticking to my skin like Velcro.

Earl tilted his head back and forth slowly as he examined me and the wetsuit.

"I didn't know I'd be doing this," I said. "So I'm wearing what I have, which is, in this case, a tee shirt and my underwear."

I glanced up, sweat now trickling down my cheeks and my neck. I tried again to slide the neoprene back hoping my hands might appear.

"That okay with you?"

"Sure, sure," he said with a huge smile on his face. "You work on the arms. I'll zip you up. Turn around."

I could feel him tugging the sides of the suit together and then I felt my chest flattened and compress.

"Can't breathe."

"Don't think it fits you."

"It's my sister's."

"This wetsuit stinks. You're supposed to rinse them out, you know. Why you going swimming...in this cold water? Maybe it's more important to ask if you can swim."

My voice came out in gasps. "Yes, I can swim. Dog paddle if I have to. I want to swim around China Camp Point. Probably walk more than swim, but that's my plan."

"Why is that?"

My breathing relaxed and I found the confining fit of the wetsuit almost comforting.

"It's about that girl whose body was found here. I'm thinking that someone brought her body down to the water, maybe on the other side of the point. Somehow moved her from one side to the other and dumped her near or on the shore. I wanted to see if that was possible and if maybe, something was left behind."

"Deputies spent all day here with tracker dogs. They didn't find anything. You think you can?"

"It's possible they overlooked something."

Earl snorted. "Okay, I'll play. So the killers came by boat?

That's a lot of work, seems to me."

"Why did you say 'killers?' Do you think there is more than one?"

"I think it would be a struggle for one person, that's all. Maybe she went swimming at night and drowned?"

I didn't respond. But then, I couldn't help myself. "The Sheriff's Department says it is a homicide not an accidental death. Anyway, who swims at night in the Bay, with all their clothes on?"

"Point made. Hold on for a moment, I'll come with. Meet you over at the edge of the water."

I grabbed a towel and crunched across the pebbly beach, past the last child on the beach, a little girl digging out chipped white shells. She picked up her head and looked at me through squinted eyes. She wrinkled up nose and started sniffing.

"Mommy, that lady smells bad," she said, looking back at her mother.

"That's not nice," said the mom.

"It's not me. It's the wetsuit," I said, walking faster.

'Smells bad,' I said under my breath, mimicking her tiny high-pitched whine. I passed the police tape moving toward the water and dropped the towel. My eyes searched the water-line. Shari's body was found at high tide. It was about 8 hours later, a little after low tide. If something was caught on a branch or rock, I might be able to see it. I walked closer to the bluff and its rocky base.

"Okay, let's go. I'll paddle next to you."

I turned around. There was Earl wearing faded red board shorts, a neoprene vest and carrying a red rescue surfboard under his arm.

"Are you a lifeguard?"

"Used to be. Frank keeps this board behind the snack bar in case anyone gets into trouble. I take it out every now and then and paddle around."

I had miscalculated the silver hair and what I thought it meant. Earl was something to see. Once out of the baggy long sleeve tee shirt and equally non-descript khaki pants, his upper body was muscular. His long arms and long legs were sturdy.

"I brought you these," he said, throwing me a pair of neoprene booties. "Rocks, twigs, probably some broken glass underwater. Hard on your feet."

I sat down, tugged them on and walked toward the tideline. Earl pushed his board into the Bay, climbed on, sat in a kneeling position and paddled with both arms about 10 feet off shore.

I stood at the water's edge and inched in slowly. The cool water seeped through the neoprene of the booties and around the edge of the wetsuit's legs. Soon, I was up to my knees. As Earl predicted, there were branches and big sharp rocks near the point.

"Now you be careful," Earl said as he paddled closer to me. "Don't bother putting your head under the water. You don't have any goggles and besides, the water is too dark to see much."

"Right."

The debris in the water made it uncomfortable to walk, so I stretched my arms out in front of me and fell. I landed with a splash, superman style. I sculled my arms back and forth moving slowly ahead and parallel to the bluff.

"Good, that's good. See anything?"

"Water is salty."

"You're supposed to be looking, not tasting."

"Got it."

My arms were only six inches below the water but Earl was right, I couldn't see them. We were already to the point and would soon be around to the other side.

"Over there. Look over there. Something shiny, looks dark blue, I think, stuck on a branch," I said pointing to the glittering object.

I put my feet down onto the muddy bottom and tried walking to the exposed branch, but they sunk down into the muck. "This mud is sucking off my booties. They're stuck."

"You're fine," Earl said. "Can you move in closer to shore?"

I pulled one foot out of the mud; then the other sunk in deeper. I lurched forward aiming for the sparkling thing. There were large boulders under the water. I bumped my knee against one, lost my balance, but snagged the blue bauble before I slipped beneath the Bay. I came up spitting out brinish water and shaking my head like a wet dog.

"It's a bracelet," I said holding it over my head like a trophy. "Ah, I can't move."

"Sure you can."

"No, I mean I'm stuck. My foot is stuck between two rocks."

Earl paddled next to me. "Here, hold on to the board. Get your balance and wiggle that foot free."

I leaned on the board and then shook, twitched and pulled until finally my right foot popped loose.

"Get on," said Earl. He slipped off the board as I climbed on. He took hold of the nose of the board and towed it about ten feet forward until we reached the edge of the narrow beach on the other side of the point. I slipped off the board and helped him pull it up on the sand.

"Well?"

I held out a bracelet, iridescent deep ocean blue balls on a stretchy band.

"Probably belonged to a kid," he said. "Not sure how it got stuck out here."

I slipped it on my wrist, watching the colors flicker in the afternoon sunshine.

"It may be more than that. Could be Shari's or maybe her killer's."

"Possible," said Earl.

"There's something else," I said.

"What?"

"The rocks right at the point have red paint on them."

"Really?"

"Looks like it was scraped off something, maybe a small boat, a kayak. Know anyone with kayak?"

"I have one, but I don't keep it at China Camp. Could be it was scraped off a surfboard, like this one," Earl said.

"I suppose."

"Well, thanks for your help. I have to think about this – the bracelet, the red paint. Could be important. Guess it's time I went home." I walked away from Earl, and headed for the trail that would take me up the bluff, past the picnic area and down to the lower parking lot.

"Come on. I'll give you a ride back to the village," said Earl, pushing the board back into the Bay. "You can paddle. I'll check out your technique."

"My technique? I don't have any technique. I don't know what I'm supposed to do." I walked over to the board now in knee deep water and climbed on. It was surprisingly stable. I sat on my knees and Earl scrambled on, kneeling behind me. I started to paddle.

CHAPTER 11

When we stepped onto the beach at China Camp Village, he said 'good luck' and then walked over to the retro snack bar and disappeared inside. I could hear laughter, probably from the other guys sitting around the counter.

I peeled off the top of the wetsuit and tugged the booties until they finally came squirting off. I'd give them back another time. The rest of the wetsuit would have to stay in place until I reached home. I spread a towel out on the front seat, climbed in the warm car and flipped down the visor, only to see my soggy hair. A quick finger comb and I was back on the twisting roads toward my end of San Rafael.

I looked at the shiny trinket on my arm. It's probably nothing, just like the scrape of red paint. After all that, I didn't know any more about Shari's death than I did an hour ago.

Lena was home working on a client's website when I walked in the door. I stopped by her room.

"What are you wearing?" she said, a big grin on her face.

"Your wetsuit."

"Why?"

"I'll tell you in a minute. Help me get out of this thing so I can take a shower."

Wrapped in a big blue bath towel with a smaller one around my hair, I shuffled into the kitchen with Mia's extra phone, Shari's semi-porn printout photos, the thumb drive, the open water files and her laptop. "Hey Lena, you need to see this."

"Can it wait?" she called out still in her bedroom studio.

'No, it can't. You won't believe what I found."

Lena appeared around the corner of the kitchen.

"This had better be good. I had no time to work today because of Mia. Not that I mind, but I'm on a deadline. I promised a client that..." The rest of her sentence was lost in the refrigerator which she had opened and was now leaning into its interior. She pulled out a pitcher of lemonade, grabbed two glasses, sat down and started pouring.

"What do you know about Shari?"

"She was my best friend, swimming buddy for years. Why?"

"Answer the question. What do you really know about her?"

"Trish, I don't have time for this. Work...deadline... remember?"

"Come on...please?"

Lena let out an exaggerated sigh. "Okay, she's a big shot lawyer. And, she's a detail person, a compulsive organizer... used swimming in general, open water swimming specifically, to mellow out. I never thought it worked. She was always the one that groups went to when they wanted something organized. Never said 'no.' That's how she got into producing the open water clinics."

I pushed the printouts of Shari over to Lena.

"Holy shit, where did you get this?"

"At Shari's."

"I can't believe it. You were supposed to go to Mia's house and get a few things. Not go snooping at Shari's condo." She picked up the one with Shari and the stranger on her bed.

"Who is this guy?"

"That's what I wanted to ask you. Have you ever seen him before?"

"No."

She picked up the other photo of a nude Shari, hand lost beneath her waist as she stared into the camera.

"I don't believe it. Straight-laced lawyer Shari is a porn princess?"

"I'm taking it that you don't know about this part of Shari's life."

Lena shook her head.

"No, the Shari I know was almost a prude when it came to sex, or at least talking about it."

Lena stood up, photos in hand and started pacing around the kitchen. "Maybe she was leaving Duncan for this man, whoever he is. These pictures, this guy. Do you think he was involved with her death?"

"He could be a suspect, like anyone else." I took the photo of the man from my sister's hand and looked at it closely. "I couldn't say for sure, but I think this guy was at the open water clinic. He was the driver for the union group. I wonder if Duncan knew him."

"That would be strange," Lena said.

"I'm going to ask him," I said.

"Right. You're going to waltz into his office with this picture, showing the two of them, doing...whatever they were doing and say, 'I thought you'd like a photo to remember the love of your life. Just ignore the guy feeling up your naked girlfriend. And oh, by the way, do you know who he is?"

"You have a point." I held up the thumb drive.

"What's that?"

"It was in the shoebox in the closet with these printouts. I bet all the original jpegs are right here."

"Trisha, you are a flat out thief. Did you misappropriate anything else? Maybe ransack her pantry? Steal her gazillion dollar designer couch? You were supposed to go to Mia's, pick up Mia's old cell and some clothes, which she didn't need any way since she went home after we left China Camp."

"Don't be so righteous," I said. "Besides Mia wants my help. You heard her. I did take the open water clinic files. You told me to do that. And, uh, her laptop."

"What? Don't you think someone will notice it is missing? Like, there is a big empty space on her desk?"

"This could help us figure out who killed Shari and why."

"I thought you decided it was Mitch," said Lena.

"Still high on my list of suspects. Especially since he didn't disappear."

"And you know that how?"

I told Lena about the strange phone call while I was at Mia's apartment.

"I'm certain it was Mitch. His initials came up on caller ID. And, oh, Duncan came into Shari's apartment while I was there. He has his own key. He seemed genuinely sad. But I also had the impression that they didn't see as much of each other as he would have liked. Then one of his work friends knocked on the door and they left."

"Maybe Mia could help us with this? I could ask, discreetly," said Lena.

"Just a moment." I walked into my small bedroom and pulled a pack of 3x5 cards from the drawer, and moved back into the kitchen. "Help me figure this out."

"Your cards. How could I forget? You know we are in the days of modern technology. You can keep notes on your phone. Or you could splurge and buy a tablet."

"I like to see them in front of me. That way I can move

them around."

I took a blue one from the pile.

"I want to have a card for everyone that we know that is/ could be/might be associated with Shari and her death."

"Mitch," said Lena. "Major culprit, according to you."

"They always say, 'follow the money.' He certainly was."

"Who is 'they?' Never mind, I don't want to know," Lena said, shaking her head.

"Okay. Then Mia," I said.

"No way."

"We are listing everyone involved."

"Okay."

"Duncan and the nude guy."

I wrote cards for them.

"I can't think of anyone else," Lena said.

"In time, I bet you will. Right now we have four people. Bet this list will grow. Do me a favor, call Mia."

"What for? She was just here."

"Please. Call and say you're concerned about her. Ask if she got home okay. Say that she needs family right now...and has she heard from her brother. I want to know her response."

"Why?"

"I want to hear what she'll say about Mitch."

"I don't want to do this."

I picked up my cell phone and handed it to her.

"Humor me. Make the call."

Lena exhaled loudly, but punched in Mia's number.

"Put it on speaker," I said. Lena tapped the speaker button and the sound of Mia's ringing phone could be heard in the kitchen.

"Hello?"

"Mia, it's me, Lena. Look. I'm worried about you. How are you feeling?"

There was a sigh on the other end of the line.

"I'm not doing that well. I can't believe that she's gone and that she was...that somebody hurt her."

"You need family around right now. Have you heard from Mitch?"

"No, I don't know where he is. I've tried all his numbers, but he won't pick up. I wouldn't be surprised if he left the Bay area. He still doesn't know. How am I going to tell him? He'll be devastated."

Lena and I stared at each other.

"He already knows," I mouthed.

Lena nodded.

"Well, keep trying. What about the coroner? Anything there?"

"Not yet."

"Let me know what I can do to help. I know this is early, but will you have a memorial for her?"

"I can't even think about that right now."

"Sure, I understand. Look, call me for anything, anything at all."

"Thank you. I will," Mia said and she clicked off.

I looked at Lena. "She's lying."

CHAPTER 12

The next morning, I woke up to an empty house. I wandered into the kitchen, poured myself a cup of coffee that Lena had left brewing and glanced around. My sister's swim bag was gone which means she was probably at the 6:30 a.m. practice with her Masters swim team. I had never seen the point of swimming back and forth, following a black line at the bottom of the pool, so early in the morning. Until I tried it. Through Lena's urging I had started to swim and I was losing weight. I wouldn't call myself a devotee yet, but I always felt better when I got out of the pool. I could now connect up to four laps without stopping. Every few days I added another lap. My goal was to swim a mile without stopping. I had a ways to go, but I was making progress.

On the kitchen table was a printout of Shari's mystery lover. His head was bowed, almost in prayer; his back to the camera. I had to work a game later, but I didn't have to be at AT&T Park until early evening so I would have time to stop by Duncan's office. I put on my Giants work uniform, picked up a bottle of water, the mystery man printout, waved goodbye to the only photo of our complete family on the side table by the door and headed for my car.

There was no fog today––an oddity for mid-summer in Northern California––just eye-popping sunshine that lit up the Marin headlands to my right and the steep drop down the hills of Sausalito and Richardson Bay to my left. Once through the Robin Williams Tunnel, I was on the most photographed span in the world, the Golden Gate Bridge. When I was little, I'd look out at the Pacific hoping to see the gate made out of gold, but I never did.

As I rolled across the bridge, the city with its tall white office buildings in the financial district and its steep hills heading straight up from the Bay were postcard perfect. It would be a great evening for a ball game if the fog didn't roll in.

Duncan's office was in the Mission District. How would I explain my visit? I never met the guy until two days ago. I had about 20 minutes before I reached my destination to figure it out.

CHAPTER 13

The NSEU office looked like it might have been a small department store in another lifetime. The first floor was wide open with columns holding up a spacious mezzanine. Instead of clothing departments on the second floor, the space had been broken into small offices. A curving wooden staircase connected the upstairs and downstairs.

The receptionist asked me to wait while she buzzed Duncan. I recognized one woman standing toward the back of the spacious room talking to a dark haired man. It was Candy, the blond who knocked on Shari's door to hurry Duncan to his next meeting.

She saw me, gave a slight wave and smiled.

"Hey," she said walking over. "What are you doing here?"

"I wanted to see how Duncan was doing."

"Sad," she said.

"Very." I nodded.

"Duncan mentioned that there might have been foul play connected with her death. Is that right?"

"I don't know." Nosey little thing, I thought.

"That is so out of line. Shari was not the type of person who would be involved with,..." She stopped talking, searching for the right word. "She wouldn't be involved with people like that."

"People like what?"

"Oh, you know, gangster types."

"You knew her?"

"No, not really. Just picking up on what Duncan said about her. Never spent time with her. I have to go. Now. So much work to do. I'll remind Duncan that you're here."

I watched her walk away. Candy climbed the curved staircase and disappeared into an office at the top of the steps. That was an odd conversation. Who said anything about gangsters? And she certainly left in a hurry when I casually questioned her. I bet she knows more about Shari than she's telling. But gangsters? Really?

I opened my backpack to search for my 3x5 cards. They weren't there. Instead I found a tablet with a sticky note on the screen.

"It's time you joined the modern world. This is my old tablet. Easy to use. Just press the button to the side and follow the directions. Here is your user name and password."

Now wasn't the time for me to learn new technology. I pawed through my backpack again. The cards weren't there. I could thank my sister for that, I'm sure. I had no choice but to use the tablet. Within seconds I was looking at a video of Lena giving me instructions on what to do. She had downloaded an app called 'Closer.' It allowed me to type as much as I wanted on a virtual card. Then it would pull together anything that linked the cards. She ended the demonstration with 'even you can do this.'

My first card would be for Candy. On it I typed, 'friend, coworker of Duncan. At open water clinic. Hanging all over Duncan.' I'd transfer the rest later.

"Trisha," a voice called from the balcony directly about me. I slipped the tablet into my bag and looked at the stairs. It was Duncan. He shuffled down the steps and the office conversation on the first floor stopped suddenly. All eyes glanced up at him. Then they turned to me, curious.

Duncan had aged in the last 24 hours. His pasty skin sagged. The lines around his eyes dug craters into the side of his face and one eye had developed a tic.

"What's up," he said.

"You don't look good. I can't see how you're still working."

"It's better than sitting at home doing nothing."

He took me by the elbow and led me toward the back of the room. Everyone was watching. Heads turned as we walked by.

"Let's go into the break room," he said.

The room was small but it had a refrigerator, microwave, sink, coffeemaker and a small round table. He pulled out two cups.

"Coffee?"

"No, water's fine."

He filled both cups with water and sat down. His back was toward the door. I sat opposite him.

"Now, why are you here?"

"There is something I want to show you."

I bent over to take the photo out of my bag. When I looked up, I gasped. Standing behind Duncan was the man in the photo. No doubt about it. Same long hair pulled back into a low ponytail, same tats on his arm. His boyish face broke into a wide smile.

"I took your picture the other day at the open water clinic. You were signing people in," he said.

Words jammed in my throat with no chance of spilling out.

"Trisha, this is a good friend of mine...probably my best friend, Andrew."

I stared at him still not able to say anything.

Andrew held out his hand. I looked at it.

"You okay?" asked Duncan.

"Sure, sorry. Thanks for the coffee. You stayed in the van most of the time, didn't you?"

"Yeah, nice and dry."

I finally shook his hand.

"Where did you get that," he said pointing to the shiny blue bracelet still on my wrist. "It looks like one of our union giveaways."

"I really don't remember. Hmm, maybe the County Fair. So everyone here has one of these?" I asked.

"If they want one. They're very popular." He moved to the refrigerator and pulled out an energy drink. "Nice meeting you," he said as he walked out the door.

"Are you sure you're okay?" Duncan cocked his head and stared at me.

"Yeah."

"So what do you want?"

I stood up.

"Nothing, nothing at all. Just wanted to see if you were okay. I...I need to go."

A surprised Duncan reached out for my arm, but I brushed by him.

"We'll talk later." I threw the words over my shoulder as I walked quickly through the large open office toward the front door.

CHAPTER 14

The women's locker room at AT&T Park had that pre-game buzz to it. Women darted in and out, chatted about the dinner special that was posted on the board in the break room and the need for stadium jackets. They loaded their pockets with game schedules and water bottles. Metal lockers swept open and clanged shut.

I sat down on the long wooden bench and tried to reach my sister. No answer. Just voice mail.

"Lena. The mystery man's name is Andrew. I met him, talked to him. He's Duncan's best friend. Do you believe that?"

After I stuck the phone in my pants pocket, I reached into my backpack and pulled out the tablet. I started typing 'mystery man.' Then I deleted it and instead wrote 'Andrew. Duncan's friend. Man in pic.'

"Hey Trisha, where are you working tonight?" My friend Charlee Anne sat down on the bench beside me. Heavy mist clung to her short tight brown curls. Her carmel-colored skin was moist from the fog.

"I don't know. Probably one of the entrance gates. I haven't checked my schedule yet."

"Well, we're giving away Eddie Martinez bobble heads, so the crowd will be happy."

"This crowd is always happy."

I could hear parts of a conversation coming from two rows of lockers behind me.

"Why you working here if you don't like baseball?" said one woman.

"I needed a second job," said the other woman.

"I know better," said a third. "You like looking at young guys wearing those tight baseball pants."

The three ladies erupted in laughter. I looked at Charlee Anne.

"As good a reason as any," I said.

"I'd say so. Have a blessed day, girl," she said as she stood up and brushed a piece of lint off her jacket.

I grabbed her arm.

"Charlee Anne?"

"Make it quick, honey. We got to get to our stations."

"I have a friend, my sister's friend really. She seems, seemed to be involved with her boyfriend's best friend. Should I tell the boyfriend?"

"You know that for sure?"

"It looks that way."

"Well, until it's a for sure, don't say a word. There could be something going on you're not privy to. Boyfriend don't need to know unless it's the truth."

I nodded and stared after her as she headed for the door.

The next two hours flew by, like they always did when I scanned tickets. Fans flowed through the gates like a rushing river, doing what I called the zombie bobble head walk––eyes large, bodies leaning forward, arms outstretched, reaching for their giveaway. I hardly had a chance to say, 'welcome to the ballpark' and 'thank you.'

I glanced up once at the crowd in front of me that stretched across Willie Mays Plaza, almost to King Street. Wait...was that...no, couldn't be. I thought I saw Mia standing off to the side at the Field Club entrance.

The next fan came through my gate carrying a huge orange sign that said 'Gamer Babe from San Jose.' It blocked my view. When I could see the other entrance again, the Mia look-alike was gone. I had no chance to check her out. My hands were constantly in motion, scanning tickets and greeting fans dressed in orange and black.

Once I finished at the gates and took my break, I went to my next assignment, near the Giants dugout, between third base and homeplate. From the score, I could see this wasn't the best of games. The Giants were losing. Even with the pitching ace on the mound, the other players provided no back up. They seemed flat, out of sync.

I walked down the aisle of concrete steps to the guard rail that separated the seats from the warning track, the reddish dirt on the edge of the playing field. I was next to the Giants bullpen. Anytime a pitcher came out to warm up, the crowd would murmur his name and clap. I stood by the low wall looking up at row after row of fans. I was a visual reminder that anyone planning to run across the playing field would end up in jail and pay a hefty fine.

A security guard walked over during a pitching change.

"Everything okay here?"

"Yeah. Just one question."

"Okay."

"I'm supposed to keep fans from running onto the field, right?"

"Well..."

"Look up. There are thousands of people and just one me.

What am I supposed to do, if...say...even a few of them decide to rush the field? Tackle them?"

The guard smiled. Then he reached over and felt my bicep. "You look pretty strong."

"Tell me you're not serious."

"Just joshin' with you. It's not your job to restrain anyone. We do that."

I felt tremendous relief as he walked up the steps to the crowded Promenade. I could picture myself lunging at a fan hell-bent on running across the outfield. I'd do it if I was supposed to. I'd might even enjoy it, but more than likely I'd end up falling on my face in front of a tv camera.

With a lopsided score not in the Giants favor, fans began to stream out of the ballpark before the seventh inning. The remaining crowd stared intently to their right, watching the battle between pitcher and batter. I kept my eyes on them, scanning row after row for anything out of the ordinary. When the closing pitcher from the other team threw a sinking slider for the final strike, the crowd groaned as one, stood up and flowed toward the aisles.

One couple standing by the field, not ready to leave, asked me to take their photo. As I arranged them so I could capture the scoreboard in the background, I looked back for a second at a group of fans crowded together on the steps heading for the exit. There was a familiar face...too familiar. About 30 seats over and ten rows up was Mia. She stood up and the man next to her stood up. I couldn't quite see him until she reached back down to her seat to pick up a sweatshirt. My mouth dropped open. Standing next to her was Mitch, her brother. They inched their way into the aisle and entered the gridlock of fans near the top steps.

"Mia!" I yelled.

But the ballpark was too noisy and she didn't hear me.

I turned back to the couple in front of me.

"Sorry about that," I said. "I saw a friend of mine."

The pictures were snapped and reviewed. The couple was happy. They thanked me, stopped for a moment to check out the ninth inning seagulls cruising by for a late night snack, and then drifted into the line of fans leaving the ballpark.

Mia and Mitch were close to the top of the aisle. I walked midway into their section and called out again.

"Mia. Mitch."

It was the 'Mitch' that did it. He turned around looking for the voice. His eyes scanned the people left in their seats, the security guards on the field and the ushers, like me, near the bottom of the steps. He turned to say something to his sister and they stepped back into an empty aisle. He did a quick look around again, his glance passing over me. Then Mia turned her head and looked down at the field. She saw me, staring up at her and her brother. She put her hands on her brother's back and pushed him. They disappeared into the throng of fans.

I walked back down to the field and met the eyes of a security guard standing by the bullpen.

"Friends of yours?"

"Yeah. I'm surprised to see them," I said still staring at top of the aisle.

About 30 minutes later, I clocked out and headed for the employee parking lot. It was after 11 p.m. The marque on the Lefty O'Doul gate was still lit up with a swimming, smiling neon sea lion moving through the glowing water. I passed groups of fans laughing and talking in the darkness. As I walked across the Third Street Bridge, I angled off the sidewalk into the street avoiding the vendors, the street musicians and three men debating an umpire's call in the third inning.

I stopped for a moment and looked back at the ballpark still ablaze with lights and then at the dark waters of McCovey

Cove. The kayaks and sailboats were gone. A ferry carrying fans home signaled its immediate departure from the pier with a long deep blast of its horn. People moved past me like shadows. Mia had lied. She was in contact with her brother. I knew it but I had hoped it wasn't true.

The crowds carried me along through the darkness until I crossed into one of the fan parking lots. A security guard that I see after each game nodded as I walked by. Bright lights, guards in golf carts, police on bicycles and on foot...this parking lot was safer than my own neighborhood at night. I threaded my way through the remaining cars and walked to the far end, heading for the employee's section. I passed a van that was still in party mode with a few guys standing outside the vehicle holding beers. One yelled at me.

"Come on over. Have a drink."

"No thanks," I said with a smile and continued walking.

"The game is over. You worked hard. You deserve it," he called taking a few steps in my direction.

"No, got to get home."

He raised his beer and said, "We're a friendly group. You don't know what you're missing." But the smile on his face and in his voice had slipped. His eyes didn't leave my face.

I hurried on, looking around for the nearest security person. I saw another usher up ahead. My fast walk turned into a jog as I hurried to reach him.

"See you tomorrow," I said as I trotted by.

"You are in a hurry to get home," he said. "Me, too."

I veered off to the left and glanced up at the towering light poles with aisle numbers at the top. One more aisle to go. As I reached my car, I stuck my hand in my pocket for the key. A hand grabbed my shoulder. A quick turn and I could see it was the fan with the beer who had called out to me a few minutes ago. He was holding more of my stadium jacket then me and I was able to squirm away from his grasp.

"Keep moving, buddy. Security!" I yelled as loud as I could.

"You look like the kind of woman that likes to get involved."

"Look…go back to your friends."

For some reason, I couldn't move away. His face was mesmerizing, almost hypnotic… angular with a close-trimmed goatee and a military-style haircut, high and tight. There was a long crooked scar down his cheek.

"Hey," I screamed. "Need help! Help!"

In the distance, I saw a security officer in a yellow vest look over at me and start to jog in my direction. I waved my arm but the man pulled it down and stared intently at me. He was only six inches from my face. Then he smiled slightly, his lips pulled back over yellow teeth. He put both hands on my shoulders, leaned over and whispered in my ear, "No need to yell. A message for you, honey. Don't be so nosey."

With that he backed away and began to thread his way around the remaining cars, heading for the street. I couldn't tell for sure but I thought I saw him step into the passenger side of a van. The van took a left and disappeared.

I hurriedly climbed into my car and locked the door. While I tried to get my breath under control and stop my hands from shaking, I put the car into gear and drove across the lot heading for the security guard, now in a flat out run in my direction.

I stopped and lowered the window.

"Some fan followed me to my car and was hassling me," I said to him.

Security radioed for the police and they were soon searching for the dark van and the man with the close cropped hair.

As I sat in the car explaining what happened to the security guard—I left out the 'don't be nosey' part—a police officer walked up to my car. She was Pilipino about 5'5", oval face, almond shaped dark brown eyes and short wavy brown hair that curled around her ears. Her deep crimson lipstick turned almost black in the night light. For a woman with such delicate features, she was bulky from the waist up. It took me a minute to compute her strange shape. Bullet-proof vest.

"I'm Officer Natalie Kalaw," she said. "Tell me what happened."

I told her most of the story. She stared directly at me for a few seconds.

"If he told you not to be nosey, sounds like he knew you," she said.

"I never saw him before."

"Why would he say that to you?" she asked.

"I don't know. Maybe he thought I was someone else."

"You sure you've never seen him?" she said, leaning in the driver's side window.

"Positive."

"How about getting out of the car?"

My hands were beginning to shake again as I climbed out. Maybe I should tell her about Shari. Not a good idea. It would only complicate things. Right now, I wanted to go home. I stood awkwardly while she went over to confer with an officer standing nearby. She slowly walked back.

"Driver's license, please."

"Sure. It's in the trunk. That's where I keep my wallet during games. Don't want to bring anything inside. Too many people, you know. Easy to lose things. Do you need my registration?"

I was babbling and I couldn't stop.

"No."

She took out a pad of paper and jotted down the information from my license. The parking lot security guard stepped beside her and took out a 5x7 form from his pocket.

"Need some information for my report," he said. It took another 10 minutes to answer his questions. They were basic: what happened, where, when, who. I was relieved when he didn't push me to answer 'why.'

Security and Officer Kalaw said they'd both file a report. They suggested that I park as close to a light pole as possible and walk with someone through the parking lot. I nodded, said I would, climbed back into the car, raised the window, locked the car doors and angled toward the exit. I couldn't get out of there fast enough.

I looked in my rear view mirror once, then again, then a third time. Two police officers and three security guards were standing there in a huddle. Honestly, I didn't really know why that man stopped me. But it had to do with Shari's death. I was sure of it.

Normally I would head down the Embarcadero so I could enjoy the ever changing lights on the Bay Bridge. But tonight, I was looking for speed not beauty. I headed up Third Street and aimed for Broadway, the quickest route to Marin County.

CHAPTER 15

The next morning, I sat in the kitchen staring out the window. My Giants work jacket was thrown over the back of a chair. I wanted to hang it up, but I cringed when I felt the smooth material. That guy last night...his menacing threat...was all I could think about. He knew something about me. It had to do with Shari, her murder and my interest in it. I felt like I was standing on the edge of a ten meter diving platform. I could turn around, climb down the tower and forget all about Shari's death and most likely, the thugs would leave me alone. Or I could step off the platform and free fall to the water more than 30 feet below.

I tried to reason it out. Someone noticed I had an interest in Shari's death. Yes, she was a good friend of my sister's, but the sheriff's office was already investigating. Good reason to back off. But then, Mia asked for help. Then she lied about her brother. Was she setting me up? I had to find out. It was time to take a step off the platform into the unknown.

Last night before I went to bed, I dropped Shari's folder for the open water clinic on the kitchen table. There it sat. I suppose I could do my sister a favor and take it over. It would be a work swap. I am living here, paying next to nothing. Maybe this would square us up.

I sent Lena a text. "Okay, I'll run the clinic."

I needed to get up to speed quickly. The clinic was right around the corner. It would be held before the Open Water Carnival to familiarize the swimmers with the area, the course and the water temperature which was supposed to be in the 70's. There was a lot I had to do. I was working the Giants-Padres game tonight but I had scheduled the week-end off––time to work on the clinic and more importantly dig deeper into Shari's death.

The phone was ringing as I paged through the files.

It was Mia.

"Trisha?"

I paused. What did she want with me? If I was her, I wouldn't want to get near me.

"Yeah."

"Look, about last night at the game."

I didn't say anything. The line was quiet. I was afraid that if I started talking I would rip into her. To me, silence was more than golden; it was a way to gain some time to think.

"You there?"

"Yes. I am." Long, dead silence.

"I know you saw us. Mitch and I."

Another excruciating lengthy pause.

"I only heard from him a few hours earlier. I didn't know where he was before that. And we had these tickets. I didn't want to go but Mitch thought it would be good for us."

"Really," trying to keep the sarcasm out of my voice.

"It sounds strange. But Shari loved baseball and I thought it would be a nice way to honor her memory."

"You don't owe me an explanation," I said. I walked around the kitchen holding the phone and drifted into the living room in front of the window. The mail lady had just stepped out of her truck and was putting some envelopes into Lena's mailbox.

"I don't want you to think badly of me, that's all."

"Look, Mia. How you and your brother spend your time has nothing to do with me." I had to stop. I was ready to say, 'but.' I could feel the word forming in my mouth and it was pushing forward, about to spurt out. I tried to stop myself from speaking.

"But" I started. Shut up. Stay out of it.

"Yes?" Mia said. Her voice had grown weak and thin.

I took a breath. Don't say it. I bit my lip. Hard. I could taste blood.

"Nothing," I said. "Maybe we can get together and talk about this."

"Of course," said Mia.

"With Mitch."

"Sure." She paused. "But right now...can't focus...so upset."

I held the phone away from my ear. Then I hung up. Never even said goodbye. Mia was like a chameleon, changing colors and attitudes to match those around her. She was worse than her brother, because, with him, you knew where you stood. Was Lena Shari's only true friend? No, there was Duncan. And what about Andrew?

My phone pinged. It was a text from Lena.

"Great. Want to go to Lake Caldwell today to scope things out?"

"Can't. Leaving for work soon. Just talked with Mia. FRAUD." I hit send.

"No. Only confused," texted back my sister.

"Not so," I replied, hit 'send' and dropped the phone on the table. I purposely didn't mention last night's incident in the parking lot.

I went into my bedroom to find the printout of the bare breasted Shari and her boy toy, Andrew. Something was wrong. At first glance, the photo appeared erotic, but it wasn't. Yeah, she was undressed and he was feeling her up, but it seemed almost over-rehearsed. There was no passion, no anticipation, no surrender. They were just there posing for the camera. It didn't matter what she had on or where his hands were. This was an act and not a very good one. Maybe Andrew could tell me more. I couldn't call him at work. Too many people had seen me, heard my name, and probably listened in on my conversation with Duncan. I'd have to figure out another way. And, oh yes, I had to quickly organize an open water clinic for 150 people.

It took about an hour to contact all those involved with the clinic from instructors who wondered if the event would even happen to the regional park that supervised the venue and provided the lifeguards. To make the change from Shari to me official, I had to fill out more papers and fax them in.

Shari kept her files in a three ring binder. Everything was properly in order as I suspected it would be. But I found a sticky note that didn't seem to have anything to do with the clinics. Tucked into the front pocket of the binder was a note much like I'd seen at her apartment. "June 15, 4 p.m., Dice. Don't forget."

I did a quick search on the internet for Dice, San Francisco and found a techie job board, shops to buy gambling accouterments, and four automobile stores that sold big fuzzy dice to hang from your rear view mirror. None of those hit the mark.

Dice was either a something, someone or a somewhere. If I stopped by Shari's condo on the way to work, I might find out which. I didn't have to be at the ballpark until 5 p.m. which would give me plenty of time to look around again. I walked into my bedroom, dug through my sock drawer and found the keys I copied.

CHAPTER 16

I assumed the authorities had visited the condo, but there was no indication of it. Shari's apartment remained a neatnik's paradise. I headed for the bedroom, thinking of the photos. I turned around and saw nothing but the curtains covering the window and two paintings of the Bay area. I walked over to the paintings and carefully took them down from the wall. There was nothing behind them but empty wall space. A dust shadow marked their outline. One painting was heavier than the other. I flipped it over and ran my hands along the frame. In the corner was a small black button. I pressed it and the lint free paper attached to the outside of the frame separated from the actual painting. The frame was deep enough to support a small metal housing, just the right size for a small camcorder or a cell phone.

"Shari, Shari, Shari. What were you up to?" I pulled out my cell phone and took pictures of the camera housing. Then I reassembled the frame and painting and shot a few stills of the front and, more importantly, the back. I had to share this. I sent a text to Lena and attached the photos. "This was in a picture frame in S's bedroom!!!" Then I rehung the two Bay scenes. Shari was a very complicated lady.

I had to leave or I'd be late clocking in. Baseball was waiting. I headed for the door when I glanced over to the phone. It was blinking. There was a message. I picked up the receiver and hit the pound key. The voice said, "You have one message." It was delivered at 7:30 a.m., three days earlier.

The voice was feminine, soft, quiet. "I'll be there. Please show up this time. It's important...important to me."

I stared at the phone. There was a tinge of desperation and something else in the caller's voice...sadness? She sounded vaguely familiar. I know Lena had no inkling of Shari's other life, but someone must. It had to be Andrew. He was next on my list to talk to, but I had to leave now or I'd be late to work.

CHAPTER 17

Work went smoothly. No one bothered me either outside or inside the ballpark. The game pushed into extra innings and I didn't arrive home until almost 1a.m. The next morning when I finally woke up, a golden blanket of sun was creeping across my bed. I pulled on a pair of dark green shorts and a frayed Giants tee shirt and shuffled into the living room. I was anxious to talk to Lena. The house was quiet.

"Lena?" Then the backdoor opened and slammed shut. "What did you think of those photos? I have a theory that Shari was…" I stopped and looked at my sister. Something was wrong.

Lena moved slowly from the kitchen into the living room. Not saying a word.

"Lena?"

"The mail. There was a letter."

"From who?"

"Dad. He wants to talk."

My fingers started to tingle. I felt warm; hot, almost. Then cold and lightheaded. I bent over trying to slow down my breathing. Lena continued to talk but I couldn't understand her words. It sounded like she was underwater.

"I don't know what to say." I reached a hand up to push my hair back. My forehead was damp.

"I don't want to see him."

"How did he find us?

"Not us. He found me. I don't think he knows that you are here. But I don't care how he found me. I don't want to see him. He is not coming into this house," she said, her voice growing louder.

"Let me see the letter."

"No."

"Why not?"

"I threw it out."

"I don't believe you," I said. "What did it say?" Lena didn't answer.

"I need to take a shower," I said, glancing in her direction. She didn't toss that letter out. She never throws anything away. I was about to challenge her again, but instead said, "Let me think about this. We'll figure out what to do."

Truthfully, I had no idea what to do. When Dad walked out, he left us not only behind but alone. Each day we'd both go to the mailbox, thinking that he'd write, tell us where he was and that he was coming back for us. But it never happened. I did as much as I could to find him. I pushed and prodded the local police, but they were more interested in my living situation and Lena. So I backed off. After the first year of waiting, I gave up. I never expected anything besides monthly bills to show up in the mailbox. But Lena knew he'd come back. She was well into her teens when she finally closed that door. And when she did, the door was nailed shut, not to be opened again.

Lena never moved when I walked past her toward the bathroom. She was quiet. Not a word. I was in the shower, scalding water pouring over my head, when Lena opened the door and walked into the steamy room. She sat down on the edge of the tub.

"Change of subject," I said buying me a few more minutes of time. "Andrew, the mystery man in the photo and Duncan's best friend. He drove the van. I met him. He was there with Shari, Duncan, Mia and Mitch. And now there is someone, or something called Dice that Shari is involved with."

"So what," she said with little emotion.

I turned off the water, pulled back the curtain and reached for a towel. I walked out of the bathroom, with my sister trailing behind.

"He is not coming back into my life. Never again."

"Can I see the letter?" Lena ignored me. "Look, you don't want to see him. So we don't see him. That's the end of it."

But somehow it didn't feel like the end of anything, more like a puzzling beginning.

CHAPTER 18

A few hours later, around 1 p.m., Lena left the house, carrying her laptop and swim bag. Dad's letter didn't seem to be on her mind anymore.

I filled a glass with ice and water and sat down in the warm sun on the back steps of our house. As usual I had turned off the sound on my cell phone, but it buzzed and hopped around the back steps, indicating someone was trying to reach me. It was Dr. T.

"Hey, what's up?"

"Seriously, you and your sister are driving me nuts."

"And why is that?"

"You don't know?"

"Terrel, this has been a difficult morning for both me and Lena."

"Tell me about it. Wait...are you talking about what I'm talking about?"

"Dad's letter?"

"Who's Dad?"

"Our dad."

"Your dad? I thought he was out of the picture."

"Until yesterday."

"Okay. It is a little clearer. Lena phoned and texted me continually, but didn't say what it was about. Only 'call me.'

Then she went off the grid. I bet she turned her phone off. I can't reach her. The ER has been crazy for the last few days... summertime eating accidents."

"What?"

"Injuries I categorize in the 'summertime eating' genre.

"Like what?"

"Chopping off, not one, but the tips of two fingers while cutting watermelon; second degree charcoal burns; severe cuts from broken beer bottles with various and sundry jagged edges. Should I go on?"

"No I get it. "

"Anyway, I turned off my personal cell phone at one point before treating the guy with a concussion––seems he was the catcher in a baseball game and the batter completed his swing by knocking him out––no one was wearing a helmet."

"T. I get it. You were busy. Lena will understand."

There was a loud snort on the other end of the line, then silence.

"So your disappearing parental figure has shown up?"

"Only by mail. Lena received a letter from him. It sounds like he wanted to make contact with us. Well, her. He doesn't know that I'm here. Anyway, she is dead set against it."

"And you?"

"I don't know. I'm open to it, I think."

"Should I do some damage control with your sister?"

"Why not wait until later. Who knows when she'll turn her cell back on. You know she doesn't like to answer her phone when she's with a client."

"Right...you're right."

"Did you ever call the Coroner's office about Shari?

"Ah, yes. Seems they outsource their work. And strangely enough, I know the doctor who handles autopsies. He couldn't really tell me too much yet. There are privacy laws. But, truth be told, he likes the cloak and dagger part of this case. He didn't want to say anything out loud, but I got him to play a yes-no game. I asked questions and if the answer was 'yes', he tapped on the phone once; if it was 'no', he tapped on the phone twice. Corny, but it worked.

"My first question was "Did Shari drown?" He actually said 'yes.'"

"I thought he was supposed to answer in code."

There was a long silence on Terrel's end of the line.

"Do you want to hear this or don't you?"

I was quiet.

"My next question: "So the abrasions around her neck aren't an indication of how she died?" No answer on that one. I thought he had hung up for a minute. Then, he said, 'Next.'

"I tried a different approach. 'Was Shari strangled?' He tapped once on the phone."

"So, which came first, the strangling or the drowning?" I asked.

"He really couldn't tell me. At least not in the format of the Q&A that we had going."

"What about the hair tie?"

"No comment on his part."

"Great. Two causes of death. What do I do with two causes of death?"

"Trisha, you don't do anything. Remember? But here's another piece of interesting information for you to think about."

Dr. T paused. "I asked if Shari died at China Camp."

"Of course, she did. The sheriff's office told Mia that."

"Not so fast.

"Answer, two taps. 'No.'"

"What does that mean? Where did she die?"

"That was it. That was the whole conversation. Someone walked in and he hung up."

"I don't think you asked the right questions."

"Seriously? You're doubting my ability to question and interpret answers. As a physician, that's what I do for a

living. That's how I get information from my patients. I ask
questions. You know, this doctor and I could both be repri-
manded, if not worse, by our medical boards for this."

"You're making that up. Doctors talk to each other all the
time and not necessarily about their own patients."

"And you know this how?"

Long pause on my part.

'Well, on TV..."

"This conversation is over. O-ver."

"T."

"Tell your sister that I am trying to reach her. And in the
future, ask your own questions." The line went dead. He was
pissed. Not that I blamed him.

So Shari could have been killed anywhere between
Caden's Corner at Lake Caldwell in Livermore and China
Camp State Park in San Rafael. That's almost 100 miles as
the crow flies. Much of it borders San Pablo Bay. More bodies
of water.

The Coroner's physician knew or suspected something
that he wasn't telling Terrel. Or he told Terrel and T's wasn't
telling me. I picked up my small tan backpack and walked
out the front door. I needed to think about this.

CHAPTER 19

Parked in front of the house was a car I didn't recognize. It was rusted green with a dent in the right front fender; the two back doors were a flat gray primer. But I did know who was sitting behind the wheel. It was my father. My father who I hadn't seen in more than 20 years. He was reading a newspaper, sitting there in this clunker like he hadn't a care in the world.

I couldn't believe it. I walked over to the driver's side. He looked up shading his eyes with his hand. At first there was no recognition, then a smile. A big smile that showed empty spaces at the side of his mouth where some of his teeth used to be.

He opened the door and stepped out.

"Trisha, baby girl. What are you doing here?"

"What are you doing here?"

The sun was hot on my neck and I could feel sweat begin to dribble down my back. He stepped forward to give me a hug, and I stepped back. Couldn't say if it were minutes or seconds that passed. We stood there looking at each other, trying to see beneath the years. He was fidgeting with his car keys, dropped them, went to pick them up and almost lost his balance.

"I live with Lena now," I managed to say.

Deep lines were imprinted on his cheeks, bottomless caverns that dropped from his nose and mouth to his chin. His nose was bulbous like it had outgrown its outer layer. Little red veins crisscrossed the bridge. The bright eyes I remembered were dull, sunken beneath pale drooping eyelids. Thin receding mud colored hair was plastered to his scalp. He needed a shave; he needed a shower and he needed to brush his teeth.

"You're all grown up," he said, giving me a long look.

"Right. No thanks to you."

"Don't start, Trishy. I came all this way to see you and your sister."

"You didn't know I was here."

"Can I come in?"

"Lena's not here...and she doesn't want to see you."

"Come on, Trisha. I'm your father."

I walked toward the house and Robert McKenzie Shriver followed me.

"You can wait here on the porch. I'll get you something to drink."

He settled down on a chair outside and I went into the house, into the kitchen. My hands were shaking. Before I reached for a glass, I texted my sister. "Prepare yourself. Dad is here. Sitting on porch."

Ice cubes clunked into the glass and as I filled it with water, my phone pinged.

"Get rid of him."

I heard the front door open and Dad walked into the living room looking around and nodding his head.

"Nice place your sister has here. She must have money. That's what I thought when I found her, you know. When I learned she still lived in San Rafael. Didn't go too far did she? Neither did you. You look heavier than I remember. Packed on some pounds, I see."

"Yeah, well. I had a weight problem a while back. I'm

trying to slim down now." For years I had been waiting to see him, waiting for him to say something to me, but not that. When I daydreamed about meeting him again, I saw a look of love and warmth. A sign that he appreciated me, approved of the job I did being the parent to his daughter. But that was my fantasy, not his.

He sat down on the couch and noticed the photo of our family, mom, him, Lena and me at the Marin County Fair.

"Will you look at that? Martha was a charmer, wasn't she," he said staring at my mother.

"OK, dad. Why are you here? What do you want from Lena?"

"Do I have to want anything? I'm her father. And yours. That should be enough."

"It's not. Not anymore. Where have you been?"

"I want to see Lena."

"I told you, she's not here. And she's not coming home until you leave."

"Guess it's you and me then."

He sunk back into the full cushions on the couch stretched his arms overhead. Dark circles stained the faded yellow tee shirt.

"I'll wait," he said.

He pushed off his shoes, stretched out on the couch and closed his eyes.

"Need to get some sleep. Been driving for a while. Tired. Wake me up when your sister comes home."

With that, he burped and almost immediately started to snore. I sat down in the chair across from him.

"You can't stay here," I said.

"Sleeping. Don't bother me."

"You can't stay here," I said louder.

But he didn't answer. Unless I was prepared to roll him off the couch and out the front door, he wasn't moving.

My phone pinged again. I knew who it was.

"Gone?" asked the text.

"No," I replied. "Asleep on couch."

"Call 911."

"I can't. He's a jerk, but he's our Dad."

"On my way," she replied.

This reunion was not going to be pretty. I walked into the back of the house not sure where I was going, but I ended up in Lena's room. Maybe his letter would tell me what he wanted, why she didn't want to see him.

Lena's room was chaotic but there was a degree of order underneath. Yes, her clothes were on the floor but in a pile off to one side. Her work desk and two extra-large graphic monitors took up one complete wall. The large bed had a faded plaid quilt casually thrown across it, a quilt she had since childhood. Off to the right was Dr. T's corner. His clothes were folded neatly, shirts lined up carefully in her closet, shoes polished and placed one next to the other. From the look of it, when she wanted to put her shoes away, she slid open the closet door and tossed them in. Each shoe was there, but where was a different story. How T put up with her sloppiness was a credit to his good nature and his strong feelings for her.

Dad's letter wasn't on her desk; just notes about the current website she was developing. A few pieces of paper were on the floor. But, no letter. I shuffled through the papers in her black wire trash can...bills, bank statements and buried underneath torn up scraps of paper--Dad's letter.

I pulled out every piece I could find. Then took them into my room and spread them on the bed. Puzzles were my strong suit, but you can't put them together if all the pieces aren't there. And some weren't. I could see the *Dear Lena. Bet you're surprised to hear from me.* The next section was gone. I found a paragraph about him searching for her on the internet and finally tracking her down through her work website and an old friend.

The last piece said, 'important that I..." The rest of the

sentence was missing. The page had been ripped down the middle.

I looked at the three sections laid out on my bed. What was so important that he needed to find Lena now after so many years? I heard the front door open and a gasp. Lena was home. She walked into her bedroom and then into mine.

"Why didn't you get rid of him?" The words came out in a hissing whisper.

"He fell asleep. I think he's drunk. He was kind of staggering around."

Lena's eyes looked at the three pieces of paper on my bed.

"You've been snooping in my room, haven't you? Why can't you leave my things alone?

This is personal, you know."

She reached down and grabbed the scraps of letter and stuffed them into the pocket of her jeans. "What is wrong with you? Creeping into my room, going through the trash." She spoke so fast some words were unintelligible.

"Why is he here?" My words were slow, precise. Sometimes that was the antidote for Lena's speed talking.

She sat down on the bed. She looked at me. "I don't know. The letter didn't say."

We both walked out to the living room and stared at the sleeping figure.

"Wake him up," I said to Lena.

"Not me. You wake him up."

"No. You do it."

"You're the oldest. Wake him up and get rid of him. Please Trish, I can't do it."

Lena folded her arms and stared at the figure sunken into the couch, peacefully snoring away. "I'm going to my room and I'm not coming out until he's gone."

"Lena, be an adult for once will you. Let's do this together." But my sister disappeared. I heard her bedroom door shut. I walked over to my father and tentatively shook his shoulder.

"Wake up, Dad."

He sighed and turned over. He was now facing the back of the couch. I tried again. He felt bony. The strong shoulders I leaned my head against when he read me my favorite books were gone.

"Dad, wake up."

Before I was able to turn him over, the phone rang in the kitchen. It was Dr. T again.

"Is my darling Lena there?"

"Yes and so is our father."

"Seriously? I thought his letter just came yesterday."

"It did. His letter came yesterday and he came today."

"Interesting. Has he said why he wants to make contact after all these years?"

"No. He's been asleep on the couch practically from the time he stepped into the house."

"Is he dangerous?"

"Not really."

"Should I come over?"

"I won't mind you being here. I'll go get Lena."

"Hold on there. Got more to tell you. I found out something...let's say...an unanticipated detail about Shari's death."

"From the phone-tapping doc?"

"No from another source."

I heard Lena's bedroom door open and she walked into the kitchen. She mouthed, "Who is it?"

"T, Lena just walked in. I'm going to put you on speaker phone." We walked out the kitchen door and closed it carefully behind us not wanting to wake Dad.

"China Camp is on San Pablo Bay, right? There is salt water flowing in from the ocean mixing with fresh water streaming down from the Delta. What kind of water would expect to find in her lungs?" T asked.

We both blurted out at the same time, 'salt water.'

"Wrong," said Dr. T. "Her lungs were filled with fresh

water."

"What? Not possible."

"Fresh water. That means..."

I interrupted him. "She didn't die at China Camp."

"Right. There's more. Time of death was probably 12 hours earlier than when the body was found."

Lena counted backwards on her fingers. We both looked at each other.

"She must have died soon after we left her," I said. "And her body was moved to make it look like she had some sort of accident at China Camp."

Lena was walking around the kitchen staring up at the ceiling.

"I have to go. Patients are waiting."

"If someone moved her...," Lena continued.

"Lena, can't talk. I'm working. Patients...injuries...accidents. Gotta go. Will continue this later, I'm sure." He clicked off the line.

"So she must have been killed at Caden's Corner. Then dumped at China Camp. Someone went to a lot of trouble. Don't you think?" I said.

"I don't really know. And I don't think it matters anyway. She's dead and nothing can change that."

"Lena, how can you say that? This matters. Where she was killed is important. We know who was at Lake Caldwell and Caden's Corner. One of them is probably responsible for her death."

Right now I have a bigger problem," said Lena. "My father—who I do not want to see—is sleeping on the couch."

Lena picked up the cell phone and hit the redial button. It went to voice mail.

"T. What should I do about my father?"

She walked out of the kitchen and into the bedroom. I could hear her say, "Can you come over?" And her bedroom door closed.

Poor Terrel. When he was finally able to pick up his messages, there would be my sister pleading for help yet again. He had taken over my role. I grabbed the tablet and set it down on the kitchen table. I added the following to Shari's file under Information. 'No saltwater in lungs. Approximate time of death, mid-afternoon, following open water clinic.' Under the Questions tab, I wrote 'Why would someone move the body? How did they do it? Were they alone? Why choose China Camp?' It's almost 70 miles from one park to the other.

I remembered the smear of red paint on one of the rocks at China Camp. Earl asked me if I knew any kayakers. I thought it was a stupid question at the time, so I humored him, but in the end, he might be on the right track.

I brought up each of the e-notecards looking for Earl, the man I met at China Camp. He may have seen or heard something. I wanted to go back there talk to him again. I needed to know who killed Shari – competent lawyer, compulsive organizer, porn princess and respected swimmer.

As I clicked on each card, there was a cough behind me. Dad was standing in the doorway to the kitchen.

"Okay, if I get some more water?" he asked, leaning heavily onto the door frame.

"Let me get it for you. Sit down."

He glanced at the floor to make sure it was there and not moving. He took careful steps toward the center of the room, grabbed the back of one of Lena's mismatched kitchen chairs and moved himself to its side. Then he dropped heavily onto the wooden seat. I could almost see the fibers in the wood expand, then slowly retract and stabilize.

Haltingly my father turned toward the table, placed his elbows on the edge and dropped his head into his hands. I've seen my sister strike the same pose many times.

This was not the dad I remembered––quick with a laugh, easy with a word that could console or inform. His broad boney shoulders drooped. There was a rip at the pocket of his faded yellow tee shirt. It was hard to believe he was here———after so many years———in the same room as I was. I had trouble looking at him. So I didn't. I walked to the sink and stared out the kitchen window at Lena's small vegetable garden.

"What's wrong with you?" I asked glancing over my shoulder at the discouraged figure sinking lower in the chair by the minute. He was headed for the floor. I took a few steps and caught his arm. My hand sank through the skin like I was grabbing hold of melting butter.

"Nothing. Just tired. Long drive," he said.

If I wasn't looking him straight in the eye, I'd swear he was as drunk as I've ever seen anyone. But his grey eyes were clear. True there was some red around the edges, but they were alert and knowing.

"Here," I said. "Have some water." I handed him a glass and I watched him drink it down.

"Do you want more?" I asked. He nodded so I refilled it and handed it back to him.

"Where have you been?" I asked.

The house was unbearably quiet...just the sound of him sipping the water from the glass.

"It's not important," he said. Then a door in the back of the house opened and I could hear footsteps...hurried footsteps coming my way. Lena came bounding around the corner, her mouth set in a squeezed tight line. "You have to leave...you can't stay here go...go nownownow."

"Lena, stop it," I said.

"He has to leave. I don't want him here," she said, her voice was two octaves higher than normal.

"Sit down, Lee," Dad said. His voice was surprisingly stern.

Lena closed her mouth, but stood in the doorway.

"You can't tell me what to do in my house."

"Please...sit down."

Lena dragged a chair away from the table, placed it near

the refrigerator, almost directly behind me. She sat down and crossed her arms. I glanced from my sister to my father. Invisible blocks separating the two climbed to the ceiling—and I was stuck in the middle.

"Get out," she said.

With a sigh, I looked at Dad. "Why are you here?"

He sat a little straighter, but said nothing.

"You never came back for us. You left me to bring up Lena. I was only 18. She was 10. Mom was dead. There wasn't a letter, a phone call, anything. And now all of a sudden you're here. Why?"

I clenched my back teeth, trying to keep my anger under control. I bit down so hard my jaws hurt.

"I have no place else to go." He took a sip of the water again and placed the glass down carefully. "Things have been tough for me. Don't like telling you that. It hasn't been easy. I had a job, but..."

His voice drifted off. He was looking down at the table and lifted his eyes slowly to look at me, carefully avoiding Lena. "I hoped I could stay here."

"Oh, no," said Lena, standing up and lunging toward the table. I grabbed her arm because she was about to slug him. Her arm was muscular, firm, unlike Dad's.

"Trish, you'll let me stay, won't you?"

"This is Lena's house," I said. "I'm only a guest here, temporarily. It isn't my decision."

"I worked, saved and bought this house by myself," said Lena. "I'm leaving now—going to the pool—when I get back in two hours, I want you gone. If you're not, I'm calling the police. You don't deserve to see us, to be part of our lives."

"Okay. Okay. No need to bring in the cops. I'll go. But could I talk with Trish for a minute?"

"Up to her. But outside. Do it outside." She threw the words over her shoulder as she moved quickly into the living room, almost tripping over her own feet. She held open the front door until Dad and I walked out. She locked the door behind us; hurled herself down the walkway, into the car, almost slamming the door on her hand and drove away.

"That girl is so clumsy," said Dad with a quiet smile on his face, "She was always stumbling, falling down, scraping her knees. Your mother, bless her heart, signed her up for ballet lessons, hoping that would help. She lasted through two sessions and refused to go back. Said it was too slow for her. That's why your mama and I got her into swimming."

He sighed. "Guess I waited too long to make this visit. Not hard to understand why she doesn't want me to stay. Can't say I blame her. I knew where she was for years. Kept track of you, too, until you left Colorado. Thought you had vanished like your old man did.

"Trishy, can't you put in a good word for me? I need a place just for a few days, that's all."

"Like I said, it's not my house. I'm only staying here until I get enough money together to move out. Dad, where did you go? All those years? Where were you?"

"It doesn't matter."

"It does to me."

"You did a good job, Trishy. Taking care of Lena. Must have been hard."

"Hard doesn't begin to cover it. I gave up everything to take care of my sister. What did you do? Nothing."

He reached over and patted my arm. "That Lee. She was always like a stack of dry leaves ready to explode with a drop of a match. Just like your mama. Don't remember you being like that." He sighed. "I'll leave."

"Of course you will. That's all you ever do."

"You heard your sister. I have to go. You said so, too."

He headed for his car, turned around and said, "I'll keep in touch."

"Wait," I said. I scribbled my phone number on the back of a grocery store receipt. "Call. Let me know where you are."

He took the receipt, crumpled it up and stuck it in his pocket. I watched him walk around to the driver's side of his car baking in the sun, get in, pull down the visor and slowly drive away.

I absentmindedly moved around to the back of house and went through the kitchen door. My sister was undone...justifiably so. I was worried about her. I texted her. "Gone now.. Coming to pool. Wait for me."

CHAPTER 20

It took 15 minutes to reach the large parking lot outside of the new Marin Sports Center. This area was a dream come true for anyone involved with athletics. It housed both an indoor and outdoor pool, two neighboring soccer fields, three baseball diamonds, six tennis courts and an enormous gym with four full-sized basketball courts. I headed toward the pool's entrance and found a parking place near Lena's electric blue Mustang. She was still sitting in the car—absolutely still, staring into space—with the windows rolled up and air conditioning blasting away. She never saw me pull up or walk over to the car. I tapped on the window and she jerked around. The window glided down.

"What? He didn't come back, did he?"

"No. How are you doing?"

"Look at me. My hands are shaking. I'm a mess."

I reached through the window and rested one hand on her arm. "We'll figure this out as a family—meaning you and me. We've done it before. We can do it again," I said.

Lena climbed out of the car and I walked with her across the parking lot.

"I'm going swimming with you."

"Really?"

"Can I borrow a suit?"

"Okay."

A slender teenage boy smelling vaguely of chlorine was at the counter in the pool's lobby. "I'm bringing in a guest today," said Lena, dropping $5 on the counter.

"No prob," the kid said.

I followed my sister through the door of the ladies' locker room and was hit with moist air and the hammering of showers in the background.

"Here," she said, handing me a suit with a sunburst of orange and yellow printed on it. "It's pretty stretched out. You should be able to stuff yourself in it."

"Be nice."

"Did he say where he was going?"

"No."

CHAPTER 21

"Cookie, are you planning on getting wet sometime today?"

I was hovering at the pool's edge and I glanced down to locate who was talking to me. All I could see was a patch of blinding white hair on a skinny body.

"Cookie, get in already," the elderly male voice said.

"Sure thing," I said. But I didn't move.

The 80-something year old swimmer was holding on to the pool's gutter next to my feet. He looked up at me again. "Okay, I tried," and he pushed off the wall, and headed for the other end of the long 50-meter pool with a slow practiced freestyle stroke.

I stood there. Thanks Dad. You got me to exercise. Well, I wasn't exercising yet, but almost. I could see my sister a few lanes over churning through the water with her slightly lopsided but speedy stroke. Each time she flip turned at my end of the pool and streamlined off the wall, I could see her anxiety fade. Her freestyle stroke grew more fluid, relaxed... as if the chlorine was a neutralizer for worry and sadness.

I looked from one lane to the other. Everyone in the pool seemed to know what they were doing. I felt so out of place. This was Lena's spot, not mine. The swim suit was too tight. I had flesh bulging out of every opening. The cap hurt my head. I was getting a headache. And the goggles. Lena had tightened them for me and they were digging into my eye sockets.

"How can anybody be this uncomfortable and still swim?" I said to no one in particular.

In the lane next to me, a woman just reached the wall and said, "You can get in with me. There's plenty of room. New swimmer?"

"I don't swim very much. And when I do, it isn't like what everyone else is doing here. They all look so...so focused."

"Don't worry about it. You'll be fine. Come on, get in."

I sat down on the edge of the pool and dangled my feet and legs in the crystal blue water. It was cool and it felt great in the hot afternoon sun. And just like that, without thinking, I was in the water.

"Have fun," she said and pushed off pulling into a breast stroke with a long easy glide.

I stuck my head under the water. The sun shining into the pool was dazzling. I'd forgotten how much I enjoyed the moving colors, the light blues fading in and out as the water moved. I started to swim, thoroughly enjoying the underwater view: legs kicking by me in the next lane; arms pulling through the water; and the line of bubbles as I let out puffs of air.

I picked my head up and started to tread water. I was only ten feet from where I started. The other end seemed very far away. So, I stroked and kicked and although it seemed to take forever, I finally reached the shallow water. The woman who invited me into the lane swam by me at least once. Now she was standing up chatting to the senior swimmer in the next lane.

"This is an awfully long pool."

"You'll get used to it," and she pushed off again, leaving me standing there, my back to the warm sun, my stomach and everything below in the cool water.

The little old man with the white hair looked over.

"You know, to take advantage of exercise, you have to

move," he said with a smile.

I chuckled. "You are a taskmaster. Okay, I'll swim."

Then I tucked my feet up against the wall and pushed off, looking at the bottom of the pool. Shari's face flashed below me. Her last view was probably of water. Not like this but probably the brownish-green lake water that edged Caden's Corner. My chest tightened. I turned my head to breathe and took in a mouthful of water. I spat it out, stood up and started to cough. I inhaled deeply, then stretched out in the water again and made my way to the other end.

Thirty minutes later, I picked up a kickboard like I had seen Lena do so many times and started to kick. But I went nowhere. I glanced over my shoulder at my feet. They were moving up and down. The water bounced and gurgled around my toes. But I didn't seem to be making any forward progress.

"Hey Trish, you have to kick harder," yelled Lena from a few lanes over with a big smile on her face. "You're as slow as a turtle."

"Even slower," I said to myself. But I was glad to see the smile on my sister's face. The chlorine cure had worked again.

"This kickboard is defective. It doesn't move forward. Think I'll get out," I yelled back at her. I ducked under the lane lines one by one until I reached the ladder on the side of the pool.

"So, Cookie," said the white haired man as I passed through his lane. "You've had enough?" His dark green plaid swimsuit ballooned around him.

I nodded.

"Well, come back." With that he gave me a wave and started to breaststroke with his head out of the water, looking like a regal mallard wearing a kilt.

I couldn't let an octogenarian show me up so I decided to do one more lap. True, I was now in the family swim lane and there were kids up ahead, but I'd stay out of their way. I pushed off again angling toward the bottom of the pool. The pressure built slowly in my ears but I was in a blissful trance, head down gazing at the blue reflections of the water. Then I felt a small body on my legs, another on my back. Two kids were trying to swim over me. One tried to stand up on my back pushing me deeper. I tried to throw them off. One kid had his hands on my head pushing it down. I wouldn't be able to hold my breath too much longer. A wave of panic flooded my body. Then, as fast as they came, they disappeared. The weight on my back and head was instantly gone and a red rescue tube was in the water, in front of me. I grabbed it. Without the kids on my back and with the help of the rescue tube, I bobbed to the surface.

"You okay?" said the lifeguard.

An upset mother with two squirmy nine-year-olds in tow was at the water's edge, anxiously looking down at me.

"I am so sorry. They weren't paying attention and didn't see you."

"You need to watch your kids," I said, coughing and gasping for air while hanging on to side of the rescue tube.

"Sure you are okay?" said the guard.

"Yeah, I am. But I don't plan on drowning as a way to die."

CHAPTER 22

By the time I showered and dried my hair, Lena was in the locker room, looking relaxed.

"What was that commotion about in your lane?"

"Two kids wanted to sink me."

"What?"

"That's what it felt like. They swam over me and wanted to use my back as a diving platform. I couldn't surface and for a second there..."

"You thought you would drown?"

"It crossed my mind."

"Like Shari," said Lena.

"Yeah, like Shari." I laid my sister's swimsuit, goggles and cap on the bench next to her swim bag. "Thanks for the loan. I'm going into San Francisco."

"Why? You don't have to work. You'll get caught in rush hour traffic when you come back. It will take forever."

"I know."

She looked at me. "Then why?"

"I just have to. I want to talk to Duncan again and Andrew. They might remember something or someone from Lake Caldwell or Caden's Corner."

Lena stripped off her clothes and was standing there stark naked.

"Wrap up in a towel," I said.

"You're a prude," she said turning around and shaking her bare bottom at me. "Oh, I forgot to tell you. I had a call from a Detective Hamilton at the Sheriff's office. Mia gave him my phone number. We talked about my relationship with Shari and the day she died. I mentioned you and your growing interest in all this. Notice I didn't say obsessive interest. He wants you to phone him."

"I'll call right now," I said jogging out of the locker room.

Sitting in the parking lot, I called Det. Hamilton. I wondered if he knew about the lack of saltwater found in Shari's lungs. Probably. I bet he was zeroing in on Mitch. I couldn't wait to talk to him. Unfortunately, I'd have to. My call went to voice-mail so I headed for San Francisco, as originally planned.

The streets near the union headquarters South of Market were packed with traffic trying to leave the city. Pure grid-lock. Nobody went anywhere, not even me. When I was within four blocks of the NSEU headquarters, I spotted an empty parking space in an alley. I wasn't sure if it was legal, but I pulled in anyway, parked and started to walk.

I passed row after row of cars, bumper to bumper, going nowhere. There were long lines at bus stops and people streaming into the subway stations. I walked by shops and office fronts. I was about to cross the street when I glanced into a small coffee shop. Sitting next to the window and read-ing a newspaper was Duncan's best friend and Shari's groper, Andrew. He was alone.

I pushed open the door and was met with the inviting aroma of rich dark coffee. The quiet sound of a guitar solo filtered through the air. I walked to the counter and ordered an iced coffee.

"Hi, mind if I join you?" I said pulling out a chair and sitting down.

Andrew looked up without a bit of recognition. Then it clicked. His face lit up.

"You're Duncan's friend, aren't you? The girl from the swim clinic."

"I don't know him very well. My sister is the connection."

"Well, nice seeing you again. Was just leaving." Andrew folded his paper and stood up.

"Does Duncan know about this?" I dug into my backpack and pulled out the screen grab of him and Shari. His face went white, but he recovered quickly. He sat back down and leaned against the chair with a stupid smirk on his face.

"Where did you get that?"

"At Shari's."

"It's not what it seems."

"Enlighten me. This is you and Shari, the girlfriend of your best buddy. Did he know about your relationship?"

"Why do you care?"

"I don't care, but Duncan might."

"You've got it all wrong. There was nothing between me and Shari. Ok look, you won't say anything to Duncan if I talk about this?"

"Depends."

"I make sex tapes."

"Excuse me? I thought you worked for NSEU."

"That's my day job. But I've made videos my whole life. It's my true passion."

"And this photo is from a film?"

"Yeah, it's a screen grab, a shot lifted from the video. I put myself through college working in the adult film industry. Before you jump to conclusions, I was behind the camera."

"I'm confused. You make porn and Shari was an actress?"

"Adult films. Not porn. Let me explain. I was sitting in a bar not far from here, talking to some techie types. One guy was telling his buddy how he tried to make a sex tape of him-self and his girlfriend and what a mess it was. He said he'd rather pay for someone to come in take over the mechanics of the video while he could just...you know..."

"I think I do."

"It was an 'ah ha' moment. A void that needed to be filled. I had all the skills to shoot and edit a video. I brought in a buddy to develop a website and a mobile app."

"People actually are willing to let you into their homes and shoot them naked?"

"This is like any other business. You have to build up trust. I visit, talk to the client, discuss their vision and talk about the scope of the video and package prices."

"What's the name of your company?"

"Closed Set. It's a filmmaking term when you are shooting nudity. There are as few crew as possible on the set. We're in development currently. I needed a sample video to show the scope of my work. This screenshot is from the sample."

"And Shari was your––what would I call it––model?'

"Actress. She was big on the idea."

"That's hard to believe. My sister says Shari was straight laced, prudish even."

"You didn't know her."

"She was my sister's best friend."

"No one knew this side of her, but me and a few others. Duncan has no clue of who she really is...was."

"Tell me more about Closed Set."

"I want to offer a number of packages. The basic being shot by one cellphone at the client's home. I would operate the camera remotely, so no one else except the couple would be there. The most extravagant offer would be shot on a sound stage. Shari and I––in the screen grab you have––were working on a video for the simplest of packages. I was con-cerned about the one angle and the lack of additional light-ing. Although limited, the cellphone camera was pretty good.

Natural lighting gave it a raw 'cinema verite' look. But there was one problem."

"What?"

"Shari. She wasn't a very good actress. It didn't look like she was enjoying herself. Not the best...um...attitude for this kind of business. It has to come across that the guy is pleasing her."

"Let me get this straight. Shari was willing to be the actress."

"Yes."

"But she wasn't into it during the filming?"

"Oh, she dug it, all right. But it didn't look like it. When I saw the first clips. I knew I needed to find another actress. I was thinking of a friend from the industry. I explained it very tactfully to Shari. She didn't buy it. Since she was funding this little startup there wasn't much I could do."

"You mean, if she didn't get to be the star, she'd take her bat and ball and go home?"

"Something like that."

"Were you and she together?"

"You mean like a couple. Well, we...uh...let's just call us good friends." He chuckled. "She said that Duncan was nice but dreary. Those were her words, not mine. I like the guy; he's my friend."

I stared at him in disbelief. I do not want a friend like him. The ice in my iced coffee was long gone, but I was fascinated with this conversation. "This was your idea?"

"Yep."

"How did you get Shari involved?"

"One night Duncan and I were at her condo after a business agent meeting. She was actually making dinner. Her favorite way to cook was normally to call for takeout, so this was a big deal. Anyway, we were discussing what it meant to be creative, to be your own boss. Duncan is knee deep in this union shit, but he'll listen to anything, so I told him my idea.

I remember exactly what he said, 'Dude, not my style. But, go for it…as long as it's legal.'

"He wasn't interested, but before we left, Shari pulled me aside and said she wanted to hear more. We met a few days later. One thing led to another. We ended up back at her apartment in bed. We spent a lot of time there, together, more than her and Duncan, poor guy. He never found out what was going on. It took some time for her to loosen the purse strings on that big bank account of hers. But eventually…"

"She did?"

"Yep.

"Did she ever give you a check for $250,000?"

"Don't remember."

"Who wouldn't remember a check for $250,000?"

Andrew shrugged his shoulders. "She was generous, I'll say that. We started some advertising, asking for Beta testers. People loved the 'Closed Set' name. Got a shit load of responses. I even lined up another funding source. The sample video was the sticking point, but we were working it out. Then she died."

"Any of your beta testers named Dice?"

"No, nothing like that. Who is Dice?"

"I don't really know. I thought Shari was meeting someone with that name. After what you told me, I assumed it was a client. Guess not. Think she might have branched out on her own? Doing a little freelancing? Maybe this Dice was a private customer?"

"No." He paused. "She didn't know the first thing about filming, editing, developing apps. She was impatient to get started. Said something about paying back an account."

"Do you know what account she was talking about?"

"Something to do with the estate, I think. Anyway, I had to make sure everything was in place. And, it was crucial––absolutely crucial––that the video upload and download functions were spot on and absolutely private. No glitches.

I didn't want it to go live unless it was perfect. As smart as Shari was, she didn't understand or didn't want to understand the need for technical excellence. She just wanted to take her clothes off."

"Anyone talk to you about her death? Maybe Duncan?"

"Yeah, he did. He is so broken up about her. Told me she drowned at some beach in Marin County. Not the ocean beaches in West Marin, but somewhere off the Bay...can't remember where. Seemed odd. She was a good swimmer. Really poor timing. Ms. Moneybags. Sorry to see her go. How did you find me here?"

"Just luck. Was walking down the street and looked in the window. Out of curiosity, how much would a tape like this cost?"

"First level package, $1,000. It can go up to five figures even more, if the client wants the Hollywood treatment." His dark eyes searched my face then slowly moved up and down my body, like he was evaluating a heifer at a livestock auction. He leaned over and whispered in my ear.

"You'd be a great replacement for Shari. Interested?"

"Not a chance," I said as I pushed back from him, as far as I could without landing at the next table.

"Think about it. Here's my card. Bet you'll call me."

He smiled and winked, then slipped on his sunglasses. With that he walked to the door, glanced over at me sitting there with my mouth open, did a military salute and walked out.

"Slime ball," I said to myself. How could Shari have gotten involved with such a creep? She must have been very bored, desperate or really needed an extra source of income. My phone pinged.

"Did you meet Duncan? Where are you?" asked Lena.

"Talked to Andrew, Shari's porn partner. Not her boyfriend. Business partner." I hit send.

"Porn vids?"

"Sex tapes," I texted back.

"Same thing. BTW thumb drive is hot. You need to see it."

I fished around in my backpack, pulled out the tablet and brought up the e-notecard for 'Mystery Man/Andrew.' 'Jerk, ultimate loser. But probably not the killer. Had too much at stake.' And then switched to Shari's. "Needed money to reimburse an account."

CHAPTER 23

"If I didn't see this myself, I wouldn't believe it," said Lena. We sat on the couch in the living room finishing up a pizza. We had just viewed about 10 video clips ranging in length from 30 seconds to 15 minutes with Shari and Andrew front and center. "So this was going to be the sample sex tape they showed Closed Set's potential clients?"

"It hasn't been edited. So we are looking at scenes, I guess. It needs to be put together. You know, I understand what Andrew was talking about when it comes to Shari's acting ability. She was awful. Beautiful but stiff, uncomfortable, clinical, almost," I said.

"She probably had more fun at her gynecologist's office," said Lena.

"This is it," I said holding the last piece of pizza.

"You can have it. I'm stuffed," said Lena.

"No, I mean this video, this company––not the pizza––is at the core of her murder. I know it."

"Then Andrew is the main suspect?"

"Nope. I don't think so. He wanted to make movies and Shari was bankrolling his company. He wouldn't get rid of the goose with all her golden eggs."

There was a loud knock on the front door that made me jump.

"Yes? Who is it?"

"Detective Hamilton."

I pulled open the door and looked up. In front of me was a tall man, almost 6'7" in his late 40's. His dark hair was combed straight back and he was growing a thin salt and pepper mustache. His sheriff's uniform from the tan short sleeve shirt to the dark pants were freshly ironed. A gold badge sat above his left shirt pocket over his heart.

"Can we talk about Shari Grantner?" Both Lena and I nodded.

"Come in. Sit down," I said. He began by asking simple questions. 'When was the last time I'd seen Shari?' 'Anything unusual happen that day?' 'What was my relationship like with her?' 'Did I see anything out of the ordinary?' I told him about the hot-headed Mitch and the brooding boyfriend, Duncan. I wanted to be methodical, telling everything and leaving all emotion out. But I couldn't contain myself.

"I discovered something about Shari that I'm sure has something to do with her death."

"Oh?"

"Closed Set. It was a company she was financing. She wasn't happy about the way things were going and had threatened to stop her funding."

"Never heard of it. What is Closed Set?" asked Det. Hamilton.

"They make sex tapes and she was filmed for a sample video. Clips are on a thumb drive that I took."

"Really?" Det. Hamilton took out a small notebook and started to write.

"Bet you didn't know about that?" I said. Lena elbowed me.

"Please forgive my sister. She considers herself a successful part time sleuth," said Lena.

"Hey," I said to Lena. "Did you forget I solved a murder last year?"

"Ms. Carson?"

I turned.

"Does last year's murder have anything to do with Shari Grantner?"

"No," I said.

"Let's focus on her," he said. And I did. First I turned on my tablet and arranged the e-notecards. Then I started talking beginning with the last thing I learned––about Andrew and Closed Set––and worked backwards to the point where I interrupted a fight between Shari and Mitch. Det. Hamilton had stopped taking notes about halfway through my monologue. He just sat and stared at me.

"My money is still on her brother Mitch," I said. "He's the one who threatened her and he had a motive. But..."

"Ms. Carson."

I stopped mid-sentence.

"Thank you. This is all very helpful. I'd like the thumb drive with the videos."

I almost said 'no' out loud. I couldn't believe I had to give up that drive with the film clips. I only viewed it once. Why didn't I keep my mouth shut? I wanted to show him that I was on top of it...that I was professional, organized, a source he could depend on, lean on even. Instead I showed him that I was an overconfident blabbermouth.

Lena smiled sweetly and handed over the little drive.

"Thank you ladies. This will help in the investigation."

"Could I..."

Det. Hamilton held up his hand like a traffic cop at an intersection. "This is a murder investigation. It can be very dangerous. You need to step back. Just in case, here is my card. But please, please put an end to your investigation. We will handle it."

With that he left. I waited until I heard him drive away and then I howled. "How could I be so dumb? How..."

"Trish."

"Why did I mention that I had the drive? I could have..."

"Trisha.

"Do you realize..."

"Trish. Stop it. Now. Stop."

"I feel like an idiot."

"You are. But I'm not. I downloaded the thumb drive. We have all the videos right here." She tapped her laptop. I reached over and hugged my sister.

"You are so smart."

'Yes, I am," she said. "We make a great team, don't we Trish."

"Yes, we do. We always have. Look, I'm exhausted. Going to bed." I slipped Det. Hamilton's card into my pocket.

"I think Mitch should be your next contact," said Lena. "That's if you can find him."

"Will do. But after a good night's sleep."

CHAPTER 24

A few days later I was back at an AT&T entrance gate scanning tickets. I wondered if Mitch and Mia would attend today's game. Instead of the brother and sister, I faced long lines of elementary-aged kids. This was a mid-week day game and summer camps often brought their campers to the ballpark for the afternoon. Frazzled looking counselors kept the youngsters, all wearing the same colored tee shirts, together as they inched their way through my line. The kids were in awe of the massive open entrance to the ballpark, the constant noise, and the pushing crowds.

When there was a brief hold up, I leaned over and asked two 8-year-olds, "So who's your favorite player?" The little boy was speechless. But the girl was ready to answer. She said, "I'm a Dodgers' fan. I'm not supposed to like the Giants." With that the jam in my line was cleared and they were on their way.

Later, I was re-assigned to the View Section, the top level of the ballpark. It was a no hitter until the 7th inning, so the game flew by. That's when the Rockies put in a relief pitcher who struggled with his control. The Giants went ahead 1–0. After that it was batters up, batters down. In a blink of an eye, Tony Bennett's rendition of "I Left My Heart in San Francisco" signifying a Giants win was drifting through the ballpark.

I moved over to the escalator and stood on one side as the crowd surged out of their sections toward the exit five flights below.

"Love games like this," said a fan as he walked past me heading down the moving stairway.

"Me, too," I said, already thinking about the traffic I would hit on the ride back to Marin. I watched as a little boy and his father stepped on to the escalator. It moved downward about two feet and then stopped.

"Sorry folks," I said to the massive crowd inching toward me in a solid block. "The escalator isn't working. Please take the ramp around the corner or the stairs." A weary groan arose from the fans. While not thrilled, they took the machinery breakdown in stride and began to walk away.

I turned around to watch the little boy and his father, the last people on the escalator, walk carefully down one flight and turn to the left. A maintenance man had just arrived and was waiting for the escalator to clear before he began to fix the problem.

I faced the throng of fans, my arms spread out, blocking the escalator. Over and over I repeated, "The escalator is broken, please take the steps or the ramp." The wall of black and orange then flowed around me like they were passing boulders mid-stream in a river.

I took a quick look behind me down the escalator. I'm not crazy about heights. Looking down, the empty metal stairs began to narrow and steepen. There seemed to be a gravitational pull pushing me head first toward the stationary steps. I grabbed hold of the side rails, closed my eyes and turned back around.

"Let me walk down," said a man.

"It's not safe. I'm sorry."

"Oh, come on."

"Can't do it. Please take the ramp or the stairs."

"Ted," I called out to my co-worker who was directing

some fans.

"Ted, can you come over here and give me a hand?"

The people in front of me began to blur; the sounds faded. My head felt like it was light enough to float away from my body. Deep breath. Don't faint. Not now.

Ted couldn't hear me. There were too many people. It was too noisy.

Okay. Okay. I can handle this. I glanced down the escalator, saw the brown shirt of the maintenance man bent over the uncooperative stairway.

"I'm going down those steps," said a voice I had heard before.

I turned around and was facing the creep who had stopped me in the parking lot a week ago. He took a step closer. I took a small step back, very aware of the one story drop behind me.

"The escalator is closed, sir," I said, eyes darting around the crowd for Security.

"Ted," I called out again. But, my voice vanished into the thousands of moving, talking, laughing fans.

"You can't stop me," he said, now only inches away. "And I'm taking you with me."

I put my hands on his chest and pushed. But he didn't budge.

"Don't touch me," he said.

"Security," I called out. But my voice dissolved into the boisterous cheer from the fans as the escalator behind me started working. I glanced back at the empty moving steps.

"Give me one more minute to test them," the workman called up at me. I turned my head back and the man's face was next to my ear.

"Stay out of the apartment and stop asking questions. I told you that before. Leave it alone."

"What are you talking about?"

His arm circled my waist, holding me close. He began to squeeze. I felt a sharp point, the tip of a blade pressing through my black vest and deep orange work shirt. It rested on my stomach.

I gasped.

"Don't scream. Just listen. Leave the dead alone. This is your second warning. That's all you get."

He took a step forward. I tried not to move but I shifted one foot behind me. I could feel the concrete give way to the smooth metal of the escalator.

"Help." I yelled again, louder. "Help." I reached for the arm of a nearby fan. Alarmed, he grabbed my hand and pulled me away from the escalator.

"Whoa," said the thug, still holding on to me. "Careful little lady, you almost fell."

Off in the distance I saw two San Francisco police, I raised a hand and started waving.

Below me a voice yelled, "Okay, send them down." and the fans surged onto the escalator. The man was gone, lost in the crowd.

"Ted" I called out again. This time my co-worker heard me and threaded his way through the swarm to my side.

"You okay? You look real pale."

"I need to talk to the police. Watch this for me, will you?"

"Sure, sure. You go."

As the fans passed in front of him, he thanked them for coming and gave an occasional high-five. He looked over at me. I hadn't moved.

"Go. Everything is fine here."

I nodded and pushed through the crowds heading for the police.

"Well, Ms. Carson," said Officer Natalie Kalaw. "So, the man who harassed you in the parking lot about five days ago is back."

I nodded. Officer Kalaw and I sat knee to knee in a small windowless room of the police substation buried in a corner of the ballpark.

"He held a knife to my stomach and tried to push me down the escalator."

"Are you okay?"

"Scared."

The cop kept her eyes on my face. "What did the person look like?"

"I told you that before. A week ago. Remember?"

"Again, please."

"He was taller than me. Probably 5'9, 5'10. Average build. No accent that I could tell. A narrow, angular face and a small goatee and a buzz cut. He was white."

"Any idea of his age?"

"Thirty-five to forty, I'd guess

"Anything else?"

"He had on a windbreaker-type jacket. You know the type that crinkle when you touch it."

"What color was it?"

"Dark blue, I think."

Officer Kalaw pushed back her chair and bumped into the wall. Her thumbs were hooked into her heavy dark belt.

"And you still don't know why he has chosen you to harass?"

My face heated up. My hands were icy cold. I was holding my breath.

"Breathe, Ms. Carson."

I let out an audible sigh. My shoulders that had been hugging my ears, relaxed.

"I think I do know. This time he was very specific. He told me to stay out of an apartment that belongs to a friend of my sister's who died recently. Actually, she was murdered."

Officer Kalaw leaned in slowly toward me. Our faces were

inches apart.

"Murdered?"

"Yes."

"Is there an ongoing investigation?"

"Yes. Marin County Sheriff. Det. Hamilton is in charge of it."

Officer Kalaw called out to an associate and asked him to put a call into Det. Hamilton. "Tell me what you know about this murder."

I went through everything that had happened yet again. She asked questions, but mostly she listened.

"Ms. Carson, in the future, I'll have one of the officers or a security guard at the ballpark walk you to your car after the games. In the meantime, stay out of the dead woman's apartment and let the police handle the investigation."

She stood up, and squeezed by me, walking into the larger outer office of the substation. I followed closely behind. There was that familiar refrain again. 'Let the police do the investigating.' Maybe I'll have those words engraved on my tombstone.

About 30 minutes later, after a quick stop at my locker, then at the kiosk to clock out, I headed through the Second and King Gate along with a few remaining fans and employees.

I walked the long block toward Third Street. At Willie Mays Plaza, fans were still hanging out around the 24 towering palm trees. I dodged a man taking photos of his family all holding their Giants caps over their hearts.

"Hey, would you take a photo of us?" the mom of the group called out.

"Sure," I said and the dad gave me his phone.

"Come on folks. Get closer. Pretend you like each other."

There were a few giggles but they obeyed and squeezed tightly together. A few feet behind them, there was a man clearly in the photo. Why didn't he move? He had to see the family standing between us.

"Sir, you back there? Could you scoot over? You are in the picture," I said looking at the small screen on their smart phone. The figure began to move and then I heard,

"Only if you have a drink with me."

I looked up. It was Jon.

"OOOO," said the kids lining up for the photo. "Is this your boyfriend?"

I ignored them.

"Where did you come from?" I asked. He pointed at the ballpark.

"Right, silly question. You're still in the picture. Keep moving. Please."

He did and I was able to take a few quick snaps. The family crowded around me and pointed to the small digital screen. They agreed the photos were perfect. After a few spirited thanks, and one big bear hug that lifted me off my feet, they headed to the streetcar now pulling up in front of the ballpark.

I waved. "You guys looked good. Safe trip home. See you next time."

Jon walked over to me. "Does your job ever stop?"

"When you're in a Giants uniform, you're an instant part of everyone's ballpark experience."

"I'm in security across the city, remember. No one is thrilled to see me. By the way, last time I was here, you didn't stop by my seat during the game," he said. "You said you would."

"I said I'd try. I was probably busy." Truth be told, I was also embarrassed. I had seen him one more time after he escorted me out of my office at Fort Mason when I was fired. It was night and I had just been pulled out of the bone-chilling waters of Aquatic Park off San Francisco Bay. He was there on the beach with my sister along with the SF Police and an ambulance. Yes, I had helped the police catch a big drug dealer, but I was shaking, scared and humiliated the last time I saw Jon.

We chatted for a few minutes about the game. I tried to listen, but I kept rerunning the escalator scene over in my mind.

"I moved over for that photo so you owe me. You can pay up now. How about here?" he said pointing to the outside patio of the Public House, a restaurant connected to the ballpark.

"What? What did you say?"

"I asked if you would like to have a drink...in a roundabout way...with me."

"Sure. As long as there are chairs. I have to sit down."

Jon found two seats near the door.

"Beer?"

"No, I'm tired and need to drive. How about an iced tea?"

"Okay," and he ordered for us.

Jon looked at me, then shifted in his chair. He tapped his fingers on the tabletop and shifted again. He was about to say something, but he stopped.

"Yes?" I said.

"When did you start to work here?"

"This is my first season." Awkward pause.

"How did you get a job like this?"

"Some friends told me they were hiring. I was lucky, I guess. I've never worked in the sports industry before."

"Yes, you have. When you worked for that Masters swim group."

"It's not quite the same. I didn't have to deal with 40,000 excited fans. Are you still at Fort Mason?"

"Yeah. Are you still an amateur detective?" He smiled.

I was silent. His eyes narrowed and he stared at me with a questioning look. "That was not a trick question. And I'm hoping the answer will be 'no.'"

"Well...," is all I could muster.

He sat back in his chair. "I don't believe it. You are involved with something. Probably something that you shouldn't be. Didn't you learn your lesson? You are not a member of the police department or a private investigator," Jon said. "You know, you remind me of a rabbit I had when I was growing up. Name was Hiphop."

"A rabbit? I remind you of a rabbit. So I'm timid and shy?"

Jon shook his head.

"Pushy. Nosey. Rabbits love to explore; especially places they aren't supposed to explore. That's you."

"I'm not pushy. I'd say more like determined, focused, curious, interested."

Jon snorted.

"Why did you name your rabbit Hiphop?"

"I don't remember. I was 8-years old at the time. So, tell me what's going on."

The waiter brought over our drinks along with a big bowl of nachos. I pulled out a chip, plastered with gooey cheese. Before I stuck it in my mouth I said, "I have talked about this once today. I don't want to do it again."

"I won't let you get away with that."

"Away with what?"

"The 'I'm not going to talk about it' line."

"Look, I'm tired."

"Tell me."

I hesitated. Jon's instincts had been on target last year, but I hadn't listened to him. He wouldn't like what I had to say now. I pulled out the tablet from my backpack, pushed the drinks and the nachos to one side. I clicked through each e-card explaining as I went along. Then I told him about the man at the escalator. When I finished, he looked at me in disbelief.

"Don't...do...this, girl. Got it?"

"Jon, Shari was my sister's best friend. Her sister asked

me to help."

"Not your job," said Jon.

"Someone held her head underwater. She drowned. A horrible way to die."

"Yes, it is."

"Have you ever come close to drowning?" I asked.

He nodded.

That was unexpected. I sat up straighter in my chair. "Really, what happened?"

"I surf or I used to. I was a teenager and had gone to Hawaii for my first big surf trip. I dropped in on an overhead wave, wiped out. Was held down by the next wave. There were coral outcroppings under the water. I was about to kick for the surface when my leash caught up on something, probably the coral. I was kicking and kicking. I could see the surface right above me, but I couldn't get there. The inside of my chest was starting to vibrate and burn. I couldn't hold my breath much longer. My arms were numb and my throat felt like it was going to explode. Then my friend dove down, pulled the Velcro release on the leash around my ankle until it came free. He grabbed me by the waist just as I opened my mouth and swallowed what had to be half of the Pacific Ocean. When we surfaced, there was a lot of coughing and heavy breathing for a while, but I was okay. Then he dove back down and was able to unsnag the leash around the outcropping. My board popped back up with him. So, that's a long answer, to the drowning question."

"You surf?"

"That's what you took away from what I just said?"

"Of course not. It just came as a surprise."

"Remember the conversations we used to have?" he asked.

I nodded.

"What did I tell you then?"

"Go to the police? I did, remember?"

"Not soon enough. Put the tablet away."

I scooped it up and dropped it in my bag. I could tell a lecture was about to occur. His next line would be 'if I had any concerns––any at all––tell them to the local police. They would investigate.' My back stiffened as I readied for his chastisement.

He cleared his throat. "Would you like to have dinner?"

Not what I was expecting. "Jon, thank you, but I'm tired. I want to go home."

"I don't mean now. Maybe this weekend."

"This weekend? Dinner? With you?"

"Yes, with me. Is there something wrong with that?"

I just stared at him.

"That's what people do when they want to get to know each other. Well?"

"I'm flattered, I really am, but I have to get ready for the next open water clinic. I'm taking Shari's place as the coordinator."

"Oh."

Jon shifted in his seat again and looked past me at the fans left in Willie Mays Plaza.

"Thank you for asking. Maybe another..."

He interrupted me. "Guess this weekend won't work. Anyway, here's my phone number. Call me when you have some free time."

I let out a big sigh. "I want to go home now. I'm tired." With that I stood up and walked out, leaving him staring after me.

As soon as I rounded the corner, I wondered what just happened. Someone who I knew and trusted and liked, had asked me out and I ran for the door. No wonder I didn't have a social life. I turned around and walked back to the restaurant. Jon was still sitting there. I came up behind him.

"Dinner, Saturday night. This is where you can reach me." I scribbled my phone number on the back of a napkin. Before he could turn or say anything, I was gone again, heading for my car.

There were still a few cars in the parking lot when I pulled out and headed for Marin. The toasty late afternoon sun still warming the neighborhood near the ballpark faded into overcast dampness as I approached the Golden Gate Bridge. Dense drippy fog erased the tops of the bridge towers. A wet chilly wind blew in from the Pacific Ocean causing the flags flying near the bridge to snap and pop in the strong breeze.

To my left, the ocean was hidden beneath a flat unappealing screen of grey. A foghorn rumbled loudly beneath the wheels of my car. Startled, I almost drove into the next lane. When I reached the Marin side of the Bridge, I drove out of the wall of fog into the sun lighting up the Sausalito hills that stretched down to San Francisco Bay.

Although my radio had been on as I drove through the City and across the bridge, I never heard a word of the post-game review until now. The talk radio host shifted the conversation from the prowess of the pitcher to the feisty right fielder, Eduardo Martinez, known as Fast Eddie to his fans. I remember returning from my break seeing Martinez trotting toward first base about to argue with the umpire, who was standing with his hands on his hips staring at the approaching player. The first base coach stopped him before he reached the ump, turned him around and sent him back to right field before he got himself into trouble.

The caller that came on next was Sibyl, an astrologer who analyzed the baseball players based on their astrological signs.

"It was an Aries thing to do. You know that Aries are fiercely competitive, scrappy, willful. They tend to act first and think later."

"Fast Eddie's an Aries?" asked the talk show host.

"Of course, it is so obvious. In the heat of the moment, he can be hot-tempered, even unstoppable. But he is an achiever."

"Well, this achiever needs to dial it down a notch," said the radio host.

I wish Sibyl would look at my chart and weigh in on me. Maybe help me figure out why I seem to attract dangerous people. I drove into the tunnel that cuts through the Marin headlands. On the other side, I switched off the radio and glanced at the fog bouncing around the top of the hills waiting for a signal to tumble down and screen out the sun.

I was tired when I was sitting with Jon, but now, every nerve ending tingled. I felt alert, awake. The re-emergence of the thug was an endorsement for my persistence. I was on the right track and someone wasn't happy about it. The question was 'who?'

CHAPTER 25

When I turned in to our short street in San Rafael, I could see Dr. T leaning against his pitch black '70 Dodge Charger parked at the curb in front of Lena's house. He was coaching four pre-teens playing street basketball.

"When the ball is passed to Jaime, that's the time for you, Sue, to go to the basket, so he can pass it to you and you can shoot."

"I always miss. I never make it," she said.

"Well, you will. But first you need to get the ball and keep it, not bounce it off to someone else as if it's on fire. Don't be afraid to shoot. Think of it like this, every time you miss a shot, you are closer to making the next one."

"Huh?" said the girl, her hair pulled back in a ponytail. "I don't get it."

"You will, in time," said Terrel.

The tweens moved to the side of the street as I pulled into the driveway.

T. walked over the driver's side door, opened it and offered me his hand. "Allow me," he said, with a slight bow."

"What's with the formalities?"

"You don't remember?"

I looked at him as he pulled off his black rimmed glasses and started to clean them on his shirt.

"Oh that's right. Our last baseball bet. Something about civility."

"Correct," he said, placing the glasses back on his face. A basketball came flying our way and hit the trunk of my car.

I groaned.

"Sorry," came four voices. Terrel picked up the ball and threw it back to them.

"The bet was, as I remember it. If the A's win their next game, you have to be polite and agreeable to me for 24 hours. If the Giants win, I have to be polite and agreeable to you, etc., etc., etc."

"That's right. That means you can't yell at me or tell me what to do?"

Terrel put his hands on his lanky hips, cocked his head. "I don't yell at you or your sister, although there are times when I'm close to it. Anyway, that's the basic premise."

"Well, if you won't yell or lecture me, I'll tell you what happened today. I was..."

Lena walked through the front door talking on her phone, listening first to us, then to the caller. She hit 'end call' and came over and sat down heavily on the front steps.

"What is it, Lena? You look...strange. Who was on the phone?" I asked.

Terrel sat down next to her, took her hand and turned her face around so he could see her eyes.

"You don't look good," said Terrel.

"That was Mia," she said.

"Which Mia was on the phone? Mia, the weepy sister or Mia, the liar?" I asked.

"The police have arrested Mitch."

"If they didn't release him, that means they had probable cause," said Terrel.

"What's that?" Lena asked.

"Legal terminology. The police found something, maybe in his apartment or his car or they learned something when they questioned him that made them think he might have committed a crime."

"Mia mentioned something about his car. They found something in the car."

"That little sports car he drives?" I asked.

"I don't know," she said.

Terrel looked over at me and said, 'Well, that takes care of your investigation. The police have a suspect in custody. You know if this goes to trial and he loses, he could get the death penalty."

"That's a big jump. He was just arrested. Besides, no one dies in California. The last time anyone was executed in California was in 2006 and that was after spending 23 years on death row. The guy was 76 years old," I said.

"Seriously? That's what you want to talk about––the history of executions in California? Mitch is in very genuine trouble," said Dr. T. "He won't care if the death penalty is actually, life in prison with a possibility of execution. His life as he knows it could be over."

Lena grew suddenly pale. Terrel, who now had his hand on her wrist, checked her pulse and looked at his watch.

"Are you sick?" I asked my sister. She snatched her hand away from T.

"No, I'm not," she said. "Mia wants me to go visit Mitch with her in a few hours."

"You're not going," said T.

"I don't want to go, T. So Trisha, would you go?"

I could barely contain myself. Of course, I would go. I wanted to talk to Mitch and here he was a captive (literally) audience. However, I didn't want my excitement to tip off Terrel. As far as he was concerned, my investigation was over.

"Well, I'll think about it."

Lena gave me a strange look. "But last night we agreed..."

"Let's go inside," I said to the both of them before Lena could say anything else.

Terrel helped Lena stand up.

"You are sick," I said. "Is that why you don't want to go?"

Lena ignored my question. She sat down on the couch. "I can't believe he would murder his sister," she said. "That money she was holding for him would be his in—what did she say—less than a year?"

Terrel sat down in the big easy chair, crossed his arms and leaned back. His long legs stuck out in front of him and he looked at the ceiling. Outside, the kids' voices bounced back and forth. I could hear the dull thump, thump, thump as someone dribbled toward the basket.

"The police don't hold people unless there is a reason," he said. "Well, let me take that back. Where I grew up in the 'cheap seats' side of the Peninsula, guys hanging out on the corner would be routinely picked up and tossed in jail. A lot were gangbangers. But there were also innocent people that ended up in jail for being brown or black. My dad had many long talks with me about how to deal with the police if I was ever stopped. I pretended to ignore him...that I was too cool to listen. But all his advice came back, speed of light back, the first time the cops stopped me."

I learned about Terrel's past life in short little comments like this. I knew his father was black and had an auto body shop near Palo Alto. His mother was white. She was a teacher and from what Lena told me, his mom wasn't too fond of her. Didn't think she was good enough for her son, the doctor. His dad liked her. He even helped me out once when my car was damaged. T's dad owned an autobody shop in Pleasanton and when my car was damaged, he loaned me a bright yellow restored 1978 Checker Cab, with trademark checkerboard black trim.

"Okay, I'll go," I said. I stopped for a second and stared at the both of them. Should I tell them about the escalator incident. Not a good idea. They would tell me to step back and I wasn't about to do that.

The adrenaline that surged through me on the drive home had rapidly ebbed. Even the thought of questioning Mitch didn't help. I lumbered into my room, sank down on the bed and called Mia, arranging to meet her at the entrance to the Marin County Jail in about an hour. That gave me time to check on line to see if her brother was listed in the Sheriff's Booking Log. He was and so were his charges. One was Violation of Probation. That's interesting. I didn't know Mitch had been arrested before. For what? Then there was another listing for possession of a controlled substance.

I reread his charges a few times; then checked the penal code to make sure I understood what I was reading. Nothing was said about murder or manslaughter. He could easily make bail, I thought, but no bail was listed.

Marin County Jail is hidden in a hillside in the Marin County government complex in San Rafael, not far from our home. In fact, when Lena and I were young our parents took us to feed the ducks and geese at Lagoon Park across the street. I never knew the jail was there. I do remember seeing police cars parked next to a walkway that ended at the top of a hill, but I was too young to put the two together. During my booking log search, I came across a review–yes, a review of the jail by someone who knew jails––seems the reviewer had been in and out of them more times than he wanted to discuss. He felt our local penal institution was one of the best.

The evening sky was a deep violet-blue when I met Mia in the parking lot near the jail. Her face was a flat mask and her hands were shaking.

"Mia, are you okay?" I said putting a hand on her arm.

"I'm cold, really cold." She folded her arms and grasped her sides. "This is what happens when I get nervous," she said. Her teeth were clenched to make them stop chattering. I actually felt sorry for her. Her sister was dead, her brother now charged with her murder. She was the only one left. She had to take charge. Right now, it didn't look like she was up for the job.

We walked into the building, rode the elevator to the intake floor. The fluorescent lights cast a bluish light on the people waiting in the chairs. One mother read a book to her little girl in Spanish. Another couple sat quietly staring at the blank walls. We checked in, stored our purses and backpacks in the small lockers available, headed for a walk-through metal detector and then took an elevator one flight up.

I'd been in jail in Colorado after two DUI's when my husband left me. It was a horrible experience. Once inside, a jail is a jail is a jail and if you are on the wrong side of the glass you don't get to go home.

We walked into a closet-sized room, big enough for two chairs, separated by thick double, maybe triple paned glass. Our eyes were glued to the door on the other side, the side that Mitch would use.

Wearing a bright orange jumpsuit, Mitch walked in and looked at Mia, who immediately started to cry.

"What is she doing here?" he said through the speaker on his side of the glass.

For a split second, I seemed unbalanced. Not sure who was behind the glass, Mitch or me. I focused on the names scratched into the window, the phone numbers, and the hearts. How many people had sat here before me?

"Well?" said Mitch sitting down.

"She came, because...because," said Mia. "You tell him."

"Mia asked me to help find out who killed Shari. I want to ask you some questions," I said. "This is off topic, but you have outstanding warrants and it looks like there may be at least one parole violation. The police want to hold you, so they used these charges to keep you here. What I want to know is why?"

"Because I told the truth. When they questioned me last week, I said my sister was a controlling person. She had my money and I wanted it. A week later, here I am."

"What you said––although it doesn't sound very good––it's not a crime to have a disagreement with a family member."

"Right. This is a misunderstanding. Mia, did you call our lawyer? I'm supposed to be arraigned soon."

She nodded. Barely able to speak, she whispered, 'you said they found something in your car, something that linked you to Shari. What was it?"

"Nothing really important."

"Well, it is important enough to keep you here. What is it?" I asked.

Mitch looked annoyed. "Strands of her hair, okay? No big deal. She rides–did ride in my car––more than once."

"That's all? Only strands of hair?"

"Aren't you finished with your questions yet?"

"Please Mitch, she is trying to help," said Mia. He leaned back in his chair and crossed this arms over his chest.

"I heard you threaten your sister before the open water clinic. You were so upset. Did you see her later?"

"No, I didn't. I cooled down after I saw her...and you. I went for a long bike ride. That helped. I wanted to explain why I needed the money...why it was important to my business venture. I went back to the site of the clinic; she was gone. I packed up my bike and left the park."

"You didn't go to Caden's Corner?"

"I don't know where that is."

"What about China Camp?"

"I went home, okay. I drove home, by myself."

"Then what?" I asked.

"I put a call into my business partner to tell him about the lack of funds."

"What did he say?"

"He wasn't there. I left a message."

Mia finally stopped crying, took a big gulp of air. "I knew you didn't do it," she said.

Mitch looked over at me again, a little warily. "I didn't. And I hope the police figure it out sooner rather than later. I have a meeting in a few days for the fate of this start up. I have to be there."

"A meeting is the least of your problems. What's the meeting about?" I asked.

"Money," he said. "Now, can I have some private time with my sister?"

I stood up to leave. I pressed the button to be buzzed out when Mitch said, 'Since I didn't kill my sister, who do you think did?"

"I'm not sure."

"What exactly do you know?"

"Not as much as I thought."

"That's not going to help me," he said.

I nodded, left the tiny cubicle and headed for the elevator to take me back down to the waiting room.

According to my sister, Mitch was always an entitled, hot-headed jerk. He had no idea how much trouble he was in. But I began to doubt my iron-clad belief that he was the murderer. Maybe he was innocent. Maybe he was a liar. Back to the drawing board. No matter what Dr. T said, my investigation was far from over.

CHAPTER 26

I had to put Mitch, Shari and Mia aside the next day. I had the open water clinic to think about. Although my sister thought I was ready and capable to run the event, I wasn't so sure. So I scheduled a run through with the volunteers at Lake Caldwell.

"Lena, I'm not expected to get in the water, am I?" I asked pulling out of the driveway. I hoped the answer would be 'no.' Instead there was silence. My sister had her ear buds in and her eyes were closed.

"Lena," I said a little louder.

No response.

Finally, I reached over and pulled out one of the buds.

"What?" she said.

"I don't get in the water, do I?"

"You don't have to. But it might help if you did."

I thought about that as we drove down Highway 680 in bumper to bumper late afternoon commute traffic. We were crawling east along with half of the San Francisco Bay area, leaving me too much time to imagine the hours ahead.

"Well, I'm not sure I want to. I've only been swimming a few times in the last year."

"You could wear that old wetsuit of mine if you want," my sister said. "That way you could dog paddle without any problem. But you really should get on a paddleboard and follow us around."

"I'll think about it. Tell me about the instructors. Anything I should know?"

Lena listed the five instructors and a bit about their different personalities.

"Tim is a pleasant, easy going guy, great with the mid-level swimmers. So is Pablo; he has tons of Bay swimming experience. He can be a little cocky, but nothing to worry about. Both exude confidence in themselves and the swimmers. We've got Michelle with the more advanced group. She packs in as much information and technique as they can take. And the swimmers are grateful for it. Amy is with the beginning-mid-level types. She is direct, encouraging and funny. Trudy takes the beginning beginners and somehow gets them to be comfortable in the water."

I drifted off while Lena was talking, thinking about Dad. After that meeting with him a few days ago, Lena had calmed down. As far as she knew, he was gone, hopefully never to come back. I felt he wasn't too far away. From what he said, he had driven a long distance to find my sister and had been surprised, but pleased to see me. I know it took some effort to track Lena down. So it was strange for him to turn around and drive away.

"Lena?"

She looked over at me.

"Do you want me to move?"

"Of course not, no."

"That's not the feeling I get. You've made some very pointed comments about me not paying my share, owing you, staying longer than you wanted. Have I overstayed my welcome?"

The cars ahead of me were now moving at a steady pace. Lena turned back to her window.

"I don't want to talk about it," she said.

"Look, I'm sorry. I thought I'd have enough money to move

out by now. But at least I have a part time job. It's seasonal, but I am bringing in some money. Do you need more?"

"No."

"Do you need the room?"

"No."

"Well, what is it?"

"It really doesn't have anything to do with you. I'm trying to figure something out."

"But it has something to do with me in your spare room?"

"I guess."

"Well, tell me about it. I can't help if I don't know what it is."

"Let it go, Trish."

"But..."

"Just let it go."

This isn't the way I wanted the conversation to end. "One more thing," I said.

"I don't want to talk about it."

"No, this is something else."

She looked over at me and sighed.

"What?"

"Remember Jon, the security guard from Fort Mason?"

"Yeah. Why?"

"I've seen him at the ballpark a few times."

She perked up. "Really. So that's a good thing?"

"He asked me to dinner. But I don't think I'll go."

"Of course you won't. You don't want to get involved with him or anyone else."

"Not true. I have what I'd like to call an open door policy when it comes to my love life."

"An open door policy when it comes to psychopathic killers, maybe. From what I can tell, that door is slammed tight when it comes to normal guys. I think you'd rather live vicariously through me and T."

"Not true." I pressed down on the accelerator and we

careened off the freeway at the Livermore exit. Bitch. Bitch. Bitch. Who does she think she is? I sped along the outskirts of the busy small town, pass a few vineyards and then turned right. Up we went, winding along the edge of straw-colored hills and steep farm land falling into the valley below.

"Slow down," Lena said. "You almost drove off the road on that last turn."

"I wasn't even close."

But I lifted my foot off the accelerator and we coasted down the last grade into the kiosk at the park entrance. Lake Caldwell was off to the left. As we pulled into the parking lot, I saw some of the instructors sitting around a picnic table. Lena bolted from the car and slammed the door. She hesitated, waiting for me.

"Let's try and be civil in front of these people," I said. She nodded and we walked together down the dirt path to the table.

"Thanks for stepping in, Trisha," called out Michelle on her way to the changing rooms. "You did a great job last year. Everyone thought that Dick Waddell, one of the best open water swimmers around, had died of a heart attack, but you. You figured out he was murdered."

"Have you learned anymore about Shari?" asked a woman wearing a two-piece black work out bikini.

"Nothing yet," I said, looking over at Lena, hoping she would keep her mouth shut.

"We'll be right back." I took my sister by the arm and gave her a slight push toward the beach. When we were far enough away, I said, "Let's not talk about this. OK?"

"I wasn't going to say anything," she said, "but maybe they picked up on something you missed."

"Only mention Shari if someone brings it up and then if they ask you questions, be vague with the answers."

"All right, all right."

We moved back to the table with the swimmers and Lena

formally introduced me. I looked around and everyone was staring at me. They were curious, I could tell. With a deep breath, I pulled out the binders with Shari's meticulous notes and agenda and started to go through them. Things would run the same as Shari had planned. Dryland talk, in water drills then a short half mile swim. I passed out a timeline and everyone looked it over.

"From what I saw at the last clinic––where we need some work––is with the in-water drills. It looked like the instructor and the helper weren't communicating. I know it's hard when you're in the water. How about we get in for a while, go through the drills, making sure the two instructors are clear about what's going to happen. It's a safety thing. Last clinic, I saw one group of five swim right through another group. Nobody was hurt but it was confusing or at least, it looked confusing from the land."

"Didn't feel that way in the water," said Pablo with a towel draped over his shoulders.

"Well, I'd like to keep the groups separate. Let's divide into instructors and students. Then we can switch and the first group of instructors become the students. Okay? That way you can practice talking to each other in the water while you're teaching. How does that sound?"

The group looked at me, nodded and walked down to the water's edge. I heard one instructor say to another "I don't know why we need this. We've never had to rehearse before."

Lena looked over at me. "You were very impressive. I like that take charge mode of yours. Did you bring a whip to keep everyone in line?"

"Oh, come on. That's not funny."

But my sister was smiling. That was a relief.

Lena trotted after the other instructors. At one point, she turned toward me and pantomimed cracking a whip. I really didn't understand these mood swings. But at least she wasn't thinking about Shari or Dad. I shooed her down the beach.

Standing at the water's edge, I split the group in two: one group were instructors, the other were students. The instructors had to discuss one of their basic drills: how to swim straight. The 'students' were encouraged to act like they couldn't hear, were too scared to try, or had no clue of what they were supposed to do. I planned to stay on the shore and watch, since the group would be close by in waist-high water. They were ironing out who was going to do what, when a lifeguard came over.

"Want to borrow a rescue board and paddle out with them?"

I started to shake my head.

"Sure, she does," Lena called out from the edge of her group. "This will be helpful. Much better vantage point."

I gave her a withering glance.

"Right, might be helpful," I said to the lifeguard. "Thanks. I'll use it."

"You," I said looking at Lena, "Go get in the water. You're supposed to be of the new swimmers, remember?"

"I can't wait to see this," she said while wading into the lake. The guard put the board in the shallows.

"Should I lay on my stomach, get on my knees or stand up? What's the best way?"

"Do what is the most comfortable way for you. These boards are very stable. You can change positions without any fear of tipping over. And here's a whistle. If you find yourself in trouble, just give it a blow; one of the guards will come get you."

With that, he walked back to the lifeguard tower.

I pushed the board out into the water and then scrambled on and got to my knees. The board was wide and floaty. It was like paddling the living room couch. Very steady and solid. Stroking with both arms, I kept the front of my body leaning forward and moved toward the swimmers now in shoulder-deep water.

The 'students' were out of control. Floating on their backs, splashing one another, talking and squealing loudly; they weren't paying any attention to the teachers.

"Guys, don't overdo it," I said. "The instructor needs to communicate with the assistant. You're the next group of instructors. Remember, karma. You're going to get what you're giving." I felt like a mama duck talking to her unruly ducklings.

"Thank you," said Trudy, who was treading water at a fast clip and clearly annoyed with her group of students. "Okay, she started. "I want to show you a few different ways to sight." She had Jake, the other instructor swim about 30 yards away and stop.

"Jake is now a buoy," she said to the swimmers. She demonstrated a few ways to sight or look ahead so that the students could keep swimming in the right direction. Then the group took off, aiming for Jake.

Once they all reached him, Trudy said, "Now, see that larger tree on the other side of the lake. I want you to head for it."

"Where are we going?" said one pretend student, floating on his back.

"Which tree am I heading for?" said another whose legs were churning up the water with a fast egg-beater kick. Trudy and Pablo swam to each student and talked calmly to them until they understood. Then, off they went. I paddled slightly ahead of a group of swimmers. It was early evening and the water was a delicious 75 degrees. The air was still and warm; the lake as flat as green-tinged glass. This isn't as hard as I thought it would be. My shoulders drifted downward and I let out a sigh of relief.

At our backs, the sun was dropping behind the straw colored hills. We were headed for the tall dark pines on the other shore lit up by the sinking sun. The shoreline ahead looked much closer than it actually was. We had other drills to practice so I needed to get the group back to the beach.

I was moving through the water toward Trudy, when I saw a flash on the shore, like the sun hitting metal. It seemed to come from an area that––if I had my directions right––was next to Caden's Corner.

"Trudy, turn the group around and head back to the beach. Practice the next drill: exiting and entering the water. I'll follow you in. Need to check something out," I said.

I watched as they swam easily to the shore. Trudy was in front leading the group. Pablo brought up the rear in case anyone had problems. Halfway in, two guys decided to race each other and slipped from a smooth freestyle to an arm-churning undulating butterfly stroke.

I smiled and relaxed. Well, they were listening to me. I turned and paddled a few strokes closer to the tree-lined shore. I saw the flash again only this time it was 50 feet to the right of the original spot, moving away from me. My back hurt from bending over and my arms were tired from paddling so I sat upright for a few minutes and straddled the board, dangling my legs over the sides. I watched the flash move further to the right.

I started paddling on my stomach toward the thin line of beach in front of the flash. It disappeared; instead a long, narrow shape emerged from the trees. It was a rifle barrel. Strange, they don't allow hunting that I know of in this area of the park. The rifle moved slowly, then stopped, pointing directly at me.

"No!" I yelled."Stop"

Something zinged by my head and splashed in the water. Another bullet flew close to my shoulder. I dropped into the lake and pushed the board onto its edge making a barrier between me and the shore and the rifle.

A third bullet pierced the board less than an arm's length away. "Stop," I yelled again. "Someone help me!" The board wasn't much protection, but at least I was invisible to the shooter.

The guard's whistle hanging around my neck floated between me and the board. I pushed it into my mouth and blasted out a long high pitched screech until I was out of air. Its piercing sound echoed across the quiet lake.

"Help! Help me!"

The shooting stopped. The lake was silent except for the sound of my panting. I tried to control my heavy breathing but I ended up swallowing the cool lake water and coughing it back up. My heart thudded so loud in my ears I couldn't concentrate on what to do next. I looked back toward shore and saw a lifeguard near my swimmers. Waving my one free arm frantically back and forth, I tried for another ear-splitting blow on the whistle. The guard ran into the lake with a rescue board. His arms kicked up so much water that he was covered in glittering spray. Lifeguard on fire. It would have been beautiful, if I wasn't so scared.

It took him less than 10 minutes to reach me. Still in the water, I grabbed hold of his board. He was calm. I was the one out of breath, speechless.

"What was that?" he said.

"Bullets. Someone is shooting at me," and I pointed to the trees off to my right.

"That's what it sounded like to me, but shooting isn't allowed in this area of the park or this time of year."

All I could do was nod. "I saw the sun reflect off the barrel of something...must have been a rifle."

"Rifle?"

"Yeah, rifle. I saw it. Sun on metal. When I blew the whistle, the shooting stopped."

His eyes tracked through the trees. He pulled a radio out of the waterproof pack he had around him and called into the park headquarters. "Someone might be shooting on the far side of the lake. Check it out."

"Will do...right now," said the hollow radio voice on the other end.

"You okay?"

"Yeah, I need to get back to my swimmers."

I climbed back on my board. There was a hole big enough to stick my thumb through at the front of the board. "Look at this," I said to the lifeguard watching the lake water spurt through the opening like a small geyser. "It is definitely from a gun."

I glanced up and down the shoreline. I was a perfect target if the shooter came back. I wanted desperately to stand on the far off beach, preferably behind a tree near the parking lot.

"You go back and get all of your swimmers out of the water until we figure this out. I'm going to take a look," said the guard.

"Okay," and I started to paddle feeling exposed and vulnerable. From my vantage point in the middle of the lake, I could see a dust cloud coming from the ranger's office barreling around a corner heading for the lake and then disappearing.

Most of my swimmers were already out of the water when I paddled in. Another lifeguard was off to the side holding a radio, listening to the conversation between park headquarters and the guard, now on the far shore by the trees.

I could see Lena inching forward into the water as I approached the shore.

"What happened?"

"I'll tell you in a minute," I said, scrambling off the board, pushing it to onto the pebbly beach. I looked up. A row of 10 adult swimmers still in swim caps with goggles pushed to the top of their heads were staring at me.

"We're done for the day," I said, as I led the group away from the water to the picnic table with our swim bags.

"What was that all about?" asked Pablo with a striped towel wrapped around his waist.

"Why were you blowing the whistle?" Trudy asked. "What were those pops?"

I wasn't sure what I should say. "Someone has really bad

vision. Maybe they thought I was a deer."

"Do deer swim?"

"Those were gunshots?"

"I think so." When I started to say more, I saw a figure walking through the parking lot toward me. Toward the swimmers. Toward Lena. It was Dr. T.

"Oh, no," I said in a barely audible voice. He was going to be unhappy, extremely unhappy with me. I glanced hurriedly at my sister.

"What?" she said.

I looked at the group in front of me.

"There might have been...could have been a disoriented hunter on the other side. Not a big deal. Anyway the lifeguards and park rangers are checking it out."

"Someone really shot at you?" said the woman in the bikini. I took a step away from them, cleared my throat and put my hands behind my back. They were shaking.

"Back to the clinic," I said to the group, who were looking across the lake. "I think we ironed out some of the problems that I saw before. So we can all go home, now. Thanks for coming. Next time won't be as exciting."

"I hope so," said Trudy.

The group was quiet. Then they picked up their swim bags and headed for the changing rooms. They walked off in small groups, heads together, voices low.

Terrel stood in front of me and Lena, his hands on his hips.

"Seriously, a disoriented hunter? The season for shooting deer is the fall and it is never--got that--never near a populated area. You are in 100% denial if you think this is an accident."

I sat down on the picnic table bench and watched the guard paddle back from across the lake. Then a ranger's truck pulled into the parking lot, passed the cars and drove right up onto the concrete walkway next to the lifeguard's office.

It would only be a moment before someone came over and started asking me questions.

Here we go again., I thought. Well, they hadn't been in contact with the SF Police, so as far as they knew, the shooting was an accident. That was what I was going to say.

Terrel looked at me closely. "Are you okay?"

He continued staring at my face.

"Your pupils are the size of Frisbees. Bet your blood pressure is through the roof."

"I'm fine," I said. "Stop being a doctor all the time, okay?"

"You are a magnet for trouble," he said.

"What are you doing here?" I asked Terrel.

"Didn't I mention he was going to pick me up?" said Lena.

A park ranger came up to the three of us and asked to speak to me. I walked with him to the snack bar. Out of the corner of my eye, I saw Terrel move closer to Lena and put his arm around her. Then he bent over and said something to her. I was too far away to hear it, but Lena shook her head and rested her face on his chest while she continued to stare at me.

The conversation with the park ranger didn't take too long. I gave him my name and phone number and told him what had happened. I showed him the hole in the board. Other than that, I didn't have much to say. He promised they would check into it. With that, he handed me his card, walked over to his truck, climbed in and backed off the concrete into the parking lot. He was soon lost behind the curving road and the rolling hills. I watched until, at the far end of the lake, I saw his truck cross over the bridge and onto a dirt road. His vehicle was soon smothered by a curtain of dust. The cloud disappeared behind a bend in the road that led to Caden's Corner.

Lena and Dr. T approached me slowly, arms around each other. I was struck by how in tune they were with each other even though they were so different. T, with his clinical sharp mind and very big heart; Lena, with her artistic sensibility and emotions close to the surface. They were always one click away from boiling over. But the bond they had was based on trust and a firm grip of reality; they liked the good and the bad about each other. I particularly think they enjoyed the bad more than most people. Terrel often said, 'perfection is overrated' when Lena complained about not getting things just so––whether it be in the pool or with her web design work or even her garden.

"Are you done here?" asked Terrel.

"The ranger seems to think it was an unfortunate accident," I said.

"You don't agree with that, do you?" he asked.

"If it was the first time something like this happened since Shari died, I'd say, yeah, an accident. But let's see, I've been threatened twice at work and now here in a regional park. Does that sound accidental to you?" I said.

"Twice?" Terrel and Lena said at the same time.

"Yeah, there was this thing near the escalator at the ballpark. I didn't want to worry the both of you so I didn't mention it."

"This stops now," said Terrel. His voice was quiet but firm. His dark eyes held my gaze. I couldn't look away if I tried.

"If someone was brazen enough to shoot at you in a very public place, they are getting desperate. In case you didn't notice, there were at least ten other swimmers close by, including Lena. Do you think risk-taking is––I don't know–– fun, exciting? Look, you can do what you want with your life, including going after the perceived bad guys. I've tried to talk sense into you before and it didn't work. But, and it is a big but, when it begins to involve others, including your sister, I'm going to step in. No more. O-ver. Done with."

"T, let me talk to Trish for a minute, okay?" Lena asked.

"I'll meet you in the car. Remember we have to be at dinner in the city in a few hours."

"Right," she said.

We watched Terrel walk to his shiny black Dodge Charger. Two teenage boys were in the parking lot and they stopped to admire the car. Terrel got behind the wheel, fired up the engine. The deep throaty rumble of the muscle car scared away the ducks waddling past on the edge of the sidewalk. The teens laughed. They were impressed. T climbed out of the car raised the hood and the three of them disappeared as they peered into the engine.

"He loves that car," I said. "Almost more than you. Look, I understand his concern. Maybe you shouldn't be involved."

"Trisha, I have to tell you something." She stopped.

"Okay. What?"

She glanced out at the water and down at her feet.

"Is everything okay?"

"Yeah. It's just that…"

"What?"

She shook her head, swallowed and sighed. "It's just that… uh…Shari was my friend and I don't really agree with Terrel on this. I want to know what happened to her, as much as you do." She stopped.

I nodded, urging her to continue. "Okay."

"That's it. That's all. I have to go." She turned around and walked toward the car, now surrounded by a small crowd of men and boys.

"Lena," I called after her.

The lake in front of me was deceptively calm––a long swatch of greenish water with mallards walking along the pebbly beach. I didn't understand what is going on. With Lena. With Mia. Even Mitch. It seemed just beyond my grasp. All I knew was someone took a shot at me. More than once.

The drive home was tiresome, seemingly endless. I headed into the setting sun and even the car's visor couldn't protect my face. I tried to shield my eyes from the glare with my hand, but it didn't work. The sun lit up every smeared bit of dirt on the windshield. It was impossible to see through it. I turned on the window wipers but they spread the dirt around. My phone buzzed a few times indicating a call or a text. It could wait. I wanted to go home, but I'd never make it with this windshield and its curtain of dust and grime and dried bugs. The phone kept buzzing. The annoying phone, the filthy windshield and the fact that I was almost on empty made me pull off Highway 580 and into a gas station. As I filled up the tank, I checked my messages. There was one from Duncan.

"Can you meet me at Shari's apartment tomorrow around 4?" I couldn't get away from that place even if I wanted to.

"Sure," I texted back.

I thought I'd take a detour before heading home. Although it was almost 8, the evening was warm and I really wasn't ready to go back to my small bedroom in Lena's house. I took the Central San Rafael exit as always and instead of turning left, I turned right and headed past a long linear shopping center and the high school. I was on my way back to China Camp.

I parked in the upper lot and walked down the hill to the remnants of the old shrimp-fishing village that hugged the shoreline. Off to one side, families of deer grazed on the green grass near a point of land sticking into the Bay. The afternoon Mommy-and-me crowds were gone from the beach and the seagulls inched their way across tiny pieces of cracked clam shells looking for tidbits of left behind sandwiches and cookies. A few sailboats bobbed at anchor in San Pablo Bay, just off the Village.

To my left was the point that I paddled around with Earl. A few men were cleaning up the area, probably park rangers. The snack bar that I visited was closed for the evening. Cool shade stretched across the beach and edged its way down the fishing pier. I could hear voices laughing in the distance. The sound came across the water from the sailboats anchored in the warm sun. Smoke drifted into the air from their barbecues. I watched as another sailboat came up alongside. Two men ran lines from the cleats of one boat to the other until they were rafted side by side. The incoming tide moved the boats as a unit. They drifted slowly around the anchor line.

I had just completed the trip that Shari made the afternoon or was it the night she died. What if someone brought her body to China Camp by boat, maybe anchored the same place as those sailboats? Then slipped a kayak or paddleboard into the water, took her body, paddled into this cove and dumped it. I walked over to a picnic table at the edge of the beach and stared at the sailboats, so lost in thought, I never saw the two men drifting in my direction.

"Trisha, what are you doing here?" I knew that voice well. It was my father. I stared, not trusting what I was seeing.

"What are you doing here? I thought you were leaving." About ten yards away was Dad and Earl. "I don't understand. You two know each other?"

"Old friends," said Earl. "But I hadn't seen your dad for years until he showed up here."

"We're fishing buddies," said my father. "Trish, stop glaring. That's not polite."

"This is where you came after you left Lena's house?"

"Yes. Earl was here and said I could stay with him for a while."

Dad's friend nodded to confirm my father's story.

"I come here and help him most days."

"Like a volunteer?" I asked.

"Kind of."

I had a feeling that Dad hadn't gone very far when Lena kicked him out of the house, but I never imagined he was less than 10 miles away.

"Hear you're trying to find the key to a girl's death?"

"You told him that?" I said to Earl.

"I figured out who you were when your dad here said one of his daughters was named Trisha and he described you... ah...as the sensible one, among other things."

"I have a theory," said Dad.

"About what?" I asked.

"Me and Earl have been discussing this and actually doing some on-the-water recon."

"You know that red scrape we saw on the rocks near the point?" said Earl.

"Trisha," said dad, "you're still staring."

"Of course, I'm staring. I didn't know that you two were friends, that you were so close, that..."

"Enough," said dad. "Listen for a minute."

"The red scrape on the rocks," Earl said again.

"Okay." I nodded.

"We found some identical scrapings a few beaches over," said Dad.

I squinted at him. Was I really having a rational conversation with my father?

"Trish?"

"Oh, yeah. Sorry. You were saying?"

"The scrapes might have something to do with the girl's death, don't you think?"

"Maybe. Could be. But I'm pretty sure I saw something red over behind the snack bar the last time I was here. There was a tarp covering most it. It didn't register at the time. But it could be the thing we are looking for. Earl, could you ask around about it? First, where is it? Check it out. See if there are scrapes on it. Could be someone rented it, didn't know what they were doing and kept running into the rocks."

"Unless it was used during the murder," said my father.

"Easy to find out."

Earl laughed. "The apple doesn't fall far from the tree, does it?"

I don't know what surprised me more, running into my father at China Camp, his interest in Shari's death, the re-kindled friendship with Earl or the fact that he looked 100 times better than the last time I saw him.

"Wait right here," Dad said. "Getting chilly. Need a sweatshirt. Then he turned around and walked over to his car parked at the far end of the lot.

I turned to face Earl. "So, you and my dad are fishing buddies? You knew him before?"

"Oh yeah and I knew you and your sister and your mother, too."

"Why didn't you say something the day I was here?"

"I didn't recognize you. The last time I saw you...you were maybe 10 years old, your sister was two. Your mom used to pull your hair back in a ponytail, but there wasn't much she could do with sister's mop of curls." He chuckled. "You were a nice little family. And you liked this beach. More than that you respected it...respected its history. Your dad made sure of that.

"When I saw you and your sister that day...here...well...I never had an inkling of who the two of you were. That is until I heard Lee call out your name. 'Trisha.' It didn't register at first. Not until your dad showed up. Messed up, he was. I took him home. He's been with me since he walked out of your sister's house. He's doing okay...not great...

but he's trying. This isn't the first time he's had problems, you know. And not the first time, he's bunked in my spare bedroom."

"I had no idea." He, obviously, knew more about my father and his whereabouts over the last twenty plus years, than I did. I stood up and walked toward the water. The sun had deepened into a rich warm gold; the water, like a chameleon, had shifted colors, from the silt-filled greenish brown near China Camp shore to an endless marine blue in the middle of the Bay.

Dad had reappeared pulling on a dark blue sweatshirt.

"I think two or more people were involved with Shari's death," I said as I turned around to face both men. "Maybe she was brought here by car to some kind of boat or paddleboard and thrown in the water at China Camp Village."

"Could be one person doing the job. But it would have to be a strong person. So you're looking for a man," Earl said.

The image of compact, well-built Mitch filtered through my mind. Then I remembered the strong female swimmers that were friends of Lena.

"Not necessarily. I know plenty of strong women," I added.

"Point taken," he said. "Let's say it was two people. Maybe two girls. Maybe a girl and a guy."

"Women," I said softly to myself. I hadn't thought of that. Mia? I didn't see a motive, except she was connected to her brother in a way that only twins can be. Maybe their bond was stronger than the one she had with Shari. Duncan was surrounded by girls with his union work. Nobody stood out as someone who saw Shari as a threat. Maybe, Duncan's faux best friend, Andrew, had a girlfriend that was jealous of Shari and her aspiring porn princess role.

"Two people," I said out loud.

"What did you say?" said Dad.

I turned to look at the two of them standing there, looking at me.

"Two people. So the murderer confided in somebody because, he or she needed help with the body. Maybe this other person is having second thoughts about their involvement. That's the person I have to find. Maybe Duncan will have some insight when I talk to him tomorrow."

CHAPTER 27

It was 7 a.m. and the sun was streaming through the small window of my bedroom. I could see the profile of Mt. Tamalpais––2,571 feet of sloping uneven curves that separated me and most of Marin County from the Pacific Ocean. Its black silhouette was pasted flat against the clear blue sky. Deep green pines marched up the hillsides and disappeared into a dark ravine. A shard of fog coated the top.

I lay there thinking of last evening's conversation with my father. His parting words were 'take care of your sister.' By the time I reached home, it was past 9 p.m. I collapsed on my bed and decided I was too tired to get undressed. Lena had come in later than me. I had heard the thundering grumble of Dr. T's muscle car take over the street. He parked in front of the house and let my sister out. Was I dreaming or did I hear him say, 'Tell her. Don't wait.' Then there was a pause and my sister's words were smothered by the power plant under the hood.

I wondered if Lena was having problems with a client. She mentioned that one woman who hired her to design a website for a new swimsuit company was a pain in the neck. No, that couldn't be it. Dr. T wouldn't be that concerned over a business deal. Could she be sick? Maybe it was serious and she didn't want to worry me. Whatever it was, Lena was off kilter. Normally she was over-the-top active, funny, sarcastic, straight-to-the-point and unflappable. But during the past few months, the Lena-o-meter was in the red zone. Abrasive, snippy and obtuse were now her go-to modes of operating. Talking to her about my chance meeting with our father wouldn't improve her disposition, so I stored it away.

I wandered into the kitchen and she was still there, rearranging things in her swim bag.

"Late start?" I said. No comment. Normally, she was off to swim practice by 5:30. Her tangled curly hair hadn't been combed and deep shadows lingered under her tired eyes.

"You look awful."

"Too much work; not enough rest."

"So cut back. Your health is more important."

"You don't understand."

"How can I when you won't tell me what's going on," I said. My voice was a combination of concern and frustration.

"Another time...we'll talk another time." And then she left.

Once I heard the car pull out of the driveway, I walked into her room, heading directly toward the trashcan. That's where I had found Dad's letter. Maybe I'd find something that explained my sister's strange behavior.

The trashcan, in fact, the whole room, was clean. How unlike her. Now I knew something was wrong. Lena thrived on clutter, organized clutter. It brought her comfort and peace of mind.

Her bed was made. Papers were organized on her desk; no clothes draped over chairs or left on the floor. Usually there were three or four pairs of shoes scattered around the room. Not today. Maybe she picked everything up and stuffed it in her closet, because...Terrel had had enough of her sloppiness? She couldn't find something important and was compelled to clean up to find it?

I slid open the door to her closet. No piles of clothes or shoes spilled out. Her clothes were hung up and shoes were lined up in pairs. On her desk were job folders for different clients. From what I could see, she was branching out of the aquatic market. There was a folder for a small landscaping firm; a jewelry maker and for a doctor's practice.

Nothing out of the ordinary. "Come on, Lena. Talk to me. Please talk to me," I said to the empty room. "I can help."

CHAPTER 28

Traffic from Marin to San Francisco was light as I drove into the city. So light, I was 45 minutes early for my meeting with Duncan. I parked outside of Shari's apartment. I knew that he would be there.

No one––not one single person––walked into Shari's building. A young woman jogging and pushing a stroller for twins trotted by. Technicians for a cable company stopped, set up orange cones around their van and began climbing a towering telephone pole at the corner of the building. Surveillance is boring. Glad I didn't do this full time. Getting shot at or threatened is not boring. Dangerous, yes, even an adrenaline rush...and addictive...not that I would say that to anyone.

I turned on the radio and pulled out my phone to check email messages. I didn't have to worry about work. The team was on the road. I took a quick look over my shoulder. Nobody hanging out in a doorway or hunched down in the driver's side of a parked car––except me.

Ten minutes before my appointment, a car pulled up and Duncan climbed out of the passenger side, front seat. From this angle, although her face was obscured, it looked like Duncan's assistant was driving. I heard him say, "Wait in the car. This won't take long." She drove slowly down the street looking for a parking place, then she turned at the corner, and disappeared from view.

I sat there tapping my fingers on the steering wheel. 'Won't take long.' Well then, why didn't he talk to me on the phone? Why did I have to drive forty-five minutes for a quick conversation? Sure, it didn't matter to him. He works in San Francisco. How long would it take him to get here? So annoying. Not what I expected from Duncan.

I opened the driver's side door and took my irritation out on the door. I slammed it so hard, my car rocked back and forth. Muttering to myself, I darted into the street focused on the art deco front door of the apartment across the street. A loud, long car horn blasted followed by the sound of squealing tires. I looked to my right and saw a gray BMW about ten feet away skidding toward me. Once the car stopped, the driver, a man in a sports jacket and tie, threw up his hands.

"I almost hit you," he yelled. Then a car rammed into the back of his BMW and sent it bouncing right at me. I managed to jump on the hood before I was hit.

"Are you okay?" said the man springing out of his car.

"Yes," I said, sliding back to the pavement. My hands were vibrating, so were my arms and my legs.

The college student in the second car got out. "My father's going to kill me," she said.

The sports-coated man was a take charge sort and he and the student exchanged names, numbers and insurance information.

"You're sure you're okay," he called to me.

"Who is she?" asked the student.

"She ran into the street. I had to stop quickly."

"I am so sorry. I only wanted to get across the street. This is my fault. Here's my name and number. Call me if you need any verification of what happened."

The sports jacket and the student started taking photos of their respective bumpers. Luckily, no one was hurt and the car damage was slight. But I knew that even slight damage could amount to large repair bills. I walked over to the curb and sat down.

One of the cable guys walked over.

"Everything okay here? Want me to call the police."

"I wasn't looking," I said. "He could have killed me and it would have been my fault."

"You were lucky," said the cable guy.

"I know," I said.

Both drivers climbed into their cars and moved them closer to the side of the street letting traffic now piled up behind them, pass by. I recognized one of the cars. It was Duncan's ride. I tried to get a closer look, but the fender bender cars blocked the view.

'Probably couldn't find a parking place,' I thought.

"I'm okay," I said to the cable tech. "A little shaky." With that I headed into the building

Duncan had left the door to Shari's apartment slightly open. I gave it a push and took one step in, "Hello? Hello? Duncan?"

There was no answer. The apartment was quiet. The sliding glass door off the living room was closed. The apartment was stuffy so I slid the door open and walked out. I remembered the first evening I was here. Lena and I were standing at this same spot, admiring the sparkling LED light display from the Bay Bridge to the left and the glow from the ballpark to the right. I looked down to the street. There was my car on the other side of the road. Almost directly below me, I could see a group of people gathering. They were looking through the ornate black gate at the side of Shari's building.

I stepped back in and slid the door shut.

"Duncan, where are you? I moved past the kitchen into the bedroom. Nothing was out of place. The bedspread was smooth and unwrinkled. The paintings of San Francisco still hung in place. But, the sliding glass door in the bedroom was open. A cool breeze tinged with leftover fog pushed the filmy curtains around. I walked over and took a step outside. Shari's bedroom overlooked an inside court, complete with wooden benches, graceful green ferns, an intimate landscaped lawn with full grown palm trees.

Across the court, a few people stood on their decks, pointing and looking down. My eyes followed their arms and gestures. There, three stories below next to the tastefully landscaped grass, was Duncan. His head had hit the pavement and the side of his face was resting in a halo of thick red blood. The rest of this body was on the lawn. His legs were curled up like he was lost in the middle of a soft dream. I grabbed hold of the patio rail and hung on. Heaviness was creeping up my neck and my vision began to narrow, like black curtains closing on a stage. I was going to faint.

"Duncan," I managed to call out, looking down at the figure on the lawn. Across the courtyard, the eyes of the other tenants snapped from the body on the ground up to my face. Their arms pointed at me. 'There. Over there,' they said. I stepped back into the bedroom, and sat down on Shari's bed, breathing heavily. The darkness drifted away.

Did he jump off Shari's balcony? Was her death too much too take? Was I supposed to be there to watch? I shuddered.

Or...or was he pushed? If so, who did the pushing? And was that person still in the condo? Need to leave. Now. I sprinted out of the condo into the hall and punched in 911. I told the dispatcher what had happened.

In the distance, the wail of an ambulance grew louder. I moved toward the elevator. Unless someone was hiding in the closets––and I had no intention of opening them to find out–– the apartment seemed empty. I leaned against the wall and slid down to the floor. I wrapped my arms around my knees and blankly stared at Shari's door, a few feet down the hall.

I closed my eyes and saw the image of Duncan, his head wearing a crown of crimson. A thought shot through me. Was that supposed to be me down there? For once in my life, I had a simple straightforward thought that took me to the authorities, not away from them. I pulled Officer Kalaw's card out of my backpack and called her.

"Kalaw," said the voice.

"I'm so glad you're there," I sighed.

"Who is this?"

"Trisha Carson...the person threatened at the ballpark... remember?"

She was silent for a moment. "What's up?"

"I came to my friend's condo. She died."

"Died? Right now?"

"No, she died a few weeks ago. I told you about her... remember? Just listen. Her boyfriend asked me to meet him at her apartment. I did and when I walked inside. I saw his body."

"What do you mean 'body?'"

"The sliding glass door was open off the bedroom. It's about three stories up. I went out to the balcony and looked down and he was lying on the ground. There was blood all over. He's dead. I'm sure. It was too far a fall..."

"Trisha, did you call 911?"

"Yes."

The elevator door opened and four policemen came out. They saw me on the floor.

"In there," I said. "That's the apartment. I was the one that called you."

One officer crouched down next to me. Before he said anything, I handed him the phone.

"Hello?" There was silence. "Okay...uh huh. Sure. I will."

He hung up and handed me back the phone. "You know Officer Kalaw?"

I nodded.

One of the policemen stuck his head out the door. "Clear... there's no one here." He looked at me still huddled, holding my knees, slightly trembling. "Mam, can you tell me what happened?"

"Duncan, the man out there on the grass, called me and asked me to meet him here."

"Did he say why?"

"No, his girlfriend died, was killed actually, a few weeks ago. I thought it might have been about that. Before I came into the building, I heard him tell his driver that he wouldn't be long."

"Where were you?"

"Still in my car across the street. I was early so I waited."

"Anything else?" said the officer.

"She's a friend of Officer Kalaw," said the policeman to an officer walking into the apartment. I could hear him talking on his radio. The crackling echo grew less distinct as he moved away through the condo door.

"Looks like a jumper," I heard him say.

One cop stayed next to me in the hallway.

"This man's name was..."

"Duncan Bartholomew. He is a business agent for the National Service Employees Union."

"How do you know him?"

"His girlfriend, Shari, this is her apartment...is...was...my sister's best friend. I met him a few times. He was an acquaintance, not really a friend."

"Well, why would he ask you to meet him if he was only an acquaintance?"

"I don't know."

The officer in charge looked over his notes, made sure he

had my name and contact information. Then he handed me his card.

"Give me a call if there is anything else you can think of."

I nodded. Now I had cards from three different police personnel. I moved toward the elevator, laid my forehead against its cool doors and closed my eyes. Two policemen were talking to one another by the apartment, but I could hear them.

"The workmen from the cable company had a conversation with," and he nodded in my direction. "Seems she caused a fender bender...right outside the building. She entered the building, when one of the workers saw the victim midway down––falling. He didn't see anyone on the balcony, but about five minutes later, she walked out and stood by the balcony railing and then moved back into the apartment."

"So she wasn't here when he jumped or fell?"

"Doesn't look like it. One workman saw her standing in front of the elevator on the ground floor, while his buddy watched the guy fall."

CHAPTER 29

Outside the building, I crossed quickly over to my car, stumbled in and watched the growing commotion on the street. Four police cars, an ambulance, and a crowd gathered behind the orange cones and yellow crime scene tape. From the conversation I overheard, they seemed to think Duncan jumped. I was not so sure.

I watched the police guide traffic around the cars and the ambulance. I sat there looking for Duncan's driver. By now, he or was it a she—I couldn't tell—would wonder where he was. Duncan ran on a tight schedule. Meeting after meeting. I remember Candy knocking on the door the first time I saw Duncan at Shari's apartment. She was the force that kept him moving to his appointments. If she was his driver today, the NSEU office would know.

"National Service Employees," said the male voice on the other side.

"I'm trying to reach Duncan. Actually, I'm really trying to reach his driver."

"No one has a driver here." There was a chuckle. "But

Candy does often drive Duncan to meetings, since they are going to the same place."

"Can I speak with her?"

"She isn't here today."

"Do you happen to know who was with Duncan this morning?"

"No, I'm sorry. Can you tell me what this is about?"

"Could I speak with Duncan's supervisor?"

"Sure thing. Is everything okay?" The warm chuckle on the other side of the line had shifted to serious concern. I didn't answer.

I was transferred to an office, but it went to voicemail. Not sure what to say about something so serious to someone I didn't know, I hung up. The SF Police would be in touch and so should the person driving Duncan.

My trip back to Marin was quiet. Somehow I had to tell Lena about another death. And I had to get ready for dinner with Jon this evening. After today's events, I didn't feel like going.

Lena was working on a website in her room when I walked in. As I told her about Duncan, her face became one big 'O'; her eyes, her mouth reached Grand Canyon proportions.

"Did he jump?" she asked.

"I don't know, but I don't think so. Why would he jump?"

"Shari?" Lena suggested.

"In my conversations with him, he was truly sad, despondent, even, but never suicidal."

"So what happened? Did he slip?"

I shrugged my shoulders. She looked carefully at me.

"You think he was pushed?"

"That's the way I'm leaning."

"By who? You said there was no one else in the condo. I...I

just can't believe it. Both of them are gone. The deaths have to be connected, don't you think?"

"Yes, I do. What interests me is 'why'? Why would someone want to kill him?"

"Or," said Lena, "What did Duncan know that someone wanted to keep quiet? Maybe he knew how Shari died."

"I never thought of that. How does that fit in with my 'follow the money' theory?"

"I don't think it does. From what I know, Duncan didn't have much money," said Lena.

"I need to relook at Mitch, even Andrew. Poor Duncan. He didn't know how to pick buddies or girlfriends."

"You'd know something about that," said Lena.

"What do you mean?"

"Your colossal crush on that nutcase last summer."

"Don't start that again. Not now."

"That guy almost killed me and a few other people. You were in love with a murderer," she said. "Changing the subject, when is Jon picking you up?"

"I think I'm going to cancel."

"No you are not."

"Lena, I don't feel like it. This has been a horrible day. I can't get the image of Duncan out of my head."

"I understand. I do. All the more reason to go and do something that will get your mind off Duncan and Shari. So when is he picking you up?"

"He's not. I didn't want him here so we decided on a compromise. I'm supposed to meet him at this restaurant in Sausalito, the Following Sea, at 6:30 p.m. Ever hear of it?"

"Yeah, it's a fixture on the waterfront. Great seafood. Wonderful view of Richardson Bay. Been there so long, it's beyond trendy. How come Jon's not coming here?"

"It was my idea. It's not that Jon is sketchy, far from it. But I've learned over the years to have my own transportation nearby."

I left Lena's room and headed for my small bedroom at the back of the house.

"What is that supposed to mean?" she asked following me down the hall.

"I don't think I ever told you, but last year, I listed my profile on an on line dating site."

"You never said a word."

"There were many responses. I was picky and slow, but I finally started a conversation with a guy from Palo Alto. He talked a lot about his stuff, like expensive cameras, laptops, sound systems, even boats and his rich friends. That type of showiness never appealed to me but I thought he might be nervous and not sure what to say. We decided to meet for dinner, somewhere between his house and mine. We ended up at a waterfront restaurant in Pacifica."

"Waterfront restaurants seem to be a theme in your love life," said Lena.

"Are you interested in this or not?"

"Go on, go on. Sorry to interrupt," she said.

"The dinner, the actual food, was good. But the conversation was a repetition of the phone calls. He talked about himself and his things, again, and his rich friends. My part of the conversation was easy. All I had to do was listen and nod. I was thinking of making an early departure when he looked at me and said, 'Okay, you'll do. Do you want to get married?' I nearly choked on my scallops."

"No. He didn't say that."

"Oh, yes he did. I told him I didn't plan on getting married again. That I wasn't even divorced yet. I remember that he looked at me oddly. You know what he said then? 'I can take you anywhere in the world. Tell me where you want to go. Name a place. Any place."

"I can't believe this guy."

"It got stranger. He asked me why I wouldn't marry him and I told him that I didn't even know him, that we only met

35 minutes ago. I said we didn't have anything in common. His response was, 'Never mind we could go out a few more times and that I'd see how likeable he was.'

"I was creeped out. I kept thinking about the parking lot overlooking the ocean. What if, when he walked me to my car after dinner, he was upset that I wouldn't marry him. He might give me a push, right over the rail guard into the water."

"Like someone did to Duncan," said Lena, "except for the water part."

I looked at her. "I never thought of that. Anyway, it was December and it was dark and cold out there. I didn't want to end up in the Pacific Ocean, so I excused myself and went to the ladies' room. I was going to sneak out of the restaurant and make a quick exit. But that didn't feel right.

"So, I walked back to the table and picked up my jacket. I thanked him for dinner and told him I was going home. He looked surprised and asked me why. 'Didn't you like the dinner?' he asked. He stood up. I was moving into panic mode when he said something real, finally."

"What was that?" Lena asked.

"'This didn't go so well, did it?'" I said 'No, it didn't. It's not a good idea to propose to someone so soon after you meet them.' He sat back down and I left. I never saw him again."

"How come you never told me about this date?" asked Lena, now lying on my bed, and watching as I pulled out the clothes I was going to wear tonight. "You need to tell me when you're going out. That way if you disappear, I'll have a starting point to find you."

"Hopefully, that will never happen."

"Well, your choose-o-meter when it comes to men has never worked well. Your husband disappears and goes, god knows where. Last year, you develop a full blown obsession on a schizoid and somewhere in between, you go out with this pathetic 'I'm the king of the world' guy. Jon, by far, is the most normal."

"Yeah."

"That's it...yeah? Don't you like him? I do. He strikes me as a thoughtful, caring guy. I'm not worried that he will murder you."

"Gee, thanks."

"You know what your problem is?"

"You're going to tell me, aren't you?"

"You like the challenge of the bad boy."

"Oh, spare me. I'm not sure I am going to be good company tonight. All I can think about is Duncan. Duncan and Shari. Shari and Duncan."

"Understandable," Lena said. "This will be a good break for you. Give Jon a chance."

"I am. We are having dinner. Now I need to get dressed. But, I don't know what to wear."

"Want me to help?"

"No."

Lena stared at the Levi's and long sleeve light green sweater that I had laid out on the bed. She picked up the sweater with her thumb and fore finger as if it was one of the rags Dr. T used to wipe his hands on after working on the Charger.

"You're not wearing this are you? Where is the hotness factor? He'll think he's out with his brother."

"He told me to dress casually and bring a warm jacket."

"For dinner at The Following Sea?"

"That's what he said. Can you help me make this look attractive?"

"You don't want attractive; you want hot. There must be something in this closet that says sexy."

She began digging around in the back of my closet.

"How about these?" she asked holding up my one and only pair of 4" heels.

"No. I don't think that's the right thing to wear."

"Well, it will make even these clothes look good."

She stuck her head back in the closet and then looked back at me.

"Your clothes are pathetic. When is the last time you went shopping? You lost all that weight over the past year but you're still dressing like you are four sizes bigger."

"Move out of the way. Let me do it," and I grabbed the waist of her shorts and pulled her away from the closet. She stood there with her hands on her hips.

"I have one piece of advice for you."

"I'm not listening."

"Tonight...when it comes to dinner conversation, don't talk about murders, suspects, drowning or people falling off balconies."

"I'll try not to. Now, leave."

CHAPTER 30

There was a steady stream of customers walking into The Following Sea. They were wearing shorts, cute little sundresses, and classy (if there is such thing) tee shirts...while I sat on the bench outside the restaurant dressed to work on an Alaskan fishing boat.

A white Ford truck pulled up in front of the restaurant. Jon rolled down his window.

"Come on, get in. I'm running late."

"Late for what?" I said as I climbed into the passenger's side.

"I'm...make that, we...are delivering a boat."

"What? We are going to take a boat on a trailer somewhere?"

"No. This is on the water. We're taking the boat from Sausalito to the Berkeley Marina."

"You mean like on the Bay?"

"Yep," said Jon. He pulled on to Bridgeway and headed north about five minutes to a dirt parking lot. Once he parked, he reached behind the front seat and pulled out two yellow sailing jackets. "This will be big for you, but it's the best I could do," he said, handing it to me.

"Why do I need this? It's warm out," I said.

"Not for long. Look up there," he said pointing to the thick fog bank beginning to inch its way down the Sausalito hills.

"It is going to get chilly. Fast. We gotta go."

He climbed out of the truck while I sat there for a minute looking at the jacket. So much for the hotness factor. Good thing I didn't wear the spike heels my sister picked out.

Jon opened my door, took my hand and helped me down. Then he reached into the back of the truck, pulled out two grocery bags and handed me a small cooler.

"This is our dinner." We walked over to the gangway. He unlocked the gate and we headed down to the dock.

"Tide is still coming in. So that should make this a quick trip and we won't get stuck in the mud."

"I've never been on a motorboat before."

"It's a sailboat, an Islander 36. There's an ODCA race tomorrow off the circle. The skipper wants his boat as close as possible."

"You're talking in code."

"Sorry, I forget sometimes. ODCA is one-design sailboat racing. That means all the boats are exactly the same. The circle is the Berkeley Circle. It's sometimes called the Olympic Circle. It's basically a race course for sailboats between Berkeley and Angel Island. And at low tide, it is shallow."

Water sloshed around the dock as we moved toward the end. A man stood in front of a very big, white hulled sailboat.

"Terry, this is a friend of mine, Trisha Carson. Trisha, Terry."

Terry was a deeply tanned man in his early 60's. He nodded and shook my hand. The wrinkles around his blue eyes were significant and his hands were rough as sandpaper.

"Pleased," he said. I stood off to the side as the two men spoke. Then Terry walked by me, "See you in Berkeley. You'll have the better trip...no traffic," he said with a smile.

Jon climbed on board and I followed him. He went into the cabin and I watched him stack the grocery bags on what looked like a table by the galley.

"Come below," he said, reaching up for the cooler.

I ducked my head and climbed down the short ladder.

"This is lovely," I said, looking at the varnished wood and the ocean blue bunks off the small galley in the narrow cabin. Jon was on his way back topside, before I even turned around. He looked down at me and said, "I'm going to need some help getting out of the slip. Want to lend a hand?"

"Sure," I said, following him up to the cockpit. "But I don't know what to do."

"Right. Go up to the foredeck and unwrap the lines from the cleat and throw them on the dock."

"Okay." Not sure what a cleat was, but I figured it would be clear once I found the foredeck. Jon pointed forward and I followed the direction of his arm.

"The boat can be unsteady even at the dock, so hold on to something as you go forward."

I did, grabbing on to the mast and various lines as I moved toward the front of the boat. I reached down for the line wrapped around a metal piece of hardware on the deck. It stretched to a similar piece of metal, only larger, on the dock.

"Don't do anything yet. Just get yourself ready."

I loosened the line and held it. I heard the diesel start-up and Jon said, "Okay, drop the line on the dock and when we clear this pier, pull those fenders up."

Holding on to the rigging, I looked over the side and saw two blue bumpers between the hull of the boat and the dock.

"Fenders?" I yelled back to him, pointing to the bumpers.

His response was swallowed up by the noise of the engine.

I pointed down at the fenders again. This time he gave me a thumbs up.

"I can do that," I said, more to myself than to Jon as the boat began to move slowly forward. When we were clear of the dock, I knelt down and pulled the lines attached to the fenders.

"Just leave them on the deck," yelled Jon. "Come on back."

Within minutes, we were moving slowly down the Sausalito waterfront, past seagulls and houseboats. I could hear music and laughter coming from inside one of the boats that was docked at the next marina.

"You did good."

"Thank you.

We motored at a leisurely pace until we were almost out of Richardson Bay. The water ahead of us looked like someone had taken a rake to it. I could see choppy little waves moving east toward Berkeley.

"The wind will pick up in a few minutes and the temperature will drop." Jon reached for his jacket, slipped it on and motioned for me to do the same. Before I had a chance to zip it up, the boat began to bounce to one side, straighten, and then jerk to the other side. A light wall of spray flew over the side where I was sitting and was now dripping down my neck. Cold. I slipped the hood over my head. I could see a smile pass over Jon's face as he glanced at me. But he didn't say anything.

"How can waves that small toss a boat this big around?" I asked Jon.

He smiled. "It's more than the waves, it's the direction of the wind, which right now is coming from the Golden Gate. It should lighten up as the sun goes down. Anyway, once we turn toward Berkeley, it will all smooth out. Should even feel a little warmer."

We headed for Raccoon Straits, the body of water between the shores of Tiburon and Angel Island, a small island less than two miles around. The wind dropped off and the choppy little waves moved from the side of the boat to the rear, pushing us toward our destination.

I took a deep breath and stared out at the scenery around me. The afternoon and the unspeakable tragedy of Duncan's death began to lessen.

Behind us, the orange sun was growing larger as it dipped low in the sky, hanging out back of the Golden Gate Bridge. The brownish-green water of San Francisco Bay was transformed into a sparkling deep blue. Every now and then, pelicans soaring overhead would fold their wings close to their bodies, abruptly turn and head straight toward the water in a kamikaze dive, barely making a splash as they disappeared into the Bay.

"Dinner time," said Jon.

"Looks like it. Think he caught his fish?" I asked watching other acrobatic pelicans swoop and dive in an aerial performance that should be followed by applause.

"No, I mean for you and me. Take the wheel and just keep the front of the boat pointing to the East Bay."

"You sure about this?" I slid down the seat toward Jon and the large wheel that seemed to grow in proportion the closer I came.

"You'll be fine. We're just motoring so as long as you stay in the middle of Raccoon Straits and don't hit any other boats...a piece of cake."

I stood and grasped either side of the wheel. Jon stood behind me. Close behind me. His hands were on the wheel just below mine.

"Okay. Now steer. It's like driving a car. Steer one way; you'll go that way."

I turned the wheel to the right and boat headed toward Angel Island.

"Not so abrupt. Gently. Straighten out and head back on course."

I could feel Jon's head lean in against the top of mine.

"Relax your hands. Nothing to be nervous about." His voice was quiet in my ear.

"Got it?"

"Yeah, I do. This is fun."

"That it is. And it's about to get better." He clambered up next to the mast and started grinding on a winch. A huge white sail lifted above me, blocking out the sky. It flapped, popped and crinkled in the wind coming from behind.

"What do I do?" I called out.

"Just what you're doing. Head straight."

Then he jumped back into the cockpit and adjusted the sail and the boom so they were almost 45 degrees from me and the side of the boat. The popping sail smoothed out. With the wind pushing on the sail, the boat accelerated.

"Good times," I said.

Jon turned off the engine and the quiet was startling.

"What a difference."

"Like it?" he asked.

"Yes," was all I could manage to say as I concentrated on adjusting the wheel in tiny increments so we kept moving in the right direction.

Although the engine was off and we were sailing, it was far from quiet. The wind had a different tone as it picked up, then dropped back down again. Sometimes the boat creaked and halyards not in use clunked against the metal stays.

"Now for dinner." Jon went below and brought up sandwiches, a container of coleslaw, a bottle of red wine and some glasses. Once he laid everything out on the seat, he came over behind me again.

"I'll drive for a while."

Truth be told I didn't want to give up the wheel. I liked to watch what the wind did to the sail when it blew harder or eased off. Even the balance in the boat felt different.

"Okay, back to you," I said and Jon moved in behind me as I took a seat. I reached for a sandwich, poured myself a glass of wine, and then poured one for Jon.

"You are a natural," he said to me. "A toast. To a following sea."

"To a what?"

"Sailors often wish each other 'fair winds and a following sea.' It means they want them to have a safe and comfortable voyage."

I raised my glass and touched his. Then took a sip. Then a bite of the sandwich. Turkey on a sour dough roll had never tasted so good.

"You are full of surprises," I said to Jon who had reached forward to adjust the mainsail as we moved out of Raccoon Straits. The shadow of Angel Island blocked the wind and we slowed down.

"I feel like I've been let in on a secret," I said. "What a different way to see the world."

He smiled. "Maybe I uncovered a water person."

"Could be. But you know, as peaceful as it looks, it can be dangerous."

"Very true."

"I don't think we are thinking about the same things," I said looking over at him. Jon's eyes were on the sail. They moved back and forth from the sail to the location we were headed, one that only he could see.

I was thinking about Shari. Although it wasn't the water that killed her, someone used it as a weapon.

"Jon?"

"Mmm."

"I need to talk something out." I had a feeling my sister was eavesdropping, maybe floating in with the wind, saying 'Don't do it. Big mistake...big mistake.'

I started slowly. "Remember I told you about Shari?"

He nodded and for the first time in a while looked over at me. "You're still involved."

"Yes, very much so."

CHAPTER 31

We were tied up at a side dock in the Berkeley Marina, sitting in the cockpit and I was still talking. Although I told him about Shari's death the last time we met, I went through it one more time, in depth. I described her sister and brother. I told him about the man threatening me at the ballpark; the porn entrepreneur, Andrew, and what the medical examiner had told Terrel. I finished with Duncan's flight off the third floor balcony. Then I started up again and talked about my father showing up at Lena' house and running into him at China Camp.

Jon never said a word. He nodded every now and then, but that was it. Finally, he reached over, patted my shoulder and said, "Let's get out of the wind. I'll make us some Irish coffees."

How long had I been talking? Thirty minutes? Forty-five minutes? I had no idea. I wasn't quite sure when or how the mainsail was dropped or when we motored into the marina. We both climbed below into the cabin and I sat on one of the bunks, legs stretched out in front of me. I pulled a pillow up and put it behind my head. Telling the whole story to someone not involved was what I needed. A plug had been pulled and all the tension trickled out of my body. I sunk lower onto the bunk.

"You look like you're going to fall asleep. You tired?"

"No...just very relaxed." Jon reached over and gave me the

225

drink, warm, smelling of coffee, and tasting of sweet cream and strong Irish whiskey. He sat down on the bunk at my feet. I pulled in my legs.

"You're fine," he said, stretching them out on his lap.

Shari, Duncan and their collective problems were slipping away with each sip of the drink. Maybe Jon was right. Maybe I was going to fall asleep.

"Do you want to know what I think?" he said looking over at my half-shut eyes.

I managed to shift myself into more of a sitting position. "I already know. It's your mantra. It's everyone's mantra. 'Leave it to the police.' Well, you will be glad to learn I called one of the officers…I have cards from three of them now, a blossoming collection…and explained everything more than once."

"Really? I'm impressed. I figured you would try to bulldog your way through this puzzle, as you've been known to do in the past. That's an improvement from last year."

I felt a hand on the side of my face. When I opened my eyes, Jon was less than an arm's length away. He smiled and leaned over to kiss me.

"You taste good. Like an Irish coffee," I said.

"Really."

I closed my eyes again. "With a touch of cream."

"Trisha. Look at me."

I opened my eyes. Jon had shifted back. The warmth of his breath and body faded.

"I know you're involved. I can say, 'stay out of it,' but I know you won't. Just promise me that you will let the police know if anything––and I mean anything––happens. Okay?"

"Okay. But, I am going to find out who killed Shari and Duncan." I sat up straighter, shifted my legs off his lap and dropped them to the floor. My sister was right, this discussion of death, killing and falling off of balconies was a mood breaker.

Jon leaned over again, wrapped his arms around me, his

face in my hair.

"I don't want you to get hurt."

I wasn't sure if I was pleased or annoyed. That was my line, time and time again as I mothered my sister into adulthood. I didn't need anyone to take care of me and I didn't want to talk about this anymore. He could feel the change of mood and he pulled back.

"One more thing," he said looking at me.

"What?"

"This."

He pulled me close and kissed me again. For a minute I held my breath, then I let my hands move up to his face. We sat there in an embrace for few seconds and then that old awkward feeling that I had when I liked someone began to buzz through me. I was about to go into my 'I'm not ready for this" speech when he moved back from me.

"You're cute. Obstinate at times, but still cute. Come on. It's time to get you back on the other side of the Bay."

With that he moved toward the cabin steps and started to climb up to the cockpit.

"Obstinate. No, you're the one who's obstinate." I said as I followed after him. "You're also repetitive. The same message all the time. Just like everybody else. 'Talk to the police, talk to the police.' Well I did, but nobody seems to hear me."

Jon began locking up the boat. I, on the other hand, instead of helping, kept talking.

Jon reached out a hand to help me off the boat.

"No, that's okay, I can do it myself," I said as I pushed his arm away.

As he double-checked the Islander to make sure everything was buttoned up, I finally closed my mouth. When did I become the chatty sister? I felt a warm flush creep up my neck. I did not believe I had gone off like that.

"Got everything?"

"Yes...Look, Jon," I said, when he stopped at the white

dock box at the end of slip. "I'm sorry. I don't know where all that came from. Well, I do. I want to find Shari' and now Duncan's killer. I could use some help."

He was crouched next to the box coiling a thick heavy line.

"The police. They can help."

"No, you. I mean you. Please."

"Don't you ever give up?"

"No. I don't."

With that he laughed. "I'll think about it."

I nodded my head. "Okay, okay, great. We can work on this together."

"That's not what I said."

I just smiled and finally stopped talking. We walked down the dock toward the yacht club, where Terry was waiting to drive us back to Sausalito.

CHAPTER 32

Robert Gonzales, Duncan's supervisor and the president of NSEU, left me a message on the home phone requesting that I meet him at the union office. So, the next day, I drove, yet again, across the Golden Gate Bridge at the tail end of the morning commute...in fog––thick, gun metal grey fog. There was no ocean to my right, no San Francisco Bay or even the skyline of the city to my left. I was driving in a dingy, drippy cotton ball. I switched on the windshield wipers and my headlights. Just ahead of me, mid-span on the bridge, the deep, startling blast of a foghorn spread into the greyness. A few seconds later, a chilling two-toned foghorn detonated under my car. My pulse soared from relaxed to panic at the sound. No summer on the bridge this morning.

I zipped by the empty toll booths at the end of the bridge. The Bridge District eliminated all the toll takers and motorists mostly used a transponder or a cellphone-size gizmo that electronically withdrew money from a special account every time they crossed the bridge. The advantage was a $1.00 reduction in the bridge toll.

The melancholy grayness hung in the sky as I made my way to the union office in the Mission District. I was looking forward to my conversation with Mr. Gonzales.

The man across the desk was in his 50's, a fringe of grey hair circled his temple like a wreath. Deep purple circles hung beneath his eyes. There was a slight stubble on his chin. When he rose to shake my hand, the grip was warm and soft, completely opposite from the tight straight line of his mouth. He wore a black sweater vest over a highly starched black and white checked shirt.

"Sit down, please." He motioned to the chair across from him. He didn't say anything. One, two, three seconds went by. I started to squirm in my seat. Finally, he cleared his throat.

"Duncan...I was his supervisor." He stopped. He seemed unsure of what to say next.

I nodded.

"The police tell me that you were going to meet him. Is that so?"

I nodded again.

"Yes, he called and asked me to stop by his former girl-friend's apartment."

"Do you mind telling me why?"

"The police asked the same thing. He never said. I don't know why he wanted to see me. Did you know?"

Robert shook his head and leaned forward.

"You must have some idea what the meeting was about."

"No, I don't. I was curious, that's why I agreed to meet him."

Robert stood and began pacing around his office. His hands were clasped behind his back.

"Duncan was more than an employee. Although he had been on the West Coast only a year or so, he made his mark. He has...had...a natural ability to connect with his union brothers and sisters as well as the toughness to negotiate with very difficult adversaries. I was beginning to groom him for my position. I'm the president of this union. My decision wasn't well liked by some of our more senior and often vocal members."

Robert sat on the corner of his desk.

"I hesitate to ask this but do you think someone here––a rival––maybe someone who was jealous––could be responsible for his death?"

"I don't know. I hope not," he said. There was a pause. "You may have been the last person to see him alive."

"I don't think so. When I came into the apartment, he had already fallen over the balcony."

"Fallen? So you think it was an accident? But the police are treating this as a suicide."

"Well, the police would know more than I."

"It sounds like your next word could be 'but.'"

"Okay. But, another possibility is that––and I'm sorry to be so straightforward–– he was pushed. If that is true, whoever pushed him was the last one to see him alive."

Robert didn't look as shocked as I thought he might. He nodded his head and stared into empty space.

"Did you talk to the person in the car with Duncan, the one driving yesterday? Maybe they had a conversation about why he was going there."

"Very briefly."

"And?"

Robert looked uncomfortable. "She was unclear on why he wanted to stop at Shari's."

"What about Andrew? He was his best friend."

"Again, it was a brief conversation. He had no idea Duncan was going to the condo."

"Would it be possible for me to talk to his driver? Maybe even Andrew?"

"You think you can find out more than the police?"

I smiled. "It's worth a shot."

"I haven't seen Andrew today; Megan was with him

yesterday." He stuck his head out the door and called down the steps, "Is Megan around?" I couldn't quite hear the answer.

Robert came back into the room. "She was very upset with everything that happened yesterday so she is coming in late. Look, I asked you here because I wanted to know...want to know...why Duncan was meeting you, especially at Shari's condo. If he had plans for the future, it is unlikely that he would take his own life."

"That's what I think, too. Duncan was sad and upset about Shari but not suicidal. I don't think I can help you. I don't know why he wanted to see me."

"Okay," Robert said. He reached over to shake my hand again. "Thank you for coming in. I'm sorry it was a waste of time. The police will handle it from here."

"I was wondering," I said. "Could you give me Megan and maybe Candy's phone number?"

Robert shook his head. "Sorry, but we don't give out personal information."

"I understand. I wish I could have been more help."

I headed for the stairs that took me down to the first floor and passed a skinny long-haired blond woman dressed in jeans and a union sweatshirt. Someone called out from below, "Megan, how're you doing? Sure you should be here?"

Megan's long thin fingers twitched and quivered slightly as she gave a slight wave to the voice. She was chewing her bottom lip.

"You were Duncan's driver yesterday, weren't you?" I asked.

"Yes. Who are you?"

"I was the person Duncan was going to meet at the condo. Did Duncan say why we were meeting? I never really knew."

Megan stared at me. "No, he didn't. All he said was that he wanted to stop at Shari's for about ten minutes...said he was picking something up and meeting you. He said that he had work to do and would I mind driving. I didn't care; I was filling in for Candy. She was out yesterday. Lucky for her. Anyway, he was quiet on the drive the apartment. Candy once told me that when she drove he was usually on his cell phone or tablet, but yesterday, all he did was stare out the window, like he was daydreaming."

"One more thing, why didn't you go back for him?"

"Oh, I tried, but the police had the whole block shut down, said there was an accident. I called to tell him where I was parked. Then I waited about 30 minutes. I called again and left a message, said I had to leave. I was going to be late to the meeting. But he didn't call back."

"So you left him there?"

"I'm new here and I didn't want to be late to the meeting. I did call the office to let them know what I was doing." With that she slid past me and scampered up to the next floor.

I slowly walked down the rest of the stairs, past the middle-aged receptionist to the main entrance. I nodded as I walked by. She smiled and nodded back.

"You've been here before, haven't you?"

I looked around. She was talking to me and fishing...fishing for information.

"Yes, I have," I said walking over to her desk. Behind her was a display case of union swag, colorful bumper stickers, pins, and tee shirts that the members wore to the open water clinic. Next to a row of union visors were bracelets of iridescent deep ocean blue balls on a stretchy band. Just like the one Earl and I found at China Camp.

"You came to talk to Duncan, right after Shari died. How tragic this is. Both of them. One right after the other."

I pulled my gaze away from the display case. "Nice stuff. I like the bracelet," is all I could stammer.

"It's a favorite with our staff, that's for sure," she said. "Everyone has one."

"Like Candy or Megan?"

"Pretty sure they do.

"Andrew?"

"Maybe."

The receptionist wasn't interested in chatting about jewelry. "Do the police know what happened to Duncan?" she asked in a quiet voice, looking around first to make sure no one heard her.

"They are leaning toward suicide."

Her hand flew to her mouth. "He was so depressed over Shari's death...sad...so very sad."

A co-worker walked by heading for the front door. He nodded to both of us.

"Sorry, I'm forgetting my job. Did you park in the lot? I can validate your ticket."

"That's great," I said searching for the parking ticket in my backpack. I had it in my hand and was about to pull it out when I had an idea. "I must have left it in the car. I'll be right back." I sprinted toward the entrance, and instead of turning right where my car was parked, I headed left to a coffee shop on the corner. Maybe a fresh latte and a cinnamon bun could be swapped for some information.

I balanced the coffee and roll while I pulled open the front door and headed back to the receptionist.

"I found the ticket. Here this is for you." I put the goodies on her desk while I pulled out the parking ticket from my backpack. "I didn't know what you liked. Hope this will do."

"My goodness. Thank you." Before she opened the bag, she pulled out a stamp and stuck it on the ticket. I stood there sipping from my bottle of water as she munched and sighed over the roll.

"You know," I said. "I thought it was odd that Candy wasn't

in the car with Duncan yesterday."

"She called in sick. Said if she felt better, she would meet Duncan and Megan at the meeting."

"From the few times I saw them together, they seemed to get along very well."

The receptionist laughed. "You are right about that. Candy would have liked them to get along even better than they did, if you know what I mean."

"Really?"

"She had the biggest crush on Duncan. Poor thing. She must be devastated."

"Was he interested in her?"

"No. Not at all. Candy told me that he was going to ask Shari to marry him."

"I didn't know that."

"She didn't like Shari. Said she wasn't who she seemed."

"What does that mean?"

"I don't know. You'd have to ask her."

"Maybe I will. You know I have her phone number on the application for the open water clinics your group has attended––I've been helping with that––but I wonder, if you might give it to me now. I'd like to call her and I'd rather not wait until I went home."

The receptionist smiled a very big smile. "I don't see why not." She wrote the number down on a piece of paper and started to hand it to me. I grasped one end and she still held on to the other.

"You know, you didn't have to do that."

"Excuse me?"

"I appreciate the coffee and roll, but you didn't have to do that. I would have given you Candy's number without the tasty incentive."

My face turned a bright pink. "Too obvious?"

"As a seeker of general information, I know all the tricks," and she let go of the paper with Candy's phone number on it.

I sat in my car in the parking lot and pulled out my phone. I punched in Candy's number. No answer.

"Candy, this is Trisha Carson. I was so sorry to hear about Duncan. Can you give me a call? Thanks."

CHAPTER 33

On my way home, I took a quick right before I reached the Golden Gate Bridge and drove toward the Marina Green, 74 acres of well-used open space that borders San Francisco Bay and several coveted marinas. Even in the damp, heavy fog, joggers keeping pace to the music only they could hear pushed down the sidewalk. Tourists walked by in shorts and tee shirts, chilled to the bones, and a soccer team for girls about seven or eight years old practiced their passing skills on the wet grass.

I drove slowly through Fort Mason's parking lot looking for Jon. I didn't see his patrol car or him. Would it seem odd, me showing up like this? Without any particular reason? My internal response...yes it would. This was a mistake. If I ran into him, I'd say I stopped to call Mia and see if she was home––which was not a bad idea.

I punched in Mia's number on my cellphone. She didn't answer. That didn't mean she wasn't there. I'd find out soon enough. I drove out of the lot and headed for her house a few blocks away.

Mia's street was quiet. Maybe the fog was keeping everyone inside. Only one car drove by with its lights on and windshield wipers working. The curtains were closed in Mia's house. I parked, walked over, rang the doorbell and waited. No footsteps. No dim sound of a radio or television. I reached into by backpack for the keys to her place, when Mia threw open the front door.

"Yes?" she said, her eyes barely open. She was still in her pajamas.

"I'm sorry to startle you. I tried to call."

Mia let out a sigh. "I was asleep. I've been awake most nights, and, well, this morning...oh, excuse me, come in...I actually fell back to sleep. I have no idea what time it is."

She wandered into the kitchen. Shutting the door behind me, I tagged along behind.

"Coffee?" she asked.

"Sure."

"So why are you here?"

"I wanted to see how you were doing."

"Not great. Mitch is a mess. He has trouble keeping his temper on the best of days and he––as you know––he hasn't been having the best of days recently. His charges were dropped for some reason that he isn't telling me so he is out of jail, thank goodness. With Shari gone, I have to take over managing our parents' estate. It's a lot of work. I never realized how much my sister did. And then there's her funeral. I've taken a leave of absence from my job. That's the only way I can do this and remain somewhat sane."

"Have they released the body yet?"

"No, but it should be soon."

"What about the autopsy?"

"They're not telling me anything, yet, except that Shari's autopsy was delayed."

I listened to her talk. Although she just woke up, she was clear, forthright and dealing with the stress and new obligations better than I thought. According to my sister, Mia usually was two steps behind Shari, rarely raised her voice, and never did anything to stand out. Looks like this added responsibility has helped her grow up, whether she wanted to or not.

Mia handed me a cup of hot coffee and pushed a bowl of sugar and a milk carton in my direction. I held the warm mug in my hand and took a sip.

"Mia, did you hear about Duncan?"

"No, he was supposed to call me yesterday. I never heard from him and when I came home, I turned off the ringers on both the home phone and my cell. Why?"

My description of what happened to Shari's boyfriend was brief.

"I don't believe it," she said. "It almost seems like a death pact. Only they didn't decide to kill themselves."

"I hadn't thought about it that way."

"Is that why you are here? To tell me about Duncan?" She turned around and stared at me. "Do you think that I or Mitch had something to do with Duncan's death?"

"No." I was startled. I hadn't thought of that, but now that she brought it up...

"First you think he killed our sister. Then you didn't. Now you think, he killed Shari's boyfriend. When was that supposed to happen? Before he went to jail?"

"No. That's not..."

"Then why are you here, really?"

"I was curious about Mitch's startup."

"What? Why?"

"Was he working with one of Duncan's friends, a guy named Andrew?"

"I know Andrew."

"Do you know if they were working together?"

"I don't want to talk to you anymore. You come in here pretending to care about me. But you don't, not really. I want you to leave. Now."

"But, Mia, I'm trying to help. You asked me to, remember? Maybe there is a connection that I'm missing."

Mia walked over to the front door and opened it.

"Goodbye."

"Okay. Look, I'm sorry..."

The door slammed behind me.

"...I upset you," I said to the closed door.

CHAPTER 34

When I reached our home, my sister was sitting on the couch, still in her robe. "What is it with today? No one wants to get up and get dressed?"

Lena looked drugged. "I don't feel well."

"This is your annual summer cold. Just sit there." I walked into her room, grabbed the quilt from the bed and spread it over her.

"Do you have a temperature?" I reached to feel her forehead and she pushed my hand away.

"No. I'll be fine. Where did you go so early this morning?"

"The union president, Duncan's boss, asked to see me. He asked what I knew about Duncan. I couldn't tell him anything. I had no idea why he wanted to meet me at Shari's."

"I cannot believe they are both gone." She sighed and closed her eyes. "So, how was your date?" Before I could answer, Lena's phone pinged.

"A text from my sweetie," she said. "Aw," then she smiled.

Her fingers flew over the phone's keyboard as she wrote him back. Another ping and a sigh.

"No," she said with emphasis as she typed in the two-letter word and hit send. Then she stuffed the phone under the cushions of the couch.

I watched her with a smile. At least I was dealing with

241

the nice 'Lena' today. Or maybe she was too sick to care. "You must be under the weather if you didn't go to swim workout this morning."

Lena didn't respond.

"I met an interesting person today," I said. "Want to guess who?"

"No, I don't." She slid down on the couch and pulled the comforter over her head. Then she stuck her head back out. "Who?"

For the first time, Lena looked interested.

"A woman named Megan. She was Duncan's driver yesterday and..."

"At the open water clinic. Skinny, right?"

"She was at the clinic?"

"Yes, Ms. I Never Forget a Face. She and that other blond, the one talking to Duncan, stuck together."

I stopped for a minute. "You mean Candy and...wait, I remember...you're right. That's right."

"I had her in my teaching group. Major lack of attention. Always moving, squirming around, tugging at the sleeves of her wetsuit, twiddling with her cap, constantly readjusting it, fussing with her goggles."

"She left him there at the condo. Can you believe it? She drove off to attend a meeting. It's possible that Duncan would still be alive if she had checked on him. Maybe this Megan person knows more than she's letting on."

I was pacing around the living room by this time. "And you know what else? That bracelet with the blue balls are union giveaways. I saw a bunch of them today at their office."

"So you think Shari's killer was wearing the bracelet and therefore is connected with the union?" asked Lena.

"It's possible," I said. "I have to connect with Candy and that sleaze, Andrew."

I walked down the hallway to my room.

"You do that," called out Lena. "But first, tell me about

your date. Please. Are you going to hang out with him again? Did he kiss you?"

"Need to make some calls," I shouted over my shoulder. I was about to close the door when I said, "Date report: We delivered a sailboat to the Berkeley Marina. I'm glad I didn't wear those heels you picked out. Let's see...I learned how to steer a boat. He made Irish coffees. Yes, he kissed me. Yes, I will see him again."

Lena let out a loud whoop.

Then quietly to no one in particular, I said, "I think."

I closed my bedroom door. But from the living room, I heard.

"Pigs do fly."

I tried Candy again, but she still didn't answer. Neither did Andrew. I left messages for both.

The blue bracelet rested on the top of my dresser. I slipped it on my wrist and lay back on my bed. I looked out the window at Mt. Tamalpais. It was a hulking, dark profile against the startling blue sky. Both Candy and maybe Megan had something to do with Duncan's death. I was sure of it. But were they involved with Shari's? And where did Andrew fit in?

"Awwwgh," I yelled out loud. I threw my phone at the door, turned over in bed so I faced the window and could see Mt. Tam. Then I closed my eyes and drifted off into a deep sleep.

CHAPTER 35

I woke up to the sound of my phone ringing. Where was it? I rolled off the bed and tried to remember what I had done with it. Still half-asleep, I groped around the floor, until I had it in my hand. Jon's name popped up on the screen.

"Oh," I said with pleasure, then "oh" I said, confused. It rang again and again.

"Oh hell," I said out loud. "Answer the phone." And I did.

"Hey," I said.

"It's Jon. Saw you earlier today," he said.

"Right, I drove through the Fort Mason parking lot."

"You didn't stay too long. I was walking out of one of the buildings when I saw you disappear. You were on your way out to Marina Boulevard."

There was a pause.

"Did you need anything in particular?"

"Are you still at work?"

"Yes," he said.

Another pause.

"Trisha? Hello?"

"Sorry, I just woke up."

"Lucky you, a nap in the middle of the afternoon."

I didn't know what to say.

"I wanted to tell you about my visit with Duncan's boss

245

this morning."

That was only one of the reasons I drove to Fort Mason. The other reason... I wanted to see him.

"Tell you what," he said. "Why don't I meet you for coffee? I can leave in about 20 minutes."

"That won't work. I am...um...I have to go to China Camp again...to check up on my father. I told you he is hanging around there, didn't I?"

"You did. Let me know when you have some time. We can meet up later."

"All right."

Jon's tone was all business now. The smile in his voice had vanished.

"Trisha, it's all right. We can just be friends."

"I'm not sure that's what I want. I gotta go." With that I hung up. I stared at the phone. Then at the doorway. Lena was standing there, hands on her hips, the comforter slung around her shoulders like a shawl.

"What was that all about? Did you make that up about checking on our father at China Camp?"

"Not really."

"You mean he is still here?"

"Yes, I ran into him when I went back to look at the area where Shari's body was found. He's doing good, Lena. Really."

Lena had a fierce grip on the comforter and her face was turning red.

"You never told me," she said, almost sputtering.

"And that is a surprise? Why would I want to do that...with an attitude like yours?"

She was about to say something. Then she stopped.

"Okay, you have a point. Change of subject. You said, not more than two hours ago that you were going to see Jon again. The conversation that I just heard was not encouraging."

"What do you mean? And, by the way, don't eavesdrop. It's rude. Anyway, he was the one who said, 'we can just be friends.' I'm not sure that's what I want. I think I want more than that."

"Dear sister, let me repeat what I heard." Lena stood up straight, dropped the quilt and folded her hands together at her waist. "This is you. 'I'm not sure that's what I want.'"

"So?"

"You're thinking. 'I want more, but I'm not sure what that means.'"

"Right."

"Well, I bet he's thinking, 'that's not what she wants.' She doesn't even want to be friends. She doesn't want to spend time with me."

I stared at Lena who was walking back and forth like a teacher giving a lesson in a classroom.

"Understand now?" asked Lena.

I closed my eyes and nodded my head. "I never thought of it that way."

"Yeah, well, if you want to see this guy again, you better let him know that you're interested."

I fell back on the bed. "What a moron I am. You're right."

"Of course I am. So do you want to tell me more about Dad?" She sat down on the end of my bed.

"I don't know too much. But it seems that years ago, when we used to visit China Camp as a family, he met a man named Earl and they became friends. Even though Dad didn't stay in touch with us; he stayed in touch with him over the years. All I can figure is that the other day, when you threw him out, he went looking for Earl. The guy took him in. Dad's staying in his spare bedroom. Last time I saw the both them was a few days ago."

"A few days ago?" Lena said.

"Yes. The two of them have been searching the grounds around the Village, for—I don't know—for something that may relate to Shari's death."

"Seriously?"

"You sound like Dr. T. Yes, seriously."

"Well, I don't know if I want to see him."

"He gets that. It doesn't seem like he is going to intrude on your life."

I moved over to sit next to her.

"Lena, do you still have Shari's laptop?"

"Yeah," said Lena stretched out on the bed wrapping the comforter around her. "I stuck it in my closet."

"Remember this appointment with Dice that was supposed to happen a while back?."

"I do."

"Well, Dice never showed up. I was there in Shari's condo, just in case, this Dice person––if it is a person––came by. I now think that Dice is a company or a business. It has to be on her computer. Would you see what you can find?"

"I'll do it. On one condition."

"Keep it a secret from Terrel?"

"Yes. He doesn't need to know."

"Deal."

"I promised I would cut my hacking career short after last year's mess. But this shouldn't be so bad. I mean, after all, I knew Shari and I have her password. I am on it!"

"Don't forget," she called out from the hall.

"I know. Terrel will never hear about it from me."

"And, call Jon."

CHAPTER 36

Actually, I texted him.

"Forget everything I said. Was sound asleep. Will be at China Camp in an hour. Bringing a picnic." Then I typed. "Pls come" and hit send.

There. That should smooth things over.

I stopped at the Mission Street Farmer's Market and picked up some bread, cheese and apples. I took the long way to China Camp today, driving out past the ground-hugging Marin Civic Center designed by Frank Lloyd Wright. Its warm soft pink stucco walls and its UFO-styled weathered blue roof were a local treasure, a national landmark that caused quite a stir when it was built in the 1960's.

I drove up a small stretched out hill and San Pablo Bay opened up before me. The deceptively thick carpet of brownish-green grasses in the saltmarsh followed the contours of China Camp State Park, then faded away at the pilings off Buckeye Point. Since I didn't expect Jon to arrive for 30 minutes, I decided to take a short hike up in the hills that overlooked the shoreline and the Bay. I parked on the side of the road, grabbed a pair of binoculars I kept in the glove compartment and started up the hard dirt path. The hills I passed were a tinder-dry light brown. Crackling leaves turned to dust when I stepped on them. Occasionally, I'd hear a rustle in the brush at the side of the trail. It could have been a bird or a squirrel, but I never saw the foraging animal digging among the parched leaves.

The trail I took was high enough for a seagull's view of the calm waters of San Pablo Bay, stretched out like a flat blue mirror. Miniaturized picnic sites were tucked into the shallow coves below.

Two mountain bikers came up from the rear.

"Behind you," said one. I took a few steps to the side of the narrow trail and let them pass. "Thanks," said the other as they continued on. There was no one else around. Quiet and peaceful. I walked along the path moving from the warm afternoon sun to the cool shade of the dry oak trees. I overlooked Bullhead Flat, not far from the Ranger Station.

This was the only spot close to China Camp Village where boats can be launched. So if a vehicle was carrying Shari's body, this is where they parked, unloaded their kayak, or canoe, even a paddleboard, put it in the water and rowed to the Village, a half-mile away. I turned the binos to look at the stump of rock 100 yards offshore called Rat Rock Island. Maybe someone anchored at this island? No. They would be too visible, even at night. Maybe they put their boat in at Bullhead Flat, paddled around the point to Rat Rock Cove to pick up someone or someones, then staying close to the land, ducked into China Camp Village and dropped the body near the shore.

That made sense to me, although I couldn't prove it. Now I had to figure out who was involved and why.

I was waiting in the parking lot that sits above and between China Camp Village and Rat Rock Cove when Jon's truck pulled in and parked next to my car.

"We're having a picnic," I said, grabbing the farmer's market bag and heading for the path down to the beach at Rat Rock Cove.

"Wait," Jon called, locking the truck.

I was halfway down the dirt path when Jon caught up to me.

"Lady, please slow down," he said.

He dropped his jacket on the clamshell beach and looked out across San Pablo Bay. "You know, I have lived in this area for more than 10 years and I've never been here." He watched as I unpacked our food from the market bags.

"This is nice," he said looking at the spread of apples, cheese and bread.

"Welcome to the scene of the crime," I said withstretched arms.

"Now, I get it. I thought you wanted to find your father," he said with a sigh. "But, you are still in detective mode. Well, at least the food looks good."

"Oh no," I said staring at a white egret standing in the goopy mud near the shore.

"What's wrong?"

"My 'launching the boat from one cove over' theory is shot."

"What are you talking about?"

"It is all mud out there. Twenty yards off shore and it's mud. Someone would have to drag a body across these mud-flats before tossing it into a boat of some kind. These coves are back further from the water than I thought."

"Trisha."

"Wait. Never mind. I figured it out. It's low tide now. It was probably high tide the night of Shari's murder. Do you happen to have a tidebook so I can check?"

"You are obsessed with this aren't you?"

"I wouldn't call it obsessed. Focused, maybe."

"Way beyond focused."

"Well, I wouldn't..."

"Trisha, drop it. Do you have any wine?"

"I do. A very nice chardonnay, so says the clerk at the wine shop." He nodded. For a few minutes, we sat in silence enjoying the view and sipping the cool white wine. Out in the deeper water, two sea lions barked at each other.

"Bet they are soaking up the last bit of sun on that little island," said Jon.

"I want to run a theory by you."

"Have you ever heard of small talk? Sometimes it is nice to say, 'hello, how was your day?'"

I avoided looking at him. I wasn't sure if he was smiling or not. My sister was right, I thought, I have limited social skills, especially when it comes to men. But I couldn't stop. The two killings and the threats had taken over my life. And, it was easier to talk about them than about me.

"Thinking about the deaths again, are you?"

"To tell the truth, I don't think of anything else these days."

"Okay, I give up. Last year, I thought you were naïve. Maybe had seen too many television detective shows. Now I think you're...I don't know." He was tapping his fingers on the blanket that doubled as a tablecloth. "What's the theory this time?"

"I think the killers launched their boat one cove over at high tide, then went around the cove to drop off the body."

"Where does Mitch fit in?"

"I'm not so sure any more. Unless he is connected to some-one with the union."

"Duncan's union? Why would someone in the union want to kill Shari?"

"I don't know, but Duncan's boss said he was grooming him for his job which did not make some of the other business agent types happy."

"That has no connection to Shari," said Jon cutting off a piece of cheese, placing it on a hunk of sourdough bread and handing it to me.

"It could."

"It doesn't. It might connect to Duncan's death. But Shari's...not likely."

I took the bread and stretched out on my stomach, my chin resting on my fists.

"Wanna brainstorm?"

"Eat the bread and cheese."

He reached over and stroked my hair.

"What goes on in that head of yours?" He leaned over and kissed the back of my neck. A tingle shot through my spine. For a moment, I lost my train of thought.

"Concentrate," I said.

"I am. I'm concentrating on you."

"I was really speaking to myself."

"Trisha, for a few minutes, let it go. Let's sit, eat these nice things that you brought. Enjoy the view."

I tried. I really did. But the brainstorm idea wouldn't go away.

"Just for a few minutes, I want to think of the most outlandish ideas that connect the two murders and why."

Jon sighed and pulled back. "Sure." He looked weary.

Finally, there is someone that I like and that seems to like me. But I am pushing him into a back corner while I focus on someone else's problems. This is bad.

"Go ahead," he said crossing his arms and staring at me.

"Well, what if Candy was in love with Duncan and she killed him and Shari? Or what if Andrew and Mitch were partners, Mitch being a silent partner. Mitch wanted money for Andrew's videos. When Shari said no, he killed her in a fit of anger. Or maybe Duncan got wind of the porn project, confronted Andrew and they got into a fight and Andrew killed him."

Jon shook his head, cut another piece of cheese and apple and gave it to me.

"Are you listening to yourself?"

"Maybe Mia was the one in love with Duncan? She had plenty of time to get to know him. She tells her sister about her feelings for Duncan. The two sisters have a fight and Mia accidently kills her. Now Mia is in charge and she can give her brother the money he needs. And..."

"I'm not even going to get into this except to say, in most cases, there is a simple answer. Stop thinking so much. Give your unconscious mind a chance to work on it," said Jon.

"That's it?"

"Yes."

"That's really not brainstorming."

"Well, I think your brain is brainstorming all by itself and not in a good way. All synapses are firing at the same time... but no communication is happening. Step back. Think about something else for a while."

Jon was right. My mind felt like a pinball machine in play. My ideas were redirected from one flipper to a bumper to the rubber sides like that little silver ball trying to rack up points before it disappeared. With each direction change, my idea changed. I nudged the machine to score more points, but I came up with nothing. The bottom line...I was trying too hard.

Toward the center of the cove, two photographers were setting up tripods, aiming at Rat Island, the squat little island 100 yards from shore.

"Do you think that's an interesting subject for a photo?" I asked. I glanced over at Jon. He looked at the tiny island. "I wonder why they are taking pictures of that. Think I'll go find out."

"Trisha, it's not necessary. Let's stay here and eat."

But by that time, I was walking over to a man and woman pulling out camera gear.

"Hey."

They both looked up and smiled. "Hi. Are you here for the photo shoot?" said the woman.

"No, my friend and I decided to have an early evening

picnic. What's the photo shoot about?"

"We're setting up to make some images of Rat Rock," said the man pulling out a long lens.

"What's the attraction of the rock?" Jon had walked over and was listening to the conversation.

"It's a full moon tonight," the man asked.

"That's the attraction," said the woman.

"Do you come here often to take pictures?" I asked.

"My first time was about a month ago," said the woman, "but my friend here comes on a regular basis, especially in the fall."

"The moon will rise right over the island...killer images," he said.

Jon and I looked at each other. "You were here a month ago?"

"Was there anyone else on the beach?"

"I don't think so...," said the man.

"Wait a minute. Don't you remember?" said the woman. "There was a girl, sitting back there," she pointed to the spot where the small cliff met the beach. When I went back up the trail to get to the parking lot––I forgot my jacket...it gets cold when the sun goes down––she stopped me to ask the time."

"You're right," the man said. "You know, she was still here after we had finished taking the photographs."

"Did you talk to her again?"

"Briefly. I think I said something like, 'we have to go. You going to be all right by yourself?' She said that she was waiting for someone."

"Do you remember what she looked like?"

"Not really," said the man.

"Men have no sense of detail," said the woman. "That's why we make better photographers." She gave him a playful nudge.

"She was small. She sat with her arms wrapped around her knees. She had blondish hair tucked behind her ears."

"Right," said the other photographer. "She was fiddling with a bracelet of some sort. Cheap–those kind you get at the fair. I couldn't really see the color."

The woman continued, "I did. It was dark when I dropped my whole camera case right by her feet. I pulled out my cellphone to use the flashlight and make sure I picked everything up. Then I saw the bracelet clearer. The beads were a shiny iridescent blue. Why are you asking?"

"There was a murder close by."

"You mean that girl on the beach?"

"No, someone else."

"She didn't stay, you know," said the woman. "When I was gathering the things I dropped, she stood up and said something like, 'This doesn't feel right' and she almost ran up the trail to the parking lot. Seemed like she was anxious to leave."

Jon and I looked at each other. "By any chance could I take a look at the images from that night?" I asked.

"Sure," they said in unison. Both clicked on their files and brought up lovely photos of the small island and the huge white moon hovering above it. Jon and I watched over their shoulder as they went through each one.

"Very nice," I said. "Thanks."

"Did you see anything that might help?"

"No, but the police might," I said. "Could I get your names and phone numbers? I'd like to pass them along to the detective investigating the case."

"Well, I don't know," said the man. The woman standing next to him rolled her eyes.

"Of course. Let me write them down for you."

Jon and I walked back to our picnic site.

"Megan. She was here. She knows something," I said.

"It does look that way," Jon said.

"Based on what she said when I met her and the fact that she's relatively new to the NSEU, she is the weak link. I need to talk to her again...outside of the office and away from her colleagues."

Jon helped pack things up and we walked toward the dirt trail.

"This is the break I was looking for," I said climbing up the trail. He was surprisingly quiet. Jon waited until I had everything bundled in my car and was sitting in the driver's seat.

"Before you head out to corral Megan, think about it. If she is the weak link, others know that, too."

"You mean, if someone learns that I'm talking to her, I am putting her in danger."

"Possibly. From what you've told me, these aren't nice people. Pass your information along to the officer in charge of the case."

"I need to give this some thought."

Jon's face was one of concern.

"I'll do it, okay. I'll do it," I said.

"Okay. Thanks for the picnic. Drive carefully," Jon said. He wasn't smiling.

He stood near the car door, but he didn't lean down to talk or to touch me. He stepped back and watched while I drove out of the parking lot, headed for home. One look in my rear view mirror and he was still standing there, but he had turned around and was focused on the water.

As I drove the twists and turns that skirted the cliffs of the state park, I couldn't believe my luck. Megan could be the key to one, maybe two murders. She was so jittery when I saw her, I bet she wanted to talk to someone about it. That someone was going to be me.

Lena and Dr. T were watching television when I walked in. Lena looked over at T. "We are now going to discuss Trisha's date and probably her lack of social skills."

"I'm outta here," said T, moving back toward Lena's room. "Let me know when you're through."

Lena waited until she heard Dr. T close the door to her bedroom. "I had an interesting call today while you were off canoodling with Jon."

"We weren't canoodling."

"That's not surprising."

"Who called?"

"Mia."

"And?"

"Well, it seems that she went to her sister's condo today and met up with a neighbor, one of Shari's swim buddies. Shari had given her a spare key. So, as the neighbor was offering her condolences, she mentioned that she didn't get to tell Mitch how sorry she was for his sister's death. Seems that he was there the day Duncan died. She saw him in the hall in the afternoon...that he was in a hurry."

I took T's place on the couch. "That brother of Shari's keeps popping up in the wrong place at the wrong time. He must have been out of jail by then. Maybe he was involved with Duncan's death. Although that sounds far-fetched, even to me." I pulled out the tablet, clicked on the e-notecards and added a note on Mitch's page. "Did she say anything about Megan?"

"No. Why?"

"I learned some things at China Camp," I said leaning toward my sister. With that I took her step by step through the evening––the photographers, the Megan sighting, tides and Rat Rock. When I finished, I sat back and looked up. Terrel was standing in the hall.

"What did Jon think?" he asked.

"I thought you wanted me to forget about all this."

"I knew you wouldn't. Lena told me she wanted you to keep investigating. So, against my better judgment, I'm listening. What did Jon think?"

"That I could be on to something. But he's concerned about me and now, Megan."

"You said you wanted to talk to Megan?"

"Right," I said.

"Why would she talk to you?"

"She's afraid. I could tell that. Somehow she was sucked into Shari's murder. Maybe someone paid her to help––downplayed what she needed to do. Now she's an accessory to a murder; she wants out."

"Possibly. It's worth checking," he said.

"I knew you'd agree," I said.

"On the phone. Talk to her on the phone."

"That was my plan," I said. Actually, I want to see her and discuss this face-to-face, but T didn't need to know that.

He stood there with his hands on his lanky hips. "Keep me abreast of what is going down."

"Sure thing," I said.

"Absolutely," said Lena. "Anything else about the double murders?" Lena looked over at me.

"Nope."

"Okay, now we are really going to talk about her date. So you can leave––or if the state of my sister's love life is of interest, you are welcome to stay," said Lena.

"My cue to exit stage right," he said. "But I'm leaving the door open. One mention of Shari or Duncan and I am back out here."

"Got it," I said. Lena and I watched as Terrel slowly turned around and strolled to the bedroom.

"Lena, I made a mess of things. I can't talk about anything else but––you know––when I'm with him. He's patient to a point, but ..."

"You never could put the brakes on that mind of yours.

Look, Jon's a great guy and he is going to walk, and soon, unless you show some interest in something besides murders and suspects. Ask him about himself...his job, that's where you two met, right? He likes baseball. You like baseball. A common interest...talk about that. Let's make this simple. Three steps. The first you know how to do...ask questions. The second is the most important. Listen to what he says. One more thing. Since all you can talk about is death and suspects, don't say more than 'oh,, so, or 'tell me more about'...whatever he is talking about. If you feel you can't do that, keep your mouth shut and nod. Got it?"

"I guess."

"Pretend you're talking to Dr. T."

"I heard that," Dr. T called out from the bedroom.

"That doesn't help," I said. "Okay, I'll try." I paused for a moment and lowered my voice. "Sounds like you're feeling better."

"I am. I'm a little behind in my work, so I'm going to put in an hour before I go to sleep. Sorry, but I haven't looked at Shari's laptop yet." With that she walked down the hall into her bed room to join Terrel.

Any sympathy for my malingering sister evaporated. She agreed to look at Shari's computer. 'I'm on it,' is what she actually said. But she wasn't. So irritating, that's what she was.

"Do it soon," I called out. Didn't she realize that I was waiting...that this was important. Think I'll do it myself. Just open up the laptop and search. Oh, I can't. That's right. I don't have the password. I wondered if Jon was home yet. I checked my messages but there was nothing from him. However, Candy had called me back. She could meet me tomorrow late in the afternoon at Pt. Richmond. Her directions were simple. Drive through the tunnel at the end of the little village of Pt. Richmond and find a place to park. She would be at Keller Cove, swimming with a group of people in the Bay, and she'd look for me when she got out of the water.

CHAPTER 37

I'd made this drive to Pt. Richmond many times with my sister. Keller Cove was the site of Lena's favorite open water swim. It's one of my favorites, too. I liked it because although it was only 30 minutes from home, the historic small town seemed a world away from everything else in Northern California.

The dark two-lane Ferry Point tunnel took me to a regional park next to San Francisco Bay. I stopped along the side of the road overlooking the calm water stretched out below. The car parked in front of mine had a union sticker on the back windshield. Candy was down there some place. I could see across the Bay to Marin County with the outline of Mt. Tam in the background. Between Tiburon and Angel Island was Raccoon Straits, the wide passage of water that Jon and I sailed through to the Berkeley Marina. While it was sunny and warm here in the East Bay, fog was hunkered down on the Golden Gate Bridge hiding it from view. Off to left was the skyline of San Francisco, layered with strings of fog spreading down the waterfront. This was a million dollar view and I was the only one––except for a few seagulls–– here to enjoy it.

In the water below, I saw a group of five swimmers moving toward the shore. Two swimmers lagged behind. One, a man, seemed to be pacing the other, a woman in a black wetsuit. He would stop, float on his back, take a stroke, and float some more, making sure he stayed at her side. The first group jogged out of the water and on to the pebbly beach disappearing beneath a cliff. Finally, the pair made it to the water's edge. The woman had trouble standing, keeping her balance. The man grabbed her arm offering support as they walked to join the others.

Was that Candy? I climbed out of the car and walked down a dirt path to a patio area with picnic tables, a shower and restrooms. In ten minutes, a few people now dressed in sweatshirts and long pants climbed up the trail. The water was probably in the mid-60's, cool enough to chill the athletes. I, however, was warm in the sun. I recognized one of the men. He was another union member, the tall one, who attended the open water clinic and was signed up for the next one, the one I was leading.

"Hey, I remember you," he said walking over. "You were at the reg table at the clinic a few weeks ago."

"That was me. Is Candy with you?"

"She's changing. She'll be up in a minute or two. Everything you guys discussed in the clinic was very helpful."

"Thank you. I'm glad it was."

He continued walking up the winding path to the street.

A few minutes later, I saw Candy. She looked frozen. Her blond hair was stuffed under a royal blue beanie with a union logo and she was wearing the ever-popular swimmer's stadium jacket, thick black tights and warm boots. She clutched the coat at her neck.

"You...you...came," she said through chattering teeth. Candy moved stiffly toward me and sat down. She stretched out her hand on the warm wood of the picnic table. "First time swimming in water this cold. Not sure I like this. Couldn't see the bottom. No black line to follow." She bit off each word as it came out of her mouth. She unzipped a swim bag and pulled out a thermal cup.

"Tea," she said, taking a sip. Her hands shook and the

tea began to splash out along the edges. "Not that warm any-more." She held it next to her face. "Can we talk in my car?"

The car had been baking in the sun while she was swimming and now it was uncomfortably warm for me. Candy turned the car on and then pushed the heater up to high, blowing air straight at us. Sweat collected near my hairline as Candy began to thaw out. She pulled off the beanie, reached over to the glove compartment and pulled out a brush. She looked in the mirror on the sun visor and started to brush her hair. The car was silent except for the whir of the heater fan throwing out hot hair.

"Mind if I open the window a little?" I asked. "I'm begin-ning to melt."

"Sure, sorry, about that."

She turned the heater off, unzipped her jacket and looked at me.

"Okay, you wanted to talk to me. Here I am."

"I'm sorry about Duncan."

She turned her head to look out the window, but didn't say anything.

"How come you weren't in the car with him the other day?"

"I had a doctor's appointment in the morning. I was going to catch up with him and Megan at a meeting."

"Did you know Shari?"

"If you knew Duncan, you knew Shari."

"Did you like her?"

She shrugged her shoulders. "I don't think she was good enough for Duncan."

"What do you mean?"

"She appeared all goody-goody, a hard working lawyer, swimmer and organizer. But she was a fake."

"Really."

"Yeah, really. You could ask anyone and they'd tell you the same thing."

"Why was she a fake?" There was no answer. Candy kept brushing her hair. "Is that what Andrew would say?"

She looked out the window again. "You'd have to ask him."

"There is no way to ask the next question, but just say it. Were you interested in Duncan?"

"Sure, we worked together. He was a friend. I hated to see him being used."

"I mean romantically."

"I don't know what you mean. Duncan was going to ask Shari to marry him. I don't get involved with men who are serious about someone else."

"But what if Shari was out of the picture. Would you be interested?"

She shrugged her shoulders.

"If Duncan hadn't died, would he be someone you'd like to know better, outside of work?"

"I don't know why you are so interested. But, yes, okay. Yes, I liked him. His death is painful. I hurt inside because of it. If Duncan had listened to me, he'd still be alive. I tried to tell him Shari wasn't the right one for him, but that stupid woman had him wrapped around her finger. Do you know that––. She stopped abruptly. "It doesn't matter. There's nothing more to talk about. I've got to get home."

"What were you going to say?"

"Look, the only reason I'm talking to you is that my boss asked me to be courteous. He said that..."

She stopped again.

"What? He said what?"

She sighed. "It might help figure out what really happened to Duncan."

"Okay, so what were you going to say about Shari? Your answer could be the key."

"I don't like to talk about someone who is dead. But Shari

wasn't true to Duncan. I tried to warn him."

"She was seeing other men?"

"Andy, Duncan's best friend."

"You're sure about that?"

"Pretty sure. When I asked Duncan about Andy and Shari's relationship, he said they were in business together. But it was more, a lot more. I've seen the photographs that prove it."

A breeze blew off the Bay into the car, cooling it down.

"What kind of photographs?"

"Porn-type things. Just disgusting."

"How did you happen to see those photos?"

"Andy. He thought I'd make a good substitute for Shari. He said she was quitting. But I said, 'no way.'"

"Do you think Andrew and Duncan might have quarreled about Shari? Got into a fight. And then somehow Duncan fell or maybe...ah...was pushed him off the balcony in Shari's apartment?"

Candy whipped her head around faced me directly. "Are you suggesting that Andy pushed Duncan and that killed him? You are crazy."

"It could have been an accident," I said.

She slipped out of the stadium jacket and glanced into the mirror once again. "Not possible. Andy doesn't get into fights. He wouldn't hurt anyone. Look, this is very difficult to talk about and I have to get back to the city. We're done aren't we?"

She turned on the car.

"One more thing. Do you have Megan's phone number?"

"Why do you want to talk to her?"

"Never mind. Yeah, we're done. Thanks for your time. I'm sorry for your loss. You really seemed to care for him."

Candy sat quietly for a moment, her head down.

"Will you be at the clinic next week?"

"I'll try, but I don't feel like doing much of anything right now." Her smile was flat and as cool as the Bay she had been swimming in.

"Well, thanks again," I said as I got out of the car. She pulled into the road quickly, did a tight U turn and headed into the tunnel. I saw her glimpse into the rearview mirror. There were no cars around so that glance was meant for me. Then, she was sucked into the darkness of the tunnel.

That was interesting. I leaned against my car, pulled out the tablet and started typing on the e-notecards. Candy was in love with Duncan and seems to be miserable about his death. Maybe these crimes were a combination of follow the money and a broken heart.

Another swimmer reached the top of the path and walked by my car. "You a friend of Candy's?"

"Not really. More a friend of Duncan and Shari."

"I remember you. You came to the office to meet with Duncan right after Shari died."

"That's right. Looks like Candy really cared for Duncan."

The woman stopped in front of me and snorted.

"Cared for him? She was in love with him. Obsessively so, to the point that she was making a fool of herself at work. Duncan had requested that they not travel together anymore. She was so pissed when she heard that."

"What did she think about Shari?"

"No love lost there."

"Do you think she'd hurt her?"

"She probably would have liked her to disappear. But Candy wouldn't do anything to hurt anyone. Not really. Why all the questions?"

"Your boss asked me to look into Duncan's death, discreetly. It's hard to talk about one death without bringing up the other."

"I get it. Look, I don't want to get Candy in trouble. She's a nice girl, friendly, cooperative, hard working. You know how it is sometime. You love someone. They love someone else."

"A never-ending sad circle."

"Exactly."

"Do you have Megan's phone number?"

"Sorry, no. Call the office."

CHAPTER 38

"Have you had a chance to look at Shari's computer yet?" I asked Lena as we walked down Fifth Street to the corner store. We were treating ourselves to dinner out, in this case, pizza and a couple of cold drinks from the local neighborhood market.

"Have been really busy with clients, but it's the next thing on my list."

"This is so frustrating. I don't know who killed Shari. I don't know who killed Duncan. All I know is that they are dead. I have a bunch of suspects. More people than I know what to do with."

"You are thinking too hard. The answer is probably right in front of you."

"Jon said something like that to me once."

"Has he called you."

"No."

"Not surprising. He probably wants a normal woman not a detective for a girlfriend."

"Give it a break," I said lightly punching Lena in the arm.

We walked for a while not saying a word. It felt good to spend time with my sister. We used to take this same route when we were kids. I walked into the market to order our food while Lena found a table outside.

"How are those Giants doing?" said the tattooed college student behind the deli counter.

"Out of town for a few more days," I said.

The kid pulled two pieces of pizza out from under the warming light and boxed them. I picked up some drinks, paid for everything at the front counter and headed outside.

Lena sat there, eyes closed, head facing the warm sun that was dipping behind the hills.

"Here you go," I said putting the food on the small round table. "How are you feeling?"

She opened one eye. "Feel fine. Why do you ask?"

"Well, you have been acting weird...weirder than usual. And you're not swimming as much."

"I just need a break...a little down time."

"Maybe you should go to a doctor?"

"I'm fine."

"I don't think so. Swimming usually stabilizes your weirdo moods and you're not swimming with the same gusto you usually have. I think you need a checkup."

"I said I'm fine. You are the one obsessed."

"The truth be told, when I'm working on something like this, I'm focused, determined and feel...

"Like you're going to get killed? I think you are an adrenaline junkie."

"I do like the absolute clarity that comes with being..." I didn't want to say it out loud.

"In danger?"

"I guess."

Lena slapped her hand on the table and I jumped.

"What?"

"I forgot to tell you. We can't use Lake Caldwell for the clinic. They've been testing the water for the last week and the bacteria level is unsafe."

"You're kidding me. Now what do we do? Cancel?"

"No, they suggested another site in Fremont. It's not open yet for open water events but they are allowing us to use it since it would have a very low impact on the area. It's also a way for them to do a trial run on the site with a limited amount of swimmers."

"So that means I have to let all the swimmers and the volunteers who are helping know. When did you find out?"

"The other day."

"And you didn't tell me?"

"Don't yell at me. I took care of it. A few of us called and emailed all the swimmers and the volunteers to let them know."

"Well, you didn't let me know."

"I forgot."

"I thought I was in charge."

"You are."

"Don't you think that the person in charge should know about something like a location change?"

"You're making a big deal out of nothing. It's handled."

I bit down on the pizza and chewed very, very slowly.

"I haven't been to this new place. I don't know what it looks like, where we should set up. I don't know anything about it."

I glanced over at my sister who had closed her eyes again, face toward the sun.

"You're not too concerned."

"Nope."

"Well, I am."

"You're stressing over something that isn't a problem. Let it go."

"I can't believe you. I'm going home. Maybe I can find a photo or map of this place on the internet."

"Think I'll stay here for a while." She picked up the drink, turned around and started a conversation with the couple behind us.

"Unbelievable," I muttered, as I grabbed the pizza, soda and headed for home.

The map I found on the internet was too small to get a feeling of what the area was like. I tried to enlarge it, but the image wasn't clear. I searched for photos, found a few and although they looked okay I knew I needed to make yet another trip to the East Bay to see the location with my own eyes. I called the aquatics supervisor of the park and left a message. If Lena forgot to tell me about the location change, she may have forgotten something else, like the correct name of the venue and where it was located.

I pulled up the file of participants on the computer. It did look like Lena had notified them about the change of location. No wonder she couldn't look through Shari's computer; she was working on the clinic instead.

The phone rang and it was the aquatics supervisor. He confirmed what Lena had told me. The clinic had to move and they were willing to let us use this new site, called Lake Bonita. He assured me that it was ready to be used.

"Plenty of parking. Brand new bathrooms and changing areas. A good roped off area for beginning swimmers and more than enough room to set a ½ mile or longer course," he said. He encouraged me to stop by and take a look. "I'll be there tomorrow," I said.

Panic-mode was beginning to subside. I heard the front door open. Lena must be back. I should apologize for stomping off.

"Trishy." The voice jolted me out of my self-induced trance.

"Oh, no." I walked into the living room. There was Dad.

"You shouldn't be here. Lena will be back in a few minutes and I don't want another fight."

"Piece of information for you, then I'll go. A few days ago some people came down to China Camp looking for you.

These were thugs, people I don't want you hanging around. Mean, tough. What do they want with you?"

"Who were they? What did they look like?"

"Hard faces. Trish, they knew you by name. They knew you worked at the ballpark."

I was silent.

"Look, I'm not going until you tell me who they are."

I sat down on the couch and looked up at my father who seemed to relish his long-forgotten role of protector.

"I think they are connected with the murder of Lena's friend and her boyfriend."

"Two people are dead now?"

"Yes. And someone or someones doesn't want me to ask any more questions about it." I told him about the warnings I had at work and the shots fired at me during the clinic practice.

"You stop this inquiry immediately."

"Dad."

"No, this is much more serious than I thought. You could be the next one killed. Don't you see that?"

"I do agree that it has gotten a little closer than I would want. But that means I am on the right track."

"Turn it over, Trisha."

"Dad, you have to leave."

"I'm not going anywhere until you promise that this will stop."

He came over and sat next to me, put his feet up on the coffee table, crossed his arms and closed his eyes.

"Please don't go to sleep. Go back to...go back to Earl's house."

"Do you promise?"

"I can't do that. I don't want to lie to you."

I stood up and looked out the window. Still no sign of Lena. But it wouldn't be long. I could see her face when she walked in and saw Dad sitting on her couch. She would explode.

"Not going anywhere, yet," he said.

"Please, I live here because Lena is letting me, although she is getting a little wishy-washy about that. She could toss me out because I have contact with you. Then what? I don't have enough money to live alone and roommates...well, I don't want to think about it."

Dad opened his eyes and stood up.

"All right. I don't want you living on the streets."

"Thank you."

"But you must promise that you'll take extra precautions. These guys asking questions were goons...nothing but goons. They came up to me and described you to a tee. They wanted to know if I had seen you, if you'd been there asking questions. I played dumb, but they weren't kidding. Stay away from China Camp, okay?"

"That I can promise."

"I have a cell phone now." He pulled it out to show me. Then he wrote down the number. "Use it if you need anything from me or from the park."

"Yes, all right. I will. Now go."

We walked over to the door. He stared at me then gave me a pat on the arm.

"You're a good girl, Trishy, and a good sister. I knew you'd be able to take care of Lena by yourself. Couldn't have been easy. But you did a top notch job. She needs you, you know, although she probably wouldn't admit it. But she does, especially now since she's pregnant."

CHAPTER 39

Of course. That was it. She wants me to move out of the spare room so it could be remodeled into the baby's room. Baby's room. What a thought. A new person in the world. No wonder she was tired and backing off sports for a while. What I couldn't figure out was why she didn't tell me.

What was I supposed to do now? Tell her I knew? Then I would have to say who told me. I didn't really want to say that Dad had been here. And how did he know anyway? Who told him? I doubt it was Lena. What about Dr. T? What did he think about the baby? Was he going to move in? Oh, I really had to leave. I picked up my phone and dialed his number. It went to voice mail.

"Dr. Terrel Robinson is out. Please leave a message."

I texted him.

"Call me please."

I wasn't sure what to say if he did call. He might think this is about the ME report for Shari. Based on what he currently thought of me—he might or might not call back. I turned to look out the window and saw Lena strolling back toward the house. Up the steps, opening the front door. She looked over at me and continued into the kitchen. I didn't move, just watched her.

She stood at the sink filling a glass with water.

"Do you want a glass of water?" she asked, not looking at me.

I shook my head.

"Do you want a glass of water?" she said again, louder. She turned around. "Still mad that I didn't tell you about the location change? Look I'm sorry. I've had a lot on my mind."

I bet.

"Don't worry about it," I said.

I couldn't tear my eyes away from her face. I looked at the rest of her body. I couldn't help it; her face, her arms, her legs, her stomach.

"What?"

"Nothing. I've got to go do some more work on the clinic. I'm going to drive out to the new venue tomorrow and check it out."

"Maybe I'll go with you. I'd like to see it. Don't think I've ever been there before."

"You don't have to do that."

Lena came over and sat down beside me. "I apologized for not telling you about the new location. Please don't be angry."

"It just took me by surprise. It will all work out. You already did most of the work. You feeling any better?"

Lena shrugged her shoulders. "So-so," she said.

"I have some more work to do on the clinic." I got up and walked back to my room.

"I'm sorry," said Lena after me. "Really."

"Don't worry about it."

"One more thing I forgot to tell you," she said. "I talked with Mia. Shari's body has been released. She is planning a funeral for her sister. Probably within the next week or so."

"Thanks. Did she mention Mitch?"

"Just that he'd been to the condo."

"Anyone concerned that we have Shari's laptop?"

"She didn't say and I forgot to ask her. Don't know what has happened to my memory."

I do. I shut my bedroom door and sat down at the computer. I wondered when she planned on telling me; hopefully before the baby was born. I looked around the small room with the view of Mt. Tamalpais. I'd lived here for almost two years. It had been a safe port in the midst of my stormy life, but it was time to move on, whether I wanted to or not. I pulled open the drawer to my desk. There was a small white sealed envelope. Inside was my wedding ring. I ripped the edge of the envelope and slid out the ring. It was a simple wide band of brushed gold. Maybe it was time to move on from this, too. I deposited the ring into the pocket of my jeans.

I reread the email that Lena had sent to all the clinic participants. It was adequate. But I felt I could do a little better. I drafted up another email with directions and mentioned that I'd be there the next day to talk to the park supervisor if anyone wanted to come check it out. I attached a few photos of the location and made it known that I would learn as much as I could and report back.

The biggest question when it came to open water swimmers in Northern California is 'what's the water like?' Chilly doesn't really answer it, so I planned to borrow Lena's watch that measured the water temperature and go for a short swim. I walked back into the living room. Lena had her feet propped up and was watching television. I headed for the kitchen table and my sister's swim bag.

"I'm going to do a quick swim tomorrow at Lake Bonita."

"You?"

"Yeah me. What's wrong with that?"

"Think I'll come with you."

"No I can do it myself. You're not feeling well remember and you have work to do. I'm a big girl. I will be fine."

"I'm glad you're feeling more comfortable in the water. Is the venue open to the public?"

"No, not really."

"So no lifeguards?"

"Probably not."

"Trisha, you shouldn't swim alone. It's not safe."

"I'll stay close to the shore, close enough to stand up."

"Look, I'll tag along and swim next to you. You're so slow I'll probably be floating on my back the whole time."

"No. I don't want you to feel worse. I won't go into the lake...well, maybe, only up to my knees. Okay?"

"That's not swimming. You won't get an accurate temperature reading so why bother?" she said. She tilted her head and looked at me. "I'm coming."

"No, you're not. Okay, I'll ask the rangers for the water temp. Does that make you feel better?"

She nodded.

"Listen to me. You're under the weather and staying here. And you have to...let me repeat myself...have to check out Shari's computer. Besides, the drive over to the lake and back...well, that's almost three hours. I'm going to track down the park supervisor. That's another hour. Do you have a spare four to five hours?"

I was hoping her answer would be 'no.' Logic, which isn't my strongest attribute when reasoning with my sister, caught her by surprise.

"You have a point."

"I always do," I said with a smile. "Listen to your sister on this one."

"Okay. I give up. I'll stay home and work. How pathetic. At one time, I'd skip out, forget work for a day. What is happening to me?"

"You're becoming an adult," I said.

She mimicked me, "'You're becoming an adult.' Responsibilities, I hate them."

"Can I borrow your watch? The one that tells the water temp?"

"You don't need it remember? said Lena as she switched off the TV, pulled on a pair of ear buds and started humming to the music that only she could hear. She boogied back to her bedroom, shaking her hips and her shoulders to the inaudible tune.

I waited until the door to her bedroom closed before I began looking through her swim bag. The watch was in the side pocket. I shuffled through the small bottles of leaking shampoo and body wash.

"This is disgusting," I said as I pulled out the watch encased in goo.

CHAPTER 40

The highway sign describing road conditions and driving time to the nearest cities had one message on it. "High winds on Richmond-San Rafael Bridge." I hated that particular message because in a few minutes, I'd be fighting the steering wheel and probably holding my breath as I bounced across the span. The wind was whipping up the water below me as I entered the approach to the bridge. Small ill-tempered waves streamed by underneath. The scrubby chop churned the shallow water into a muddy brown.

Behind me, the Marin hills and Mt. Tam were invisible, lost in murky fog. Ahead was no different. The unhappy grey sky sank low over the land. I glanced at Pt. Richmond to my right, but couldn't see Keller Cove where I met with Candy yesterday.

'Candy and Megan, Candy and Megan, Mia and Mitch, Mia and Mitch. Andrew, Andrew, Andrew,' I said in time to the windshield wipers brushing off the moisture from the heavy sky.

Once past the tollbooths on the bridge, my phone rang. I pulled off to the side of the road, next to a big semi.

"Trisha, its Terrel. What did you want?"

"Is Lena pregnant?"

"Hello to you, too."

"Sorry. Hello. Now, is my sister going to have a baby?" There was a long silence on the other end.

"You mean you didn't know?" I said.

"Of course I know," he said. "So she finally told you."

"No. Someone else did. But you are saying she is."

"Yes, she is."

"That's wonderful." I paused. "I'm happy for her and you."

"You don't sound it."

"Why didn't she tell me?" I almost wailed into the small phone.

"You'll have to ask her, but I think she didn't want to worry you."

"Worry? What's to worry about a young healthy woman having a baby? Unless there is something wrong. Is there?"

"No, nothing like that. Who told you?"

"You won't believe it. Our Dad."

"I thought as much. I told him."

"What? What?"

"Long story and one I don't have time to tell right now. I did a little checking on him and met him...a nice guy, really. Seems to be straightening out his life. And he does love the two of you."

"You told him and you didn't tell me? I can't believe it."

"We can talk about this later. I'm at the airport and I have to get on a plane. Going to an ER doc's conference in Atlanta."

"I don't know what to do. Should I tell my sister I know or wait for her to tell me?"

"Let me handle it. I'll talk to her, mention that I told you since...hmm...I'll think of something. Anyway, you're going to be an aunt. Gotta go."

"When..." I yelled into the phone. Dr. T clicked off.

"When?" I said in the direction of the truck driver standing next to his rig. He smiled and nodded as I drove back onto the highway.

More than once I absent-mindedly drifted into another lane, causing a lot of beeping and hand waving from the cars behind me. If I keep driving like this, I won't need to find a new place to live. I'll be planted next to Shari.

Although the sun was out in the East Bay, the wind was still lashing at the trees, dropping the temperature down by ten degrees. I took the next freeway exit and breezed by a few stores and a gas station. The land around me began to climb, first gradually, then steeply. When it leveled off, I was looking at grazing land although I couldn't see any cattle. There were bales of hay placed strategically across the straw-colored meadow. The strong wind was whipping some of it in the air and carrying it across the field.

The road climbed again and oak and madrone trees began to replace the pasture. At the top of the hill, I saw the entry toll booth to the park. I stopped at the entrance.

"I'm Trisha Carson. I'm meeting the park supervisor. Our open water clinic was moved to this location. Seems that the bacteria count is too high at Lake Caldwell. Too bad, you know. A lot of people like that location." Why was I talking so much? I didn't feel nervous, but maybe I was.

"Can you let the supervisor know that I am here?"

"Sure thing," said the ranger. "The Supervisor's office is over to the right of the parking lot ahead. The work yard has a cyclone fence around it. His office is in a trailer. I'll call and let him know you're on your way."

"Is the lake open for swimming?"

"There is a roped off area, but no lifeguards. This beach hasn't officially opened yet. Your clinic will be the first to use it this season. Check with the supervisor, but I don't think it would be safe to go in. You're alone right?" he said, looking into the backseat of the car.

"I am."

"Not a good idea to swim by yourself."

"You sound like my sister," I said, as I headed toward the parking lot.

My meeting with the park supervisor was quick and thorough. He knew the event plan had been approved by the supervisor at Lake Caldwell months ago. "Since the beach is still closed to the public, this won't impact other activities or park usage. You've checked with the aquatic supervisor?"

"I did."

"I heard that your group knows what it's doing. You come highly recommended."

"Well, thank you. That's due to Shari, the woman who organizes...uh...organized these clinics."

"Everything looks good. I'll see you in a few days," he said as he walked me to the trailer door. We stood in the doorway, watching some of the park rangers wrestle with a large unruly metal sign. The wind tugged at a corner and almost lifted it out of the hands of the two men.

"This wind is something. If you don't have any other questions, I want to help my guys."

"Just one more thing," I called after him. But he didn't wait for my question about the water temperature. Jogging over to the workmen, he snagged a corner and prevented it from flying away. The three men finally were able to place the sign in a nearby Quonset hut filled with machinery.

"Thanks," I said, walking to my car. But he didn't hear that either.

When I drove out of the parking lot I turned left, heading down a dirt road that circled around to the lake. Pebbles and dried grass blew across the road. No one could see me here. I pulled onto the paved road headed for the parking lot by the beach. It was empty.

I reached around to the back seat and picked up Lena's old swim bag that now belonged to me. A quick swim, that's all I needed. If I could tell the swimmers the water temperature, I hoped the athletes would think of me as credible. The changing rooms were locked, so I could change in the car or right here, out in the open. A large towel would do the trick if it didn't blow away.

I stood close to the side of the changing rooms to block the wind and draped the towel around me. A few metal signs, similar to the one that the rangers battled with in the work yard leaned against the outside wall. Quickly, I stripped out of my clothes and tugged on my swim suit, which once belonged to my sister. It fit better than it did in the past. Swimming helped me drop some weight and firm up what was left.

This water would be much warmer than the Bay so I didn't need a wetsuit. I dug through the bag and came up with my goggles and cap.

Thick layers of gun-metal grey clouds tumbled across the sky. The deep dense green of the trees surrounding the lake were stained black. The water looked grimy. I hugged the towel around my shoulders and walked down to the shore. I'm only going to put my feet in. That's it. I tried to lay the towel on the sand, but the wind kept playing with it, picking it up and rolling it across the beach. I stuck the swim bag on top of the sandy towel. The edges kept flapping in the stiff breeze, but it didn't fly away.

The wind moaned as it skirted across the water and tossed the sand along the beach at my feet. I tucked my chin, cupped my hands over my eyes for protection and moved to the water's edge. Slowly, I walked in. The water was warm or at least warmer than the outside air. The brownish water, although visually unappealing, was actually comfortable.

I inched out until the water was splashing around my waist. I ducked down below the surface and opened my eyes. I couldn't see anything...not even my hands. This was the definition of murky. When I popped up, the hair on my arms stood straight up, cooled by the gusts of wind. Stay in, stay down and keep moving, I told myself.

I envisioned Lena on the couch saying, 'don't swim alone, it's not safe.' I hear you sister, but I wanted to get out a little further. I glanced at my wrist, but the watch wasn't there. It was still in the swim bag. I had forgotten to put it on. No way I was leaving until I had an accurate read on the water temperature.

As I moved toward the shore, I stayed as low as possible, keeping every inch of me below the surface except my face. I stood up when the water was knee level and I ran up the slight hill across the beach for the swim bag. The straps of the bag whipped back and forth in the wind. I tugged on the zipper. It didn't move. An edge of a red swim cap was stuck in the zipper's teeth. Still pulling at the zipper, my towel took off bouncing down the beach, almost airborne. I started after it, chasing it across the pebbly beach. The wind eased and the flying towel rolled to a stop, only to be picked up again by a gust and roll further along just out of arm's reach. I was out of breath, trying to run on the rocky sand. I was chilly and my arms started to shake but my focus was on that towel. It was caught at the corner of the beach where the sand met the grass. I was about 15 yards away when the wind paused.

"Perfect. Now, one last charge and I'll..." Out of nowhere, a foot in a neoprene booty stomped on the towel before I had a chance to grab it. I looked up. The foot belonged to Candy.

"What are you doing here?" I said. My teeth were chattering and I wrapped my arms around my waist to keep warm. Candy was standing firmly on the edge of the towel.

"You said you'd be here. You said we could check it out. So here I am. Are you're going back in the water?" Candy was wearing a wetsuit.

"Yes, but I wouldn't advise getting in," I said to the young woman. "It's not that it's cold...it really isn't. But you're a new swimmer and it is awfully choppy." I bent down and pulled the towel out from under her feet almost knocking her over.

"Are you here by yourself?" I asked.

"I'm going with you," she said.

I shook the sand out of the towel and draped it around my shoulders again. The towel flew behind me like a cape. I was cold now and the towel was no protection from the wind. Another layer of lead-grey clouds scurried across the sky. I glanced over at the parking lot. I didn't see a car. How did she get here?

I tried again. "Where's your car?"

She avoided the question. "Come on, let's go." Her greenish-brown eyes were the size of dinner platters. She bit down on her bottom lip.

"You don't have to do this. I'm sure conditions for the clinic will be better."

"Can I put my wallet in your swim bag?" she asked.

"Candy, it's okay."

Her shoulders began to inch upward toward her ears. Her forearms were shaking underneath the neoprene of the wetsuit.

"My wallet. Can I?"

"Sure, if I can get it open. The zipper's stuck. I need to find the watch. Then I'm going to put the bag and this towel up there by the side of the changing rooms. That should keep them from blowing away."

"I'm going with you," she said.

We bent over as we walked into the wind toward the dark blue swim bag. Our heads were down and our hands and arms shielded our eyes. The wind picked up a notch and grains of chunky sand mixed with crushed up shells shot across the beach. They battered my bare arms and legs. The wetsuit protected Candy and she didn't seem bothered by the on-again, off-again windstorm and the lashing her body was taking. The swim bag was pushed over on its side.

"Give me your things. There are some metal signs close by the changing rooms. I'll stick the bag between them."

Candy dropped her wallet and keys in my hand and she turned to walk down to the shoreline, her hands still shielding her eyes from the debris barreling across the beach.

"Candy, wait at the water's edge. Don't go in by yourself," I called after her but she ignored me and kept walking.

"Stop. Wait, please." But she didn't. At one point, she looked back at me and over to the parking lot. My eyes followed hers, but the only vehicle I saw was mine.

'What is her problem?' I thought, grabbing for the swim bag. I gave it a strong tug and the stuck zipper slid down its track. I dropped Candy's wallet into the bag and pulled out the watch.

I was shaking so much I couldn't zip up the swim bag. My legs felt like they were encased in concrete blocks as I tried to jog back up the hill through the sand toward the changing room lugging the bag. I glanced back at Candy as she stepped into the water.

I could now see all of the parking lot. There was no other car but mine. Where did she park? I scanned the empty lot again as I kept walking. I reached the edge of the beach and left the gritty stones and shells behind. The grass was cool and damp...a relief from the sharp pebbles. I stopped walking on my tiptoes. Another glance down the beach at Candy who was up to her knees in the murky water. She bent over and put her hands in.

Okay, she hasn't drowned yet and as long as she kept her wetsuit on, she wouldn't. I was so preoccupied with Candy and her safety that I didn't see the gnarly tree root looped across the ground directly in front of me.

"Ow," I said banging my toe. I dropped the swim bag and started hopping around. "Ow, ow, ow." My clothes, hair brush, and small bottle of shampoo spilled out along with Candy's wallet, which was now wide open. Her bank debit card was on the grass, so I picked it up. What I saw written on it gave me pause. I glanced at her driver's license still in the wallet to double check the name on the card.

"Of course, why had I been so stupid?" Candy was her nickname. Her real name was Candice. This was the DICE I had been looking for. The one who had arranged a meeting with Shari. Of course she didn't show up that day when I was waiting in the condo. She already knew Shari wouldn't be there.

Candy wasn't here to test the waters. She was probably responsible for Shari's death and she wanted something from me. It took a few minutes for me to jog down the beach to reach her. My arms were still shaking, but not from the cold.

Candy had an advantage with that wetsuit. It kept her warmer in the water and neoprene would prevent her from sinking. I stood at that transitional spot between land and sea and felt the mud and sand give way under my feet. Although I was still a slow swimmer, I was confident in my ability and deep water didn't bother me. Candy was now up to her waist. Her eyes darted across the water to the other shore, back at me and out again.

"Are you sure you want to do this?" I called to her.

She nodded.

"Think I'll watch from the beach. I have a pretty good idea of the water temperature."

"You have to come in," she said

"No, I'm fine here."

"I need some help. I don't like this," she said.

"So, get out."

I folded my arms to stop them from shaking and walked into the dark water up to my knees. I either had to get in or go change. I tried to control the shivering with a deep breath.

"I'm going back. I'm too cold."

Candy started to swim into deeper water, keeping her head up. She paddled away from me for about a minute. Then she stopped. "I'm afraid. I can't stand up. Help me." Her words were those of someone on the edge of panic, but her expression was calm.

"You're fine. Swim toward me."

"No, come get me."

She started to thrash her arms around in the water. That's how people drown in the movies, not in real life, that's what Dr. T told me weeks ago. But I couldn't let her stay there even if she wasn't in real trouble. I walked into the lake and took a few strokes until I was at the drop off point.

She took a stroke closer to me. I moved back, then I dove under the water and did a breast stroke kick to get away from her. She was now standing and I was in water over my head. Not much over my head. I started to tread water using an egg-beater kick that Lena had taught me. Candy shuffled in my direction. The lake hid her shoulders and was lapping at her neck. I took a few strokes away from her into deeper water.

"It drops off there. Be careful," I said.

She lunged at me, hands trying to get to my neck. The water was too deep for her and she began to panic.

"Can't touch the bottom. Help me."

"Relax," I said. "You're wearing a wetsuit. You're not going to drown." My words meant nothing to her. She flung herself toward me again, briefly dropping below the water. She bobbed up coughing and spitting. Her arms swung at my face.

"What are you doing, Candy? Trying to kill me like you killed Shari?" I ducked under the water and grabbed onto her legs, pulling her below the surface. She started to kick and landed a foot to my chest. I let go and surfaced. Her eyes were wide with fear and anger.

"You don't know," she sputtered, gasping for air. I took a few fast strokes further out into the lake. She followed me.

"I don't know what?" I asked.

She paused for a second trying to compose herself, trying to control her breathing.

"Come on Candy, what don't I know? You killed Shari because you were jealous. Right? They were going to get married. She had Duncan. You didn't."

"It wasn't my fault," she managed to say.

She took a stroke toward me, her head out of the water and grabbed for my hair. I reached up to block her arm and she pushed me under the water. I curled up in a ball and put my feet against her stomach and pushed off. She let go and I popped up. I took a few strokes toward shore so I could stand up. She followed me, but I turned and scrambled toward her. She moved away from me, water now circling her chin.

"Somehow you talked Megan into helping you." I grabbed for her arm and she turned to swim away. I reached the long pull cord attached to the zipper of her wetsuit and yanked it down flooding her suit with cold water.

Candy yelped. "Stop. I'm sinking...help me." She tried to reach behind her back for the zipper but I was holding it. Then I tugged her closer to me into chest high water. As she got her footing and balanced, I grabbed the sides of her wetsuit and pulled them down over her shoulders and her upper arms. She couldn't move.

"What are you doing?" she yelled.

"We're getting out," I said, holding onto the back of her wetsuit, "and we're going to call the police." I pushed her toward the shore. She stumbled at the water's edge, and for a second she was quiet, kneeling there, trying to catch her breath. Holding onto the back of her wetsuit, I pulled her to

her feet and shoved her toward the changing room. I needed
to get my bag and my phone and still hold on to Candy.

"Good riddance to Shari," she said.

"So you killed her?"

Silence.

The wind was now blowing in gusts as the two of us stumbled up the incline to the side of the changing room. I dropped
my hands from the side of her wetsuit and was about to put
them on her shoulders and push her down. She twisted around
and swept her legs under mine, knocking me back against the
metal signs leaning on the outside wall of the changing room.
I covered my head as I fell to the ground, the clanking of the
metal loud in my ears. A searing pain went through my upper
arm. A sharp corner of the metal sign slashed through my
skin as I fell.

"I'm bleeding," I said watching the blood drip down my
arm, onto my hand and sink into the sand, staining it red.

Candy yanked up her wetsuit, struggled to push the signs
to one side; then, she stepped back and looked up.

"You were supposed to help me," she said to someone standing off to the side. I turned around and saw Andrew. He was
holding a knife, a long knife. I wrapped my sandy towel around
my arm to stop the bleeding. I began to struggle to my feet.
Candy pushed me back down. The metal signs covered my legs.

"Andrew, why did you and Candy kill Shari?"

"Shut up."

He turned to Candy who had her hands on my shoulders.
"Do I have to finish this up for you?"

"It's not my fault. She tricked me. The water's cold."

I stared at her. What a crybaby.

"Stop whining," said Andrew.

Candy stood up. She was weeping, reaching out to touch
Andrew with her arms, her tears, her eyes. But he wasn't buying it. I sat with my back against the side of the building. My
swim bag, forgotten by everyone, was hidden behind me. The

two of them were pre-occupied with blaming each other. I scooted forward and pushed the bag under one of the signs. Blood was beginning to seep through the light blue towel. My body was shaking so much my knees were banging against the sign. They both looked at me in surprise.

Andrew grabbed my arm and pulled me to my feet. Candy began to shimmy out of her wetsuit when he spoke, "Keep it on. You might have to go back in the water."

He pushed me along the path away from the beach and the changing room. I thought of yelling, but there was no one around to hear me.

"My arm hurts. I have to go to a hospital," I said through chattering teeth, still holding on to the towel that was turning a deeper shade of red.

"I said shut up."

We walked for about five minutes around a point of land to an empty parking lot. There under a tree was the van that Andrew had driven to the open water clinic. He opened the door. Candy started to climb in the front seat.

"Are you crazy? You're wet. Sit in back," he said opening the back seat doors and pushing me in. "Keep an eye on her."

I stayed as close to the door as I could. Candy opened the door on the other side and got in.

"Sit in the middle," she said "and keep your hands in your lap."

"I have to hold the towel."

"Don't you get blood on this van," said Andrew looking at me through his rearview mirror. He threw a necktie back to Candy. "Wrap this around her wrists."

"Why me, Andrew? What do you want with me?" I asked.

He started the vehicle and drove out of the deserted parking lot. But he didn't head for the entrance. Instead he turned the opposite direction and headed south on a road that paralleled the water for about 100 yards then started to wind up a hill and dip behind some trees.

"Shari's death was none of your business. She drowned. That was all anyone had to know."

"She was my sister's best friend. We might have thought her death was a drowning until the coroner said there were bruises on her neck that indicated a struggle. And there was a hair tie stuffed in her mouth."

Candy started to cry again and wring her hands.

"Be quiet," said Andrew.

"So you did kill her?" I asked.

"Not by myself."

"Candy, shut the fuck up."

For a minute, we drove in silence. So which one was it? Candy or Andrew? The paved road ended at a gated fire road. Andrew got out and pulled the barrier back. I turned to look at the crying girl sitting next to me. She was not made for a life of crime.

"Candy, whatever happened, don't make it worse."

"She wouldn't let him go. She laughed at me when I told her that I loved him, would take him off her hands, so she could do whatever she wanted with Andrew. You know what she said."

"No idea." I glanced out the window. Andrew was standing by the gate looking down the hill.

"That I was a groupie. And that Duncan had said as much. That he thought I was ridiculous. I knew she was lying. He never would say those things about me. Never. He liked me. I know that he could fall in love with me if Shari was gone. She wasn't good enough for him."

Andrew was coming back to the van.

"So you followed her that day after the clinic and killed her."

"It wasn't like that."

Andrew stopped and looked around again. The wind blew the dried-up leaves on the ground around his feet. Whatever he was looking for, he didn't see it. But he seemed satisfied.

He climbed in and we headed up the hill.

"Please take me to a hospital." I stared at him in the mirror. He glanced up, then back to the unused fire road. The trees closed in to the edge of the single lane dirt road. They blocked the view of the water that I knew was off to the left. I had to get out of the van. That was my only chance to survive.

"I'm going to faint," I said as I dropped my head to my chest.

"What should I do?" said Candy who started waving her hands in front of my face.

"Feeling sick...going to throw up," I said. My voice was barely audible.

Andrew hit the brakes hard, reached behind him, and opened my door. "Push her out," he said to Candy. She did and I fell like a bag of stones into the brush. A sharp pain flashed down my arm. "Don't sit there, stupid. Go with her."

"You can't talk to me like that," she said.

"Move."

I was on my side and slowly got up to my knees. Candy stuck one hand out on the side of the van to pull herself out. I was hunched over on my heels. Then I bolted to my feet and gave the door the hardest kick I could. It slammed on her hand. She screamed and managed to push the door back open with her other hand. I kicked it shut again. She let out a whelp of pain and bent over sobbing. I started to run, back down the fire road. A quick glance back and I could see Andrew running after me.

"My fingers are broken," I heard Candy wail.

I saw an opening in the brush and raced off the fire road to a small trail that headed, I hoped, toward the water. The trail was wide enough for one person and clear of debris, much too clear. Andrew would easily be able to follow me. A small almost imperceptible opening was off to my right. Maybe it was a deer trail. I turned and moved quickly between the large bushes. A branch of stickers grabbed hold of my swimsuit and ripped the material as I advanced through the thick greenery. They scraped my face, my legs, my arms. Bent over, I kept going until I could see the lake in front of me. Then I stopped and tugged at the tie still holding my hands together. The bloody towel was on the backseat in the van, so I used his designer necktie to cover the gash on the inside of my arm. Then I held my breath and listened.

I could hear Andrew and from a small opening in the brush, I saw him. He was running down the trail that led to the water. He stopped abruptly when the trail ended at the line of trees with the beach in front. He scanned the water then he walked slowly in my direction, his eyes moving through the brush around me. I flattened myself against the ground. My heart thudded in my ears.

"Trisha," he yelled. "I'll find you. You know I will. Come out." His voice was getting louder. "Let me take you to the hospital."

The wind blowing across the beach and through the trees swallowed up most of his words. I wanted to look up and see where he was. But any movement might catch his attention.

"Come on, Trisha." He was standing no more than 10 feet from me. If he saw the traces of this small trail––flattened grass leading off the path––and the blood dripping from my arm, he might come over and investigate. My arm was throbbing and my shivering was uncontrollable, so much that I shook the brush covering me. I could actually see his shoes.

"Andy, where are you?" Candy's voice rang out from halfway down the trail. "I want to leave now. My hand hurts."

"Go back to the van." He turned to walk back to the trail.

"I'm leaving," said Candy.

"No, you're not," he said.

"I don't like this," she said. Her voice growing fainter.

"Go back to the van and wait."

I heard footsteps move upwards on the trail. I scrambled to my feet and eased my way toward the opening and the water. The beach was narrow and the lake was only 12 feet from the trees. I couldn't stay in the brush forever. I had to leave the safety of this last line of trees. It was time to move. Now. I inched into the open. No Andrew. No Candy. Blood was still dripping down my arm. Lake water wouldn't help it, but it was the only route out of here.

"Well, there you are," said Andrew, standing at the end of the trail, looking at me. "Let's make this easy." He motioned for me to come closer. Instead, I began to walk backwards away from him. The wind churned through the branches above and whipped up the gritty sand once again. With each gust, it stung and my arm was pierced with pain.

"Have it your way," he said as he walked toward me. He carried a knife in one hand.

I heard it first. The van was racing down the hill. "There goes Candy," I said as I backed into the water.

He whipped around, but he couldn't see the van. He could only hear the sound of the rumbling engine growing fainter.

"Not sure how she can drive with that injured hand of hers," I said.

He smiled a smile as dark as the clouds churning over us. "You're not leaving the lake." He walked closer. With each step, I backed further into the water. Every part of me was shaking. My arms; my legs, even my head. My body was on high alert. The silhouette of the trees behind Andrew looked razor sharp. Each pebble below the water vibrated with clarity.

"Tell me about Shari," I said as I took a step closer to him. It must have surprised him because he stopped moving.

"I didn't kill the controlling bitch. She was my meal ticket."

"She knew you wanted to replace her, so the money dried up...didn't it?"

He bent over and pulled off his shoes and socks and waded into the water ankle deep, still holding the knife

"That made you angry," I said. His intense eyes held mine.

I couldn't look away.

"I didn't kill her."

I took a few steps backwards over submerged stones and branches. The water deepened quickly...from knee high to waist high. I stretched my leg out behind me and felt around the sandy bottom with my foot. The drop off was right there.

"Well, who did? Candy?"

"In a manner of speaking."

"What the hell does that mean?"

"Still can't figure it, out can you?" He took another step into the water. The wind ruffled the water around his knees.

"You are involved, I know it."

"You want to know what happened. I'll show you. He lunged at me with the knife.

"Not interested," I said as I turned and took a few steps back into deeper, safer water. The water was up to his waist and he hesitated.

"You can't stay in there all day."

I turned and swam further out. I was still shivering uncontrollably, but some warmth returned to my body after those few choppy strokes. I heard him gasp. To someone not familiar with cool water temperatures, this was a shock. He dove underwater.

Shit. He can swim.

But he couldn't. Or at least not very well. He stood up sputtering, not sure what to do with the knife. He pushed toward me until the water was circling his shoulders. I leisurely took two strokes backwards. His next step would put him in water over his head. He tried another lunge at me then dog paddled in my direction.

"Come and get me," I said, starting to swim parallel to the beach. I couldn't believe it. I finally was a more accomplished swimmer than somebody else...two somebody elses. I wanted to get him out deep enough to scare him, but I didn't want him to drown. There was too much I needed to know. I believed he didn't kill Shari but he knew who did. I had to get back to my swim bag, car keys and cellphone before he did. I angled away from the shore. That way I was in deep water and I could still keep an eye on him. I looked along the beach. There were trees and thick black roots jutting into the water.

Andrew walked backwards into shallower water. He shook the knife at me, picked up his shoes and headed for the trail back to the road. I started swimming. I knew that he could walk faster than I could swim, but he had to first climb up the trail and eventually stop to put his shoes and socks on. I kept going, stroke after stroke. There wasn't much to see from my point of view...water...trees...more trees. Occasionally there would be an opening to the road, and I took a quick glimpse. There was nothing to see.

On the other side of the lake, the side that was open to the public, I saw a small powerboat moving slowly. It was hard to tell, but it looked like two people were fishing.

"Hey," I yelled. "Over here. Help me." I waved one arm, then both arms. They didn't hear me. I yelled again, but even I could tell that it was not very loud. Add the noisy putt, putt, putt of their outboard engine and it was no competition. As far as the fishermen were concerned, I didn't exist. I was cold and tired. The necktie came undone and floated away. I held my arm above the water and looked at the gash. It was bright red and deep. I could see tissue and I wondered what kind of bacteria would set up housekeeping if it didn't get looked at soon. I caught one break, I thought. I'm not in the ocean off the Northern California coast. There are no sharks cruising these waters and the fish swimming around me don't get excited about the scent of blood.

I started to move again. My arms ached. And my kick... well, it wasn't a kick anymore. I was dragging my legs behind me. Water trickled down my face each time I turned it to take a breath. My eyes stung and my vision was blurry. I tried swimming with my head out of the water, but it hurt my back and it was too slow. Yet, I was making progress. The trees on the shore began to thin and I could see the road that had taken me, Andrew and Candy up the hill. I could make out the gate to the fire road at the top. I was getting closer to the parking lot.

Everything felt so heavy. It was an effort to lift my arms. The road curved back up a small hill and down again before it straightened out and eventually passed the lot where my car was parked. I knew that the water route was quicker and safer than the land, but I was so tired. My calves began to cramp up, first the right one, then the left. I stopped swimming again and tried to massage them. I doubled over in the water gasping through the pain. I tried to float on my back rubbing first one leg then the other.

"Deep breath in, deep breath out,' I said to myself. Slowly the knots in each calf began to relax. When I tried to kick again, I could feel the calf muscles start to tighten up. I stopped kicking, towing my legs like a heavy weight. I glanced over one more time to the winding road. There was Andrew jogging down the hill. I dove beneath the surface.

When I popped up, trees at the edge of the water were blocking my view of the road. Ahead was a point of land. If I could get beyond that, I should be able to see the parking lot. I tried to move my arms faster, but they didn't cooperate. Instead, they slapped the water with each stroke.

The point stuck further into the water than I thought. I was still a good 25 yards off shore, but the water was shallow. I tentatively reached one foot down to see if I could touch the bottom. I could. I began to walk. The knots in my calves were the size of oranges. I was almost around the corner. One curve over was the parking lot, the changing room and my swim bag.

The thick mud gave way to sharp little pebbles. Now on tiptoe, I tried to protect my feet. My legs painfully cramped up again and I fell to my knees, the tiny rocks cutting through the skin. If need be, I would crawl to my car. I saw the changing room in the distance. The metal signs buckling up and down in the wind. Where was Andrew? He needed a way to get out of the park and I was it. I had a feeling that Candy wasn't coming back for him.

I was completely out of the water in the full eye of the wind and the gritty sand bouncing down the beach. My elbows and knees were scraped and the soles of my feet felt raw. I shuffled as fast as I could and ducked behind a long hedge that lead to the parking lot. At some point I would have to make a 30-yard dash for my swim bag, hopefully still under the signs next to the changing room. I took a quick glance over the hedge. No Andrew. Now. Run.

I did. Or at least I tried to, on stiff, aching legs. My thighs burned and the run turned into a slow torturous jog. It was hard to pick my feet up and move them forward. I tripped over a small stone edge that separated the grass from the beach and I fell face forward into the gravely sand. My cheeks stung. Pulling myself up on, I started off again. The changing room was only a few feet away. I dove at the large metal sign and dug behind it. My swim bag was still there. I scratched through it hoping to find another towel. No luck, but there was an old sweat shirt. I reached up and pulled down the straps of my swimsuit and tugged the front of it down to my waist. No modesty here. My arms shook to the point that I could barely lift the sweatshirt over my head and get my arms into the right places. At first it didn't seem any warmer, but it was dry.

Crouching by the bag, I looked over to the parking lot. My car was there, but so was a man. This guy was trying to open the doors of the car. I limped toward him––a wild woman wearing a torn swimsuit, blood dripping down my arm, wet hair sticking out in all directions. I screamed. I had to get him away from my car so I could get out of here. The man turned around, a surprised look on his face. He held something black in his hand. A gun? No, a radio.

"The owner of the car is back. Get someone down here immediately. She's hurt."

CHAPTER 41

The park supervisors' office was warm, but I continued to shiver. I had changed back into my clothes and was now telling them what happened. I wasn't sure if they believed me or not.

"No one on the fire road," a radio crackled.

"So where did this guy who kidnapped you go?"

"I don't know. And I wasn't kidnapped. Andrew and Candy were going to kill me. Like they did Shari. Well, Candy was involved, and I'm sure Andrew was, too. It's awfully complicated."

One of the rangers cleaned and dressed my arm. "Keep it elevated," he said. So I rested it on the top of the bookcase next to me.

The supervisor nodded to a ranger standing at the back of the room. "Check with Jake at the entry desk. See if he remembers a blond woman in a van leaving the park."

"How come you didn't go home after we met earlier today?" he asked.

"I should have, I know. But I wanted to get in the water... get a feel for the temperature so I could tell the swimmers who are coming for the clinic."

"You could have asked us," he said. "We monitor the water temp three times a day."

"And you should never swim by yourself," said a ranger

sitting at the table with me.

"Well, now that I think about it, there was someone in the water with me most of the time."

"This isn't funny," said the superintendent who kept glancing up and out the window. Right on cue, two local police cars pulled up.

The police listened, asked questions, and then one went outside talking into his radio. The park superintendent, on the other hand, had some interesting news.

"The ranger at the entry kiosk said a young woman leaving the park in a van blasted through the exit, almost hitting him. Here's the license plate."

"Run the number," I said to the police. "You'll see it belongs to either Andrew or the union he works for."

It only took a few minutes.

"She's right. Everything checks out."

"So where is this guy?" said the superintendent looking first at the police, then at me.

I had a four-car escort as I headed to the exit gate at Lake Bonita, two police cars; one ranger car and one park truck. I'd been told not to come back to the swimming area until the day of the clinic. I knew they were doing a sweep of the hills back by the fire road. Andrew would show up someplace. He didn't have a car. Probably not a workable phone. I was supposed to call Det. Hamilton. I shuddered. Two murderers were still out there. They both had reason to kill me. Especially now.

The police escort dropped off once I reached the entrance

of the freeway. I turned onto the ramp, looked in the rear view mirror and waved. They continued on, stone faced.

Two exits down, I turned off the freeway and headed for the nearest deli. Then sitting in my car with a turkey, cranberry and feta cheese sandwich, an ice tea and two chocolate chip cookies, I called my sister.

"Where have you been?" she asked.

"It's a good thing you didn't come with me today."

"And why is that?"

"Andrew...remember the porn king and Shari's business partner. And Candy. Who by the way is Candice...get it...Can D...I...C...E."

"Are you talking in code? Just say what you want to say."

"Well, this pair of losers came to Lake Bonita. Not just to take the waters, as the saying goes. But...To...Kill...Me."

My emphasis on each of those last words stopped the snarky comments.

"You're kidding."

"I don't kid about things like that. The problem is they both disappeared. The police are looking for them. I hope they find them, before those two find me. Lena, they are involved with Shari's death."

"No."

"Yes."

"So it's not Mitch?"

"I don't think so, but..." I paused.

There was a long silence on the other end of the phone.

"I have to go to the ER," I said.

"Why? What happened to you?"

"It's a long story. My arm is cut and I probably need stitches. So I'm going to stop at the hospital before I come home. Can you do something for me? Make a couple of phone calls?"

"Sure...to who?"

"Candy had her fingers slammed more than once by the car door."

"How did she do that?"

"I helped. Look, check with the ER's in San Francisco. That's where she lives and see if anyone treated her."

"Okay, I can try. But I'm not sure they'll tell me."

"And call Mia. See if she is okay."

"Is Mia in danger?"

"I don't know. Maybe."

"I'm going to ask her to come here."

"Not sure that is a good idea. Does she have any other friends, relatives around?"

"I want her to come here. You're coming home soon, right?"

"Right after my arm gets stitched up."

CHAPTER 42

It was a slow night in the Emergency Room so I didn't have long to wait. The ER doctor reminded me of Dr. T, only he was a she and Asian. But, like Terrel, she had the same no-nonsense attitude that saw through my not-quite-right answers to her questions.

She carefully took the bandages off my arm and pulled a light closer to my arm.

"This laceration is deep. But, someone took good care of you. What happened?"

"I was at a park in the East Bay and a sign fell on me. One of the rangers cleaned it up."

I waited. She looked at me. My hair was sticking out all over my head. I looked like a porcupine ready to shoot its quills. My chin was scraped. So were my nose, knees and the bottom of my feet. There were a few small cuts on my legs.

"How heavy was this sign?"

I shrugged my shoulders.

"Did you fall?"

"No...well, yes. I...uh...was swimming and I stepped in a hole right at the water's edge and fell. I scraped my knees and chin."

"I thought you said a sign fell on you."

"That was later."

"What are those bruises around your neck?"

"I don't know."

She continued to examine me. She was shining a light in my eyes and telling me to follow her finger. Then she put down the flashlight and looked at me.

"Were you swimming by yourself or with someone?"

"A little of both."

She stared at me.

"Okay, I'm going to have one of the nurses come in, irrigate the wound and clean up the scrapes on your legs and knees. We'll numb up your arm and then I'll put in a few sutures."

She walked out and the nurse, Robert, boogied into the room. He was a human beat box with the dance steps to match. He stopped moving when he reached me.

"Okay, little lady, what's your name and when were you born?"

I told him while he checked my answers against the band on my arm. "Let's clean you up. Does the music bother you?"

"No."

So he started up his explosive 'buhs' and 'tehs' and clicks as he sprayed a stream of water on my wound and then cleaned up my knees and legs. I was so mesmerized with the sounds that came out of this mouth I never felt a thing.

"You be careful in the future, hear me?"

"Okay."

"You are going to be fine. Need some time to heal, that's all."

"Right."

With that, he nodded and shuffled out of the examination room on to the next patient. The doctor walked back in, checked to see that the area around my cut was numb and then started to stitch me up.

"I liked the musical interlude."

"Robert's great, one of the best nurses we have here. He knows when to use his beatbox routine and when to shut it down. Usually patients––even the old ones––like it. Keeps the focus off of themselves."

It was odd watching a needle go in and out of my skin without feeling a thing.

"There we go," she said. "One word of advice, keep the site clean. We don't want any infection. Arms can sometimes take a little longer to heal. Keep it elevated."

Before she left the room, she turned around. "Oh and no swimming. Got that? Stay out of the water. And stay away from falling signs. Robert will be back to talk about how to care for your arm and the sutures."

The beatbox was off when Robert strolled back in. He was in complete professional, caring nurse mode. He went over each item on my release paper and then stopped.

"Are you listening to me?"

"Yes, I am."

"Okay, what did I just say?"

"As it heals, it will itch."

"Okay...okay. You were listening, but you look preoccupied. Is all of this really from a swimming accident?"

"A sign fell on me."

"Sure."

"No it did. It's not what you're thinking. Nobody did anything to me. I was just clumsy."

"Okay...okay."

With that he left. I gathered up my things and walked out of the ER into the late afternoon sun. The wind had died down. I could see Mt. Tam from here. It was a different view than from by bedroom...bigger, broader. The trees growing up the incline were in shadow and tinged a deep dense green.

All of a sudden I was tired. I wanted to go home.

CHAPTER 43

"Lena?" No one answered. I was standing in the living room. The house seemed surprisingly quiet.

"Lena, where are you?"

My voice echoed off the walls. I stuck my head into her bedroom, then walked outside to her small garden. She wasn't here. Maybe she'd walked down to the market to pick up some things for dinner. I went back to the front door. Her car was still parked in the driveway. Oh well, she'll show up.

I headed for my bedroom, exhausted. Dropped my swim bag on the floor and collapsed on the bed too tired to even take off my shoes. Don't want to have another day like this. I closed my eyes and sank into a never-ending black hole of sleep.

It was after 9 p.m. but barely dark when I woke up. My head ached and my arm pounded in time with my head. It was a struggle to open my eyes.

"Lena," I called. "Lena? Did you get a hold of Mia?"

No answer. I turned on the little lamp on my night table. The rest of the house was dark.

"Oh. My arm hurts." I looked at the dressing covering my cut. The area around the wound pulsed.

"My knees and elbows hurt. Even my scalp hurts. Lena, where are you? Do we have any pain medication?"

The house remained still.

I lifted myself from the bed and tottered out to the kitchen, switching lights on as I went.

"Just like you to disappear and not leave a note. Bad manners. That's you, Ms. Bad Manners." Eyes half closed, I turned and that's when I saw it...a note scribbled on the flipside of a grocery receipt.

"Will be back soon. Candy treated at SF Memorial and released. Dr. T's name helped get the info. Mia and I off to pick up Mitch. Bro out bike riding at China Camp. His car won't start." I grabbed my phone and started to call Dr. T. Bad idea. He was on a plane. Then I called Jon. Another no pickup; another message. I had to get Lena home. Who else could I call?

CHAPTER 44

"Now what is it that Lena did," said Dad. He was sitting next to me in my car in the China Camp Village parking lot, looking puzzled, pleased and concerned all at the same time.

I gave him a brief recap of my day and what I had found out about Shari's death.

"Candy drove off with Andrew's van," I said.

Dad looked over at me.

"What does that have to do with Lena?"

"She is with Mia."

"So?"

"I don't think they are safe. They are going to pick up her brother. He is involved somehow."

"You're sure?"

"No."

"Great." Dad shook his head.

I sat there looking out the car window at San Pablo Bay, the water ruffled by the fading evening wind.

"Do you want to call the police or should I?" Dad was tapping his fingers on the dashboard.

"I will, I promise, but first..."

"No, buts."

"Listen for a minute. I want to see if I can reach Lena Then I'll have more information to give the police."

311

Dad tossed a side glance at me that said 'I'm not buying it."

I punched in Lena's number. It rang once, twice, three, four times. I knew it was about to go to voicemail but she picked up.

"Trisha?"

"Where are you? Don't go to pick up Mitch. Get out of there."

"Too late."

Then the phone went dead.

A shock wave blasted my nervous system. My hands started to tremble.

"She's in trouble."

"But where is she?"

"I don't know."

That's when I called Det. Hamilton.

"Do you remember anything about Andrew's van, color, make, license plate?" asked Det. Hamilton.

"I do. It's black. Has a vanity plate. Think it is owned by the union he works for, NSEU.

"Good. Give me your sister's cell phone number. We'll try and track it." I did that and there was a pause. "Trisha, are you home?"

"No."

"Well, go home. Go home and wait."

"Sure thing," and I clicked off.

"So? What did he say?"

"They are on it. Dad, reach behind you and dig out Candy's wallet from my swim bag and check out her address. I think we should drive into San Francisco and pay her a visit."

I could see my father staring at me as I drove down the freeway toward the Golden Gate Bridge. Off to our right, white fog was draped around Mt. Tam, like a thick flowing shawl. Down the hill, to the left in Richardson Bay, the sailboats were bobbing at their moorings, buffeted by the tide and the wind.

"This is my second, maybe my third trip across a bridge today," I said as we entered the span. The wind blowing off the ocean was strong enough to push the cars around and I slowed down. As we approached the unmanned tollbooths, I said, "Where does Candy live?"

"Noe Valley, off 29th St."

We were driving down Lombard, one of the main thoroughfares to and from the Golden Gate Bridge; then I turned up the mountainous Divisadero Street. Straight up, level off at the intersection, straight up, level off at the intersection. Do that a few more times, then repeat it going down.

Dad chuckled, "I used to do this is my old Ford. Manual shift it was. If I remember, I drove with one foot on the clutch, the other on the brake."

"Dad, where have you been for the last 15 years?"

He looked out the window then back at me.

"What do you plan on doing once we get to Candy's house?"

"Don't change the subject. Where were you?"

We crossed Market and were driving into the busy summer evening scene of the Castro. I turned left on Clipper Street and ended up sitting at the stop sign at Church Street. The J Church street car trundled by.

"This isn't easy to talk about." He paused. "After your mom died, I was a wreck. I needed a break, but I had planned to come back. I knew I had abandoned my two girls and it made me feel real bad. Not long after I left, I started drinking and hanging out with the wrong people. I ended up in prison."

"Why? What did you do?"

"It doesn't matter. But, you should know, I didn't hurt anybody. When I got out I was so ashamed. I couldn't...I don't want to..."

"Didn't want to what?"

"Have to tell you and Lee, so I stayed away, but I kept track, the best I could, of what the two of you were up to."

The car behind me beeped. I waved and turned right. I was only a few blocks from 29th Street. When we passed St. Paul's, the church that Church Street is named after, Dad, in his best tour guide voice said, "This was the primary location for the Whoopie Goldberg movie, 'Sister Act.'"

"Dad. Please talk to me."

"This church was almost closed in the '90's."

"OK. I get it. You don't want to talk about your past."

I pulled into an empty parking space and turned to look at my father.

"What worries me now, Trisha, is that you don't know what you're doing. I could hear that detective tell you to go home. Did you? No. Where are we? We are in the middle of San Francisco."

"Dad."

"What are we going to do? You don't know."

"Stop. Look over there. See that van. That belongs to Andrew. Candy still has it."

Dad opened up the passenger side door, got out and started to walk over to the black van. I climbed out of the car and followed a few feet behind. Halfway up the street, Candy stepped out of an entrance to a three story apartment building. Her hand was wrapped in a white bandage. I grabbed hold of my father's arm and pulled him into a doorway.

"There's Candy," I said, only she wasn't walking down the hill toward the van.

"What'd she do to her hand?" Dad asked in a whisper.

"I slammed it in the door a couple of times."

"Really," he said, never taking his eyes off the young

woman who had stopped still on the sidewalk. We watched as she turned around and stared at the doorway to her apartment building. She said something I couldn't hear. Her body language said she was annoyed.

"Well, will you look at that?" I said.

"What?" said Dad.

Andrew was coming out of the apartment.

"Who's that?"

"The guy I was telling you about. I wonder where she found him."

The two of them crossed the street and headed for a different car.

"That's the license plate number we need," I said.

"Not a problem."

Then Dad slowly crossed the street and started walking toward the couple. When he reached them, he said a few words. Andrew pointed in a direction down Church Street. Candy was shifting from foot to foot but Dad and Andrew had become instant best friends. Andrew took him around to the front of the car and lifted the hood.

Candy came up beside them and tugged on Andrew's arm. I could hear her say 'sorry, but we have to go. A friend is having car trouble. Have to pick him up.' Dad waved her off. Andrew closed the hood and he and Candy climbed into the car. Like he had all the time in the world, Dad ambled down the incline toward the corner and me hiding in the doorway. Within two minutes, they were gone, driving up the steep road.

"Like that vehicle," Dad said as he reached me.

"Come on. We need to follow them."

We scrambled into my car and started up the hill.

"Isn't this the way to Twin Peaks?" Dad asked.

"License plate, dad. Did you get the number?"

"Told the guy I had the same car, but I had tweaked the engine here and there."

"The plates, Dad. The plates."

"Never really had one like that, you know."

"Yes, you had a truck, I remember. But I need the number on the plates, so I can tell Det. Hamilton."

The street climbed straight up.

"Didn't get any numbers."

"What? Isn't that what you went there to get? All you did was talk about cars? Oh, come on."

"Didn't get any numbers, because there weren't any. He had a vanity plate. It was CLOSET1. Strange don't you think? Why would anyone name their car after a closet?"

"No Dad, it is an abbreviation for Closed Set, Andrew's company. Okay, call it in to Hamilton. I need to keep my eyes on the road."

"Won't he wonder who I am and what I'm doing?"

"You have a point. I know his voicemail number. Click on it and tell him what you found out. Tell him you're my dad."

"Okey dokey."

CHAPTER 45

"I know where they're going," said Dad, as we shadowed them onto the Golden Gate Bridge heading north.

"Sure you do."

"I do. Wanna make a bet?"

"I don't bet."

"I bet they're going to China Camp and they're going to meet up with your sister and this guy Mitch and the rest of their troops."

When Andrew's car pulled off the freeway at central San Rafael and headed east on San Pedro Road, I knew Dad was right.

I followed far enough behind them so they wouldn't see me. The warm summer twilight had turned the sky a deepening blue-black. A few stars flickered above. We drove past the brightly lit shopping center, next to the marinas on San Rafael Creek, and a few small yacht clubs. Finally, we were on the flats driving toward China Camp. The tide was in and the normally shallow muddy inlet was under five feet of black water.

There were only a few cars between me and Candy and

Andrew. One by one they turned off into The Pines, a comfortable residential area to the left. I slowed down and dropped further back. I passed the brickyard off to the right on the edge of San Pedro Bay. Then the road began to climb, past the entrance to McNears Beach. Tall dark trees lined the two lane street. Off to the right, the water was dark, but I could see specks of light across the Bay. At night, the turns seemed sharper and narrower. I slowed down even more and turned on my high beams.

"Why did you slow down?" Dad asked glancing at the speedometer.

"Too dark, trees on either side. A little scary," I said as I braked around the next turn.

"Let me drive," said Dad. He was leaning forward, reaching for the steering wheel.

"Not a chance," I said. "I don't want to get too close anyway."

"The next curve, that's the entrance to China Camp Village. Bet they turned in there," he said.

"Isn't it locked at night?"

"Most of the time. But you can get into the parking lot if you really wanted to. Or you could park on the road. We'll know in a minute what this Candy person did."

The hill crested at the entrance to the parking lot. It was chained off. I pulled up next to the chain and turned off the engine. Right ahead was a high ticket SUV with a bicycle attached to roof racks. In front of that was Andrew's car with the CLOSET1 vanity license.

"The gang's all here," said Dad.

The steep hills bordering the road quieted the wind. It was calm, completely silent and dark as a cave.

"We found the cars. But where are they?" I asked.

"Drive. Keep your lights off," said Dad."

"I'll go off the cliff." My hands tightened on the steering wheel.

"You'll be fine."

I started up and we moved at a snail's pace. "Rat Rock Cove is down there," I said. The air was so still that sound and voices traveled up the hill to our car inching along. A muffled shriek broke the silence followed by the undertone of voices.

"What if that's Lena? We have to get her out of there."

"Pull in at the next curve. At Bullhead Flat. There's a storage shed. Earl keeps a kayak inside it."

I drove less than a quarter of a mile and parked. Then I opened the car and climbed out as quietly as possible. Still sitting in the passenger's seat, Dad pulled out his phone, made a call, and then hung up. I knocked on the window.

"Come on," I said.

"On my way." He left his cell in the car and we hiked down the rocky path to the shed in the dark. It was a boxy wooden structure as wide as it was tall. Dad pulled out a key and fumbled with its lock until it opened. A few minutes later, we were carrying the kayak to the water's edge. A wave of fatigue passed through my body. The adrenalin that fired me up earlier in the day had evaporated. My legs were about to buckle underneath me. Not needing more scrapes and scratches, I flicked on a small LED light hanging on my keychain to search for rocks and exposed tree roots.

"Turn that off," Dad whispered. "We don't want to announce our presence."

That one bright glaring pass at the kayak showed me something I'd been thinking since Dad mentioned the kayak.

"It's red."

"Yeah," said Dad straightening the bow of the boat and angling in toward the water.

"Did you scrape it awhile back?"

"Sure did. Left paint all over the rocks by China Camp Village. Earl thought it was a clue in the girl's murder. But, nah, was only me."

"You could have told me." I stood there with my hands on

my hips.

"You and I aren't on the best of terms. Here, put this on." He grabbed a wetsuit from inside the kayak and threw it at me.

"Oh, no. My experience with wetsuits has not been great."

"So I've heard. Put it on."

I dropped my shirt and shorts onto the rocky beach, sat on a nearby boulder and pulled and tugged the wetsuit on, passed bruised knees and over my stitched up arm. Dad did the same a few feet away from me.

"Turn around. I'll zip you up," he said.

"Wait a minute," I said. "Take my keychain."

"Why?"

"Just take it, okay?"

He grabbed the keys mumbling the whole time. Then he took sides of my wetsuit, jerked them together, reached for the zipper cord and yanked it up into place. It was my turn to do the same for him. I watched as he pushed the kayak into the dark, chilly waters. Then I climbed in, keeping low, and sat down near the back.

"I want you near the front."

"I'm not moving." I whispered. He pointed emphatically toward the bow of the boat. I crossed my arms and shook my head. With a glare, he pulled the boat into deeper water and climbed in. I couldn't get over how confidently Dad moved in and out of the boat. Not more than two months ago, he could barely stand up.

"Where did you learn to do this?" I said in a whisper as we quietly paddled close to the shore.

"A lot you don't know about me, girl. I was a white water rafting guide for a while; even led kayak trips in Colorado."

"Colorado? Why didn't you contact me?"

"You had dropped off my radar."

"Was this before or after you were in prison?"

"Don't be sarcastic, Trishy. It doesn't suit you. Now, quiet. Let me do the paddling."

I rested the paddle across my knees. The neoprene of the wetsuit kept me warm and dry, but the incision on my arm was pounding and my legs ached. As we rounded the point, I could see small bright white lights––probably cell phone flashlights––one cove over.

We moved in close to shore, close enough to hear people talking. Three, four, maybe five voices. I could hear snippets of the conversation.

"You never should have brought here her."

And then another voice.

"Please let me go. I'm pregnant."

'Lena' both Dad and I mouthed to each other.

"Candy, you started all of this," said a male voice.

"It's not just me," said Candy.

"Andy and I will take care of it. Candy, you go with my sister. Now. You have to leave."

"What are you going to do?" said a hesitant female voice.

"That's Mia," I whispered to Dad.

"Mitch, are you involved with Shari's and Duncan's death?" Mia asked.

"Shut up. Take Candy and go."

I motioned for Dad to move away from Rat Rock Cove. He looked perplexed but he turned the kayak around and we headed away from them, around the point. I held up a hand and motioned for him to stop. I strained to listen but I couldn't hear the voices.

"Go back to shore, Dad, and pick up sticks, rock, whatever you can. Then paddle back here. I'm going to throw a handful of pebbles into the water. When you hear them hit the water, that's your signal. Turn on your flashlight and throw those big rocks into the bay. It should make enough of a diversion so I can get Lena out of there."

He nodded. "Get rocks. Wait for the signal. Got it," he said quietly to himself. I dropped into the chilly shallow Bay.

"I'm going to get Lena."

CHAPTER 46

Standing in knee deep water, I gave the kayak with Dad in it a push toward shore. My feet sank into the mud on the Bay bottom. Disgusting. I was shivering, more from fear than the cold water. I had to get to my sister before anything happened to her. I cautiously knelt down in the mud. I could feel my hands sink beneath the silt and sludge. I gritted my teeth and willed my arms to stop shaking. Slowly I stretched out. The neoprene of the wetsuit floated me easily and I began to scull my hands and arms back and forth under the water propelling me silently forward. The rocky point jutted out into the Bay. I floated into deeper water following the point's curve. I could hear voices again.

"This is all your fault. You killed the man I loved," Candy said.

"Do you mean Duncan?" I heard Lena ask.

"It wasn't me," said Andrew. "It was that jerk over there."

"It was an accident," said Mitch.

"How are you going to prove that?" asked Andrew.

"Somebody tell me what happened," said Mia.

"You don't know?" asked Candy.

"It's Candy's fault. She showed Duncan the pictures of me and Shari," said Andrew.

"He had to know his girlfriend was a slut."

"What pictures? What happened? Mitch? Tell me," said Mia.

Their voices dropped and I moved through the water a little closer to the beach.

"I was a partner, kind of a silent partner, in Andrew's video venture, Closed Set," said Mitch.

"Yeah, I was getting money from both your brother and sister––she didn't know about my alternative source of funding. But Ms. Moneybags didn't like my vision for the company. She cut me off. Then she stopped advancing money to Mitch. That was it. We owed thousands and we had nothing to show for it," said Andrew.

"Shari never told me she was involved with a film," said Mia.

"It was porn...plain and simple and your ridiculous sister was the main star," said Candy.

"No...not Shari," said Mia.

"You didn't know her," said Mitch. "Not really."

While Mitch was warming to the topic of exposing his sister, I glided into the shallows until my hands touched the murky bottom below. I grabbed the small point of rocks for balance and silently began to inch out of the water, gluing myself to the side of the cliff. With no lights and a black wetsuit, it was easy to become part of the invisible background.

"I took Andrew with me to Shari's so I could get her laptop, the checkbooks and the cameras. Only the cameras were there. Mia, you never told me you picked up Shari's things." said Mitch.

"I never picked up anything," she said.

"Doesn't matter now. So Andrew and I go to Shari's and Duncan is there moping around. When he saw Andrew, he went ballistic. He had a handful of photos that Candy had given him. He was screaming. He started throwing punches at Andy. I tried to pull them apart. Somehow we ended up out on the balcony. It all happened so fast. I ran at him and pushed him...only to get him away from Andrew. That's all. He landed on the railing on his back. Then, he lost his balance and fell. I tried to grab him but it was too late. I must have pushed him harder than I thought. It was an accident," Mitch said.

Mia gasped. Candy was sobbing. There wasn't a sound from Lena.

Andrew, Mitch and Mia stood together at one end of the cove, their faces lit by the harsh white light of the phones. Candy with her bandaged hand was pacing back and forth. Sitting behind them on the sand in the blackness was Lena. I ducked into the deep crevices of the hill.

I was now about ten yards away from her. I picked up a pebble from the beach and threw it. It landed by her side with a soft clink. She never turned her head. Then, I crept in another three feet. I found a piece of cracked oyster shell and tossed it. It hit her hand. She jerked back, lifted her hand and looked around. I threw two more pebbles that landed in her lap. They made no sound at all. This time she looked around, straining to see through the blackness of the night toward the cliff. I stuck out my hands and waved frantically. She put her hands over her mouth. Then she began to crawl silently in my direction, sliding inches at a time.

"What are you doing?" said Mitch turning around to stare at Lena. My sister moved onto her knees and pushed herself up to a standing position.

"My back hurts. I can't sit like this much longer. And I have to pee."

"Shut up and sit down."

Lena took a step toward Mitch. "What happened to you? Why would you get involved with this? Mia, help me, please."

"Listen to Mitch," Mia said. Her voice was soft and quavering. She looked over at her brother. The harsh white light from the cellphone threw black shadows on her face. "You told me you had nothing to do with it," she said.

Mitch turned to look at his sister. "I never touched Shari."

She glanced at Andrew. "You?"

He shook his head. "She was my meal ticket. I have said that over and over. Why would I kill her?"

"Candy," Mia said softly. "That leaves you."

"She was so mean to me. I followed her to Caden's Corner. I waited until Lena and her sister drove away. Then Duncan came by. I waved him down, said there was something important he should see. I showed him the pictures and told him all about what she and Andy, yes, you, Andy, were doing behind his back.

"He was so mad. I tried to calm him down, said I'd go talk to her, that he should wait for me at the other side of the lake. He agreed and drove toward the bridge," said Candy.

"Shari was surprised to see me, but all she did was laugh. 'What does the groupie want now?' She turned her back and walked into the lake. I was right behind her. She must have stepped into a hole or something underwater; she lost her balance and fell to her knees. She tried to stand up but I pushed her back down. I held her under water, telling her how Duncan really loved me. But Shari's strong. She managed to move away. That's when she saw him. She called out for help."

"Saw who?" asked Mia.

"Duncan. He must have followed me. He jogged down the beach into the lake, grabbed that long red hair of hers, pulled off that hair tie and dragged her into deeper water. Shari was crying and tried to push him away. He never said a word. He wrapped his hands around her neck and pushed her down. Her arms and legs were flailing. I could see her eyes. They were so big. She tried to hold her breath. Then he pulled her head out of the water, stuffed the hair tie in her mouth and pushed her back under the water. Didn't take long after that. There were no more bubbles. She stopped moving."

"Duncan killed her? No. It's not possible. He loved her. He wouldn't hurt her."

The beach was absolutely still. Mitch walked over to Candy.

"Why can't you keep your mouth shut? Now everybody knows everything, including Lena. We will have to get rid of her."

"This is a mistake. You know it must be. Oh, my sister. How could this happen?" asked Mia.

"Duncan was in a panic, so he called his rent-a-thug friends to move her body. Lena's sister complicated things. She started showing up at Shari's apartment. He didn't want that so he had those guys threaten her," said Mitch.

"I can't believe this. I can't believe any of this," said Mia.

Lena moved back into the darkness, closer to me.

"No more killing. I want out," said Andrew.

"That's not going to happen. It's your fault Duncan is dead. You started the fight," said Mitch.

I could see Andrew lunge at Mitch and push him down. He hit him once, twice. Mitch shoved him back. They rolled over and over on the pebbly beach. Luckily they moved away from me and Lena. I reached down, grabbed a handful of pebbles and threw them in the water. That was Dad's signal. He flipped on the flashlight and directed it at the beach. Then he started throwing. Large rocks kerplunked into the Bay. I saw a piece of wood sail into the air and land in the shallows with a splat.

Everyone ran to the waterline. They shouted at the stream of light coming out of the darkness. "Who's that?" "What's going on?"

I dashed from the outcropping of the hill, grabbed Lena's arm and pulled her. "Come on, we're going for a swim." We stayed close to the point until we reached the water. Lena looked at me like I was crazy. "I can't go in there."

"Stop complaining. Just swim around the point."

"No."

At the other end of the beach, Candy was standing absolutely still. "Who's that?" she asked squinting in our direction. She paused for a second. Then a wave of fear crossed her face. Panicking, she ran to the foot path carved into the hill that led to the twisting road above. Andrew followed her.

I heard Mia say, "Mitch, we have to leave now."

"Where's Lena?"

"Somebody grabbed her. They're heading for the water."

Mitch started to run toward our dark silhouettes. That's when I pushed my sister into the Bay and she took off, sprinting into the darkness.

"We have to get her."

"Mitch, forget it. Let's go." He paused to watch the shadow of Lena churning through the water. Then he jogged over to his sister and they followed Andrew and Candy up the trail.

The foursome was gone and I stood alone in the dark on the empty beach. Lena was headed for the cove around the bend, and Dad...oh, I forgot Dad. I walked to the shoreline.

"Dad, it's okay. Lena's fine, paddle in," I yelled.

"On my way."

The flashlight flicked off. Everything was black...the water, the beach, the sky.

"Turn that back on. Shine it on Lena," I shouted.

"Okey dokey."

The startling bright light was aimed at the shoreline around the corner.

Dad yelled, "Lee, you okay?"

That's what I wanted to know, too. The only way to find out was to get back in the water and swim to the other side. I walked in slowly, up to my knees. For a minute, I thought of using the footpath so I wouldn't have to swim. Oh, why not? I did a belly flop into the shallows, not caring about noise anymore and dog-paddled with my head out of the water around the point. Dad caught up with me and stayed by my side the last few yards.

When I could stand up in the water, I headed to the bow of the kayak and pulled it in. There was a man with a flashlight standing next to Lena. It was Dad's friend, Earl. Lena was wrapped up in long towel. I helped Dad out of the kayak. He walked over to his youngest daughter and gave her a hug. My dear pregnant sister started to cry.

Earl held a towel out to me. "Brought one for you too, if you want," he said. "Looks like you figured out how to put on a wetsuit."

I grabbed the towel and wrapped it around my head.

"We've got to call the sheriff's department."

"Not to worry," said Earl. "I made a bunch of calls before I headed out here."

"You did? How did you know what was going on?"

"Your dad called me. Briefed me, so to speak. Then I called the park supervisor and he called Detective Hamilton."

"When are the police coming?"

"Oh, they're here now."

As if on cue, three bright search lights switched on one cove over. I could see the glare moving across the top of the cliff, bouncing through the trees and finally coming to rest at street level where I had parked the car.

Then a voice yelled out, "Everyone okay?"

I looked at my sister still wrapped up in our father's arms and at the unflappable Earl.

"We're fine. Just wet," I said.

It took a few minutes for the officer to walk over to us.

"This the lady?" he said speaking to Earl, but looking at my sister. Earl nodded.

"I radioed for an ambulance," the officer said.

"Why does she need an ambulance? What's wrong?" I asked. "Lena, what's wrong?"

"She's having trouble breathing," said Earl.

Lena unwrapped herself from Dad's arms. I could see that she was shaking. Dad took one arm, the officer took the other and they led her across the rocky path to the road.

"She's pregnant," I called out. "And she has asthma." I could hear the ambulance racing around the dark curves. A policeman stood in the middle of the road and flagged the vehicle down. Within seconds, the EMT's were focused on Lena.

"All of you, come on over here for a minute. Let's have the paramedics check you out."

"I'm fine," I said.

"Me, too," said Earl. "I didn't do anything but make phone calls."

I started to walk back on the road to the next cove. The slight hill was all my legs could take. I slowed down and eventually came to a complete stop. I bent over, resting my hands on my knees.

"You okay?" asked Earl.

"Sure...well, maybe a little tired. All in all, this has been a long day."

Once we reached the peak of the wooded incline, I could see, one, two, three, four police cars parked on the road. The flashing blue light from the vehicles pulsated through the dark trees like a disco ball. Sitting on the ground were Mitch, Mia, Andrew and Candy.

I walked over to Mia, but an officer blocked my way.

"I don't think she was involved with her sister's or Duncan's death," I said to him.

"I'm not." Mia looked dazed. "They are," said pointing to Andrew, Candy and Mitch.

"Not me," said Mitch. "I told you that."

"Quiet, everyone," said the curly-haired officer. "Who are you?"

"Trisha Carson."

"Det. Hamilton alerted us about you," he said.

"Trisha, tell them I didn't do anything," said Mia. Her voice had turned into a high pitched wail.

"I think she's right," I said to the sheriff who by now was ignoring me. One by one he loaded the offenders into the back seats of the police cars and watched them as they disappeared down the road into the darkness. Then he turned and looked at me again.

"You wanna tell me who you are, why you're here and why're you're wearing a wetsuit?"

The other officer and Earl appeared out of the darkness.

"She's okay. It was her tip that brought us all here," said Earl.

He pulled out a pad and a small pencil.

"Your name?"

Here we go again, I thought. I gave him my name, address and two phone numbers as well as a brief scenario of what I thought had happened.

"We're going to want to talk to you at length," he said.

"Now?"

"No, you go home. Warm up. We'll call you."

I heard, rather than saw the ambulance pull away. The ear-piercing sirens cut through the silence and flashing lights bounced across the dark road. It took the closest route to the hospital.

"Why is my sister in there?" I asked the officer. "Are you done with me? I have to go."

The policeman held out a set of car keys.

"EMT's said they wanted her checked out because she felt faint and was starting to have contractions. Your father is in the ambulance with your sister. You can take his car."

"That's my car."

"Okay, then you can take your car. You're free to go."

Earl waved at me and walked with the policeman to his car, chatting away.

Standing next to the shed, I pulled down the wetsuit top and managed to heave myself in the car.. too many adrenaline peaks and crashes in one day. My eyes burned from fatigue.

I grabbed the steering wheel and let out a yelp. My hands. I switched on the overhead light and looked at them. Grit and pebbles had rubbed them raw. The dressing on arm was soaked and unraveling. I pulled it all the way off and wrapped a towel around my throbbing forearm. I had to change into warm dry clothes, but I was too cold to pull off the rest of the wetsuit. It would wait until I had reached home. My hands were shaking and my fingers felt the size of hot dogs. I couldn't make the car key fit into the ignition.

After what seemed like minutes, I willed my fingers to cooperate, inserted the key and turned it. The motor began to rumble. My hands started to shake again but I managed to switch on the heater and move it up to broil.

I now knew who did what to who. But it wasn't worth it if my sister lost her baby. This absurd compulsion of mine didn't matter. Not anymore. What mattered was my family. The inside of the car was finally warm. I let out a long sigh, turned off the dome light and headed for home.

CHAPTER 47

I could hear the phone ringing as I pulled into the driveway in San Rafael. All efforts to sprint from the car were a joke. I was moving through soft set concrete. But eventually, I dragged myself inside the house.

"Hello? Hello?" No answer.

It rang again.

"What?"

"Don't you usually start a conversation with 'hello,'" Jon asked.

"It's been a terrible day. I'm tired...more than tired. Two different people tried to kill me. I had to swim in the Bay. My arm is stitched up. Lena is in the hospital. She may lose the baby."

"What baby? I thought you were...she was...wanna run that by me again?"

"I have to get to the Marin hospital," and I clicked off.

I headed for my bedroom with the top of the wetsuit dangling around my waist. I tugged at the legs, pulled it down, stepped out and tossed it in the bathtub as I passed by. Every inch of me was covered in goose bumps, so I pulled out sweat pants and a long sleeve sweater. A quick look in the mirror... not a pretty sight.

Then my phone rang again. This time it was Dad.

"She's going to be fine."

"The baby?"

"It's fine or I guess I should say, 'he's fine.'"

"It's a boy?"

"So it seems. Lena's blood pressure was low, she felt faint and she had cramps when she first got out of the water. She thought she was starting to miscarriage. But everything's all right now. They gave her every test possible. That's why we know it's a boy."

"You're sure?"

"I'm sure."

He clicked off.

All the anxiety and panic slowly drained out of me. I glanced at the photos around the living room...a selfie of me and Lena down at the corner market drinking some low-cal sodas...another of Dr. T in his ER whites, a stethoscope hung around his neck. Then there was my favorite, the shot of mom, dad, me and Lena when we were kids and standing in front of the Ferris wheel at the Marin County Fair.

I would go to the hospital in a minute...just one minute. But I needed to close my eyes. I rested my head on the arm of the couch and feel into a deep sleep.

CHAPTER 48

"Why are you sleeping out here?" said Lena as she walked into the house followed by Dad and...was that Jon?

"You're back? Already?" I sat up.

"It's been a few hours. But, yes, I am."

"What about the ba...?"

"Baby's fine. I'm fine. I'm going to bed." With a wave of her hand, she turned and headed down the hall.

"Well, think I'll be on my way," said Dad.

"Okay. Wait. How are you getting home?"

"Earl."

"He went to the hospital, too?"

"Sure did."

"Everyone went to the hospital but me."

"Looks that way," said Dad. He started to walk toward the front door, but he paused, moved back to me and kissed my forehead. "Get some rest, Trishy. The police will want to talk to you sooner rather than later. Look after her, won't you?" He glanced at Jon as he headed out the door.

"If she'll let me," Jon said. He sat down next to me.

"I take it you went to the hospital also."

He nodded. "I thought that's where you were."

"Damn."

"You want to tell me what is going on?"

"How much time do you have?"

It was past midnight when Jon left. I'd fallen back to sleep on the couch and someone, maybe Jon, put a quilt over me. I woke to bright summer sun spilling into the living room and I watched little spirals of dust float in and out of the light. I looked at my phone resting on the table in front of me. It was 10:30 a.m.

Still in her bedroom, I could hear Lena talking to someone. "I'm fine. There is no need for you to fly home," she said. "The ER doc, who by the way knows you, said to take it easy for a few days." There was a pause. "T...no...really." Another pause. This one longer. "Trisha's here. She can help." Pause. "I'm not..." and then the bedroom door closed.

Terrel. I pictured his face. Dark eyes behind his old school black rimmed glasses, glaring at me. Long dark arms folded against his chest. I didn't look forward to our next conversation. I turned over on the couch and pulled the quilt over my head. An hour later I woke up. Lena sat close by in the big chair next to the couch.

"Well, sleeping beauty. I wondered how long you'd sleep."

"Lena, I am so sorry about everything."

She shrugged her shoulders. "I didn't have to go with Mia. But the combination of her brother and China Camp...well, she was not going alone. Oh, Det. Hamilton called. He wants you to call him."

"I bet he does."

Lena stretched her arms over her head. "I should have told you that I was pregnant."

"Yeah. That would have been nice. I thought you were sick...either physically sick or sick of me."

"Well, now that you mention it," she said with a smile.

I pulled a couch pillow from behind my head and threw it at her.

"I had to get used to the idea first myself," she said. "I didn't really want to talk about it...to anyone. Just ask T."

The living room glowed in the late morning sunshine. The quiet between us was comfortable...warm and relaxed. I sat up. "Do you believe that Mitch, Candy, Andrew, and Duncan were all involved. They either took part in the killings or helped cover them up."

"I finally looked through Shari's computer," said Lena.

"And?"

"Meticulous as ever."

"That's it?"

"No, her financial records show that she was dipping into both Mitch and Mia's inheritance. She'd take some money out. Pay it back. Take more out. Pay it back. She overextended her resources with that fancy condo, I guess. Anyway, with an audit coming up, she was going to get caught."

"I never would have guessed that," I said.

"What is Mia doing to do now?"

"First thing? Plan a funeral," I said.

"You were right the whole time," Lena said. "It all came down to money and love, money and love."

CHAPTER 49

One month later, the packing boxes were stacked outside my bedroom. I had cleared everything out. All that was left was a single bed and a dresser. Those would be replaced with a crib, changing table, a rocking chair and whatever else Lena and Dr. T felt a newborn needed. They'd have about five months to figure it out.

The Bay Area papers had a field day with the murders since it encompassed China Camp in Marin County, SOMA (the area south of Market Street in San Francisco) and a well-used regional park on the East side of the Bay.

Mia buried her sister in a small quiet ceremony. Dr. T drove us to the funeral and then to their family plot in a cemetery south of San Francisco. Shari was laid to rest next to her parents.

I sat on the corner of the bed looking at the soothing view of Mt. Tam. This room had been my safe spot for more than two years. I was grateful to my sister for her generosity but even I knew it was time to move out and let her continue on with her life. I was going to live with my father...and his friend, Earl. It seemed that the shaggy haired China Camp volunteer was a multi-millionaire and had a huge house in the hills behind Kentfield. I'd still be in Marin, only 15 minutes at most from Lena and the new baby.

I heard a truck pull up and Jon jumped out of the cab and walked into the house knocking on the open door.

"You ready?"

"I guess."

"Well, let's go."

He picked up a pile of boxes and carried them to the truck. I stood there, not able to move––not wanting to, really. I heard the boxes land with a thunk and then Jon's heavy footsteps coming down the hall.

"Trish? Got to get moving. You are working at the ballpark in a few hours."

"It's hard to leave here."

He slipped an arm around my shoulder. "Nothing stays the same forever. That's what my grandmother used to say."

"Smart lady." I picked up three small boxes and walked as far as the living room...the comfortable couch, the big chair, all the photos. I sighed.

"When you come to a fork in the road, take it."

"Your grandmother said that, too?"

"No, Yogi Berra."

"What are you trying to tell me?"

"That you'll be okay." He looked at me and smiled. "You'll be just fine."

CPSIA information can be obtained
at www.ICGtesting.com
Printed in the USA
FSOW02n2127280917
39268FS